THE DESIRE OF A DUCHESS
THE BEAUTIFUL BARRINGTONS

KATHLEEN AYERS

Editing by Midnight Owl Editing

Cover by Covers and Cupcakes

Ellis Aperton, Earl of Blythe, rode across the expanse of meadow, lifting his face to the morning sun. A misty haze hung over the stretch of trees to his left, hiding the thickly forested area from view. Part of Ellis wished he could escape into that forest and not come back out. Perhaps find a tiny woodcutter's cottage and spend his days in peace with no mother constantly haranguing him on duty and responsibility. He could attempt to write poetry and recite it to the trees and surrounding animals with no harsh critics to rebuke him.

A sigh left him. While he adored poetry, his writing of verse was utter rubbish.

Very well. He would take out the knife his father gave him and create a host of delicately carved trinkets. Possibly a squirrel that didn't look like a frog. Or a flower that didn't resemble a horse dropping.

Fine. Wood carving was not exactly his forte either. Unfortunately, Ellis was equally terrible at sculpting in marble.

Two years in Rome he'd tried, every moment fraught with frustration, though it had at least given him a reason to avoid

London. Then he'd attempted poetry, something he dearly loved. He'd loitered around the Piazza di Spagna hoping the ghost of Keats, who'd lived and died in the area, might inspire him to produce the sort of words that touched hearts and souls.

No such luck.

After his return to London, a little over a month ago, Ellis had decided to merely carve animals and figures for his own pleasure and to amuse his sisters, all of whom had made a game out of trying to guess what it was Ellis had carved.

Yes, he was that terrible.

They'd done the same with the previous earl, their father. Ellis's lack of artistic talent was clearly inherited. Alas, while Ellis adored sculpture, art, poetry, and music—another of his failings—he lacked the necessary skill for such pursuits.

He was quite good with a pistol, a crack shot in fact, which was a good talent to have if he ever chose to do something romantic, like fight a duel.

No one dueled anymore.

He was decent with his fists, less so with a sword. Not like his friend Haven who was adept at anything remotely piratical.

In truth, Ellis's only useful skill, in addition to providing naughty innuendo, careless flirtation, and being attractive, was his ability to grow his fortune and care for his tenants. A good thing, though a trifle boring, because being an earl required both.

His mother, Lady Blythe, was less pleased that Ellis also possessed what she called "common" tendencies. He could fix a plow, mend harnesses, and, to his mother's utter horror, had once repaired the parish pump in the small village of Larch just outside his country estate. In his shirtsleeves.

Mother had nearly fainted. Several village girls had swooned.

Ellis urged Dante forward with a gentle nudge of his heels, clucking softly.

Not Zeus, Demon, Hades or one of the other menacing, powerful, and pompous names his peers gave their steeds. But Ellis thought Dante a perfectly fine name for a horse. After all, he and Dante had been through the circles of hell together, including one over which his mother, Lady Blythe, presided.

Taking a deep breath of the fresh morning air, Ellis felt some of the tension leave his shoulders. Distance from London and Lady Blythe, though he'd only recently returned, was welcome. He loved his mother. Truly. But the role of sole heir and only son came with navigating the abundance of her manipulations. Her suffocation of him had become intolerable, just as it had years ago when he'd first fled her gentle care for the delights of London. Only nineteen years old, Ellis had engaged an excellent steward to oversee things and, for the first time in his life, had sowed every wild oat in England. He hadn't lacked for women, drink, or wealth. He still didn't. Ellis's golden good looks and charm assured his welcome. He'd had a perfectly *marvelous* time until . . . well, until his Mother had followed him to London.

That had been the *first* time Ellis escaped to the Continent to avoid the indomitable Lady Blythe. He'd returned after less than a year and been immediately anointed London's most eligible bachelor, much to his dismay. Ellis wasn't unaware of his looks; how could he be? But he wasn't overly vain about them either. After all, his appearance hadn't been his doing, but was rather a result of his parentage, much like the title he carried and the fortune he held. He'd had nothing to do with any of it. Admittedly, Ellis was an acknowledged flirt. Something of a rake. But in his defense, he *adored* women as any man with five sisters and an invasive mother must in order to survive.

His second foray abroad had been longer. Blissfully so. Then he'd returned, barely enduring a month before the petty tyrant dressed in canary yellow had forced Ellis to this remote location in Hampshire. He couldn't flee the country again. But he could hide out here—at a long-forgotten hunting lodge his father had once used.

Ellis hadn't even been able to properly take up his earlish duties before his mother had badgered him into fleeing.

Earlish.

He wasn't certain that was actually a word, but it sounded an appropriate way to describe his role in Parliament, his presence at balls, and the job of seeing to his tenants and the like.

Thankfully, while Lady Blythe knew of the hunting lodge's existence in Hampshire, she would *never* set one tiny foot in such a rustic locale. The very idea would give her fits. The nearest enclave of civilization, a kind designation, was the obscure village of Chiddon. Chiddon consisted of a shop selling necessities, a blacksmith, a tavern, and little else. At least on his last visit. Ellis doubted Chiddon had improved overmuch, though he hardly cared.

Chiddon was far away from Lady Blythe and her *constant* pecking away, which made it a veritable paradise.

Ellis closed his eyes for an instant. He inhaled the scent of the grass.

Dinner with Mother, a few nights ago, had finally compelled him to flee.

The evening had started, like so many others, with a recitation of Ellis's responsibilities to his title, the estate, his mother, and his remaining unwed sisters, of which there were two. Duty, Mother insisted, tiny fist curled at him in exasperation, had to come before his own selfish desires. No more traveling about the Continent charming the female population. Wasting his days among penniless writers and poets.

Imagining himself to be an artist, chiseling away at blocks of stone, or worse, carving like some peasant. His *sole* purpose was to marry and produce an heir.

Ellis had signaled for a footman to bring more wine. A great deal more wine.

Warming to her topic, Mother had then extolled the virtues of every young lady available for marriage this season. Her diatribe had utterly spoiled the excellent turbot in white wine sauce. She'd only paused in her recitation long enough to place a list before Ellis, written in a delicate, looping hand. Each young lady had been listed along with her lineage, best feature, and the potential of producing an heir.

How in the world Mother knew of a woman's ability to bear male children was beyond Ellis. Did such a young lady smell differently?

For his convenience, Mother had kindly ranked each of these lucky girls in order of her preference, identifying those best suited to becoming the next Countess of Blythe.

Lady Anabeth Swift appeared to be Mother's favorite. She had not one but two stars next to her name.

Ellis had pushed the list aside.

Mother had fumed, lips puckering into an angry rosette. She hadn't cared to be ignored by her only son, particularly when she was being so helpful. Glaring at Ellis, Mother had tipped her head, eyeing him with determination.

"You cannot continue to flit about and merely be charming."

No, Ellis could not. Granted, it had been amusing for a time, but well before he'd gone to Rome, Ellis had realized his own enjoyment at engaging in rakish behavior was beginning to wane. Or, semi-rakish behavior. His roguish reputation, though he'd never admit it to his mother, was largely fabrication.

Mostly.

Ellis had been blessed with a unique perspective on females owing to his complete immersion in their company. *Five* sisters. The only male in his family. As a result, Ellis was far more patient and accommodating when it came to women than the average gentleman. Young ladies, as a whole, only wished to be heard. *Seen.* Ellis merely complied with their wishes. He encouraged their pursuits no matter how frivolous he found them. Admired their talents. Watched their cheeks bloom with color when he complimented them.

Women, in return, flocked to Ellis in droves.

He wasn't a monk by any means, but overall, the tales of Ellis's exploits among the fairer sex had been greatly exaggerated. He had had numerous indiscretions with widows and the unhappily wed, but never once had he compromised a young lady of good breeding. Or any woman who was innocent.

His sisters, three older than he, would box his ears were he to do so.

Still, lavishing his attention on every young lady he met went a long way in keeping Lady Blythe at bay. It served him well for his mother to assume him nothing but a flirtatious rake. If he didn't show a marked preference for any female, Mother couldn't scheme. It was much easier that way.

Or it had been until recently. Ellis really didn't want to return to Rome.

"Middle age, my lord, rapidly approaches," Mother had continued during their dinner. "You are not exempt from the march of time, as the silver at your temples announces." The mountain of her lips had tightened. "No one cares for an aging rogue."

Ellis had put down his fork. He was barely thirty.

He'd been quite certain if he didn't get some . . . *separation* from the woman lording over his table, Ellis might well commit matricide. No wonder he'd stayed abroad.

The resolve of his mother to select the future Countess of Blythe the moment Ellis set foot on English soil had become nothing less than a military operation. One that rivaled the finest Wellington had used to defeat Napoleon. Come to think of it, Mother was a bit like the little general, except she didn't speak a word of French and insisted on wearing yellow.

"You *must* have an heir, my lord," Mother had intoned, fist smacking at the table. "Had I known you would prove so difficult in this endeavor, I might have allowed you to wed that horrid Barrington girl."

"Theodosia," Ellis had intoned, "is not horrid. I happen to like her very much." Theodosia Barrington had married Ellis's close friend, the Marquess of Haven, some time ago after being compromised during a party given for Ellis's birthday. The whole affair had happened well before he'd departed for the Continent. A scandalous event. Haven had done the honorable thing, though Ellis suspected his friend had *wanted* to ruin Theodosia for some time.

Now, the pair were madly in love. A rarity in the *ton*.

Mother had breathed out a puff of irritation, picking at the food on her plate. Lifting her chin, lips trembling, eyes filling with tears, she had murmured, "Do you not care at all for me, my lord? For your sisters? For the future of your title?" A tear had slid down one plump cheek. "Oh, to have raised a son so careless."

Ellis reached down and threaded his fingers through Dante's mane. What a scene Mother had made. So unnecessary. He'd barely had time to kick the dust of Rome off his boots before she'd begun her assault.

Could the woman not have any grace? Any patience with him? He'd been the Earl of Blythe since the untimely demise of his father when Ellis was barely fifteen. The responsibility for the entire family had been thrust upon him in an instant. Grief-stricken, Ellis had balanced the remainder of his studies at Eton with managing the estate and negotiating a marriage contract for his sister who was four years older than he. Thank goodness for Father's solicitor, a kind gentleman by the name of Firestone. Mother had been inconsolable at the time and of little help.

And Ellis? He'd been drowning.

"I realize," he said to Dante, tugging at the coarse hairs of the horse's mane, "that it was cowardly to leave Mother and the girls in London, but I am not quite ready to throw myself into the marriage mart. It is rather like being a frightened fox just before the hunt. All those young ladies racing after me like hounds. Mother has made her choice clear in Anabeth Swift. I suppose she's as good as any. Frankly, I don't care either way."

Mother and Lady Pierce, Anabeth's mother, were close friends, and the estate of Lord Pierce bordered Ellis's own, Larchmont. The match made sense.

Dante's ears twitched.

"No, there isn't anything wrong with her, at least I don't think there is. She'll suit as well as any other." It was likely true, though Ellis didn't feel even an ounce of desire for Lady Anabeth. He considered her and young ladies of her ilk to be all the same, like iced biscuits on a tea tray. Perfectly acceptable. Identical. Nothing at all to tell one apart from the other. You could sample several and not note the difference.

His eldest sister, Henrietta, would punch Ellis in the arm if he voiced such a sentiment.

The sound of thundering hooves drew his attention, destroying the near silence of the morning. A rider's shadowy form took shape in the distance, horse galloping across the grass as if the very devil were following. The rider, a woman, if the voluminous deep purple of her skirts was any indication, grabbed frantically at the reins in an effort to slow the animal.

She's going to fall.

Ellis twisted in the saddle. The pair were headed toward the thick border of forest at his left. He recalled crossing a small ravine in that direction just yesterday, a ravine obscured this morning by the thick mist coating the ground. Even a skilled rider was at risk of being thrown and might break their neck if the animal wasn't stopped. The lady in question appeared to be alone, no groom in sight. Not so unusual for the country, he supposed, but potentially dangerous given the current situation.

Urging Dante forward, Ellis raced down the slope in the direction of the rider. Sprinting alongside the frenzied animal, he concentrated on regaining control of the horse before its female rider could be unseated.

One of the reins flapped against the horse's neck as a pair of slender, gloved hands grasped for the leather without success. A thick plait of gold hair bounced against one shoulder as the woman struggled to regain control of her mount; the hat atop her head, worn at a jaunty angle, slid over one ear, and a veil floated over her features, obscuring them. Her skirts billowed up nearly to her chin as she struggled to stay in the saddle, giving Ellis a glimpse of graceful legs encased in snug trousers. If she hadn't been riding astride, she might well have already fallen to the ground.

Leaning over, murmuring softly to Dante to remain steady, Ellis stretched out one arm to take hold of the loose rein, pulling gently to turn the animal in his direction.

The lady gasped. She tried to tug the reins back.

Stubborn little fool. Did she expect he was trying to assault her? On horseback?

"Let me take it," he yelled to her.

The horse jerked in Ellis's direction, slowing into a spin, the motion pulling the lone rein from the rider's hand without preamble. Tilting to one side with a curse, she slid off the saddle, fingers grasping futilely at the leather before landing in the thick grass.

Ellis immediately dismounted and jogged back in her direction, concerned she might have hit her head or was otherwise injured.

She sat up with a lurch, legs spread wide, purple skirts puffing up around her small form like a mushroom cap. An annoyed snort came from her. Another curse. She adjusted her hat, placing it once more at the proper angle on her head. The purple velvet of her riding habit strained against what must be a spectacular bosom with every irritated breath she took.

Ellis stood back and regarded her with interest, waiting for her to push the bloody veil aside so he could get a better look at her. All he could make out was a delicate nose and chin beneath the fine lace.

"Are you hurt, my lady?"

"No thanks to you." A jerk of her fingers and the veil was flipped over the brim of the hat. She tilted her chin away, presenting Ellis with an elegant, stunning profile.

The smile waiting on his lips faltered, then disappeared completely.

Dear God. I should have let the horse run all the way to Scotland with her.

There was no mistaking the refined line of her jaw, the small, finely shaped patrician nose, or the perfect curve of her cheek. Ellis knew them all well as he'd spent hours in rapt study of her features. *Angelic* was how many in London had described her appearance.

Ellis found her to be quite the opposite.

Rose-colored lips, plump and sensuously formed, parted as she likely considered what sort of insult to hurl in his direction.

She was good at that. Insults. Disdain. That mouth had

always held a particular fascination for Ellis, though she'd never once uttered a kind word in his direction.

The shimmering pale gilt of her hair should have warned Ellis of her identity in an instant. Like the rays of the sun spun into gold. Or a dozen guineas spilling out of a gentleman's purse. The shade was burned undeniably into his memory, never to be forgotten. Strange, considering he couldn't recall the color of Lady Anabeth's hair. But *this* woman, more so than any other he'd ever known, stayed with Ellis no matter where he traveled.

Which isn't to say their association was a pleasant one. It was not.

"Your Grace," he managed in a cool, detached tone.

The Duchess of Castlemare tilted her head, acknowledging his presence but little else. She kept her features averted, pretending to stare out over the vista before them. Her shoulders stiffened beneath the velvet of her riding habit rather dramatically, as if being rescued by Ellis was the very worst thing that could have occurred this morning.

Hostile would best describe his acquaintance with the duchess though Ellis always found himself drawn to her. Like lemmings to a cliff. She was a particular sort of craving. A sweet which one longs for but after taking a small bite, realizes the filling was far too rich to be palatable.

Still, as he took the duchess in, the desire Ellis felt for her, dormant for so long, skittered along his skin.

An itch which would never abate.

"Lord Blythe. How perfectly unwelcome." Her crisp tone dripped with sarcasm, as sharp and cutting as a finely honed blade. Her lovely pouting mouth—Ellis twitched at the sudden lash of arousal—curled as if catching sight of something distasteful, which he supposed was him. Toying with the thick plait of her hair, the duchess twisted to view Ellis, and the cobalt of her eyes, still so unbelievably blue, flashed with dismissal.

She'd never viewed him with anything else.

"It seems your horse has the same opinion of you that I do," he said blandly.

"How *droll* you are, my lord." A brittle smile thinned her lips. "The matter was well in hand. There was no need for your intervention. In fact, you made things far worse."

Ellis bowed, a convenient way to hide his irritation at her words. "Gracious, as always. But you were seconds from being thrown and breaking your neck, Your Grace."

They glared at each other in silence. Ellis's dislike of her was, in his opinion, justified. Haven might have called it wounded pride that not every woman considered Ellis to be worth her adoration.

Finally, he took a step forward. No matter his feeling about this particular duchess, the decent thing, the *gentlemanly* thing, was to offer assistance. Leaning over, Ellis extended a hand.

Her Grace regarded Ellis as if he were holding out a hissing snake.

"I almost didn't recognize you, my lord, without your parade of admirers."

A slow roll of annoyance filled him.

"Aren't they usually about?" she said blithely. "Giggling and cooing at you in worship?" Her lips pouted. "Acolytes of a sort, I suppose." Her words dripped with disdain.

Ellis had always been pursued by females. It was the truth of his existence. Why it bothered the duchess that he was sought after was anyone's guess, as she was cut from the same cloth. But her opinion of Ellis, and any young woman who followed him about, was well known. Her Grace wasn't shy in voicing it. Through gossip, mostly. Never to Ellis himself. Their conversations in the past had been brief.

"I don't bring my admirers to the country," he said carelessly, retracting his fingers. She could bloody well get up on her own. "Too much trouble to feed them all."

Rolling to the side, the duchess made a soft grunt while spinning about like a turtle on its back.

Vastly amusing.

Finally, she managed to haul herself to her feet, wobbling with arms out, cursing again when the heel of her boot caught in her skirts. Her Grace had never been one to utter such vile epithets before. Marriage to Castlemare was likely the cause. The velvet made a ripping sound.

"Oh, dear. However shall you find a modiste out here?" He clasped his hands.

"Perhaps I'll simply have it sent to the Duchess of Granby for repairs."

A snap of anger touched his skin, followed by the sharp bite of arousal. They often accompanied one another when in her presence.

"She's a bit busy, at present, with Granby's heir." A thin smile crossed his lips. "Oh, and being *blissfully* happy. Not so unusual for a love match, I suppose. But then, you've little experience in that regard. None at all, I imagine."

Her cheeks pinked. "Charming as ever, I see," she murmured.

"And you are *still* a delight, Your Grace." A flood of conflicting thoughts shook Ellis as he looked at her, the fact that he still wanted her naked beneath him not the least of them. That the duchess was an *awful* creature clearly did little, unfortunately, to dissuade his cock.

She tilted her dainty chin. "I never did understand your appeal, my lord. I confess, I still do not." The cobalt of her eyes slid over him with little interest. "Your vanity, barely deserved, can't possibly endear you to anyone." The duchess walked a few steps from him, keeping her face in profile so that the sun lit a halo around her stunning features. A practiced move, no doubt.

"You might be speaking of yourself, Your Grace."

The line of her jaw hardened. Even that was beautiful. "You actually form thoughts? How unexpected. I hadn't thought you capable of stringing so many words together."

Ellis's lips tightened at the insult. The duchess wasn't the only one who assumed him to be far too affable to be remotely intelligent. What was it about handsome, charming men that immediately made others think them stupid? As if you were given an appealing countenance or brains. Never both.

"No groom with you this morning, Your Grace?" He gave no indication her slur had disturbed him. "Or perhaps the duke will be by soon?" Castlemare, the lady's husband, wasn't known for his affection or good humor. One didn't wed a duke for his amiability, especially not one like Castlemare.

Her shoulders braced at the mention of the duke before she tipped to brush the grass lingering on the velvet of her skirts. "No, my lord. I'm quite alone. If you wish to commit murder, you'll have no witnesses to the act."

There was something disquieting in her reply. It pulled at the innate protectiveness Ellis had for all women, a feeling he didn't wish to have for her. The lust tormenting him was bad enough. But—

"Are you injured?" Ellis inquired softly before he thought better of it, wondering at the sudden paling of her cheeks.

"I'm quite well, my lord," she snapped back. "Aside from being forced to endure your company."

Why had he bothered?

Haughty. Disagreeable. Good to know some things hadn't changed in the two years he'd been gone. "I only want to make sure you aren't seriously hurt."

"As if you would care." The color came back into her

cheeks. "Even if I should be injured, what makes you assume I would request aid from a prancing dandy such as yourself?" A graceful wave of her hand gestured toward him.

"Harpy." Ellis took a step back, fighting down the bolt of arousal triggered from the exchange of insults. The sensation was wholly unwelcome.

He'd hoped to never see her again. That this strange, unnatural longing for her would abate.

Instead, Ellis found himself imagining the duchess naked, on her hands and knees while he took her roughly from behind. Tearing and biting at the pristine, creamy skin of her shoulder while she screamed his name.

An animal. She made him want to be a *bloody* animal.

The duchess walked over to her horse, oblivious of his lustful thoughts. Patting the animal's nose gently, she murmured in a soft tone, "There now, Cicero. I forgive you for being startled by that flock of birds. It was very sudden, I admit. And frightening."

Cicero?

Castlemare must have named the horse. He doubted the woman before him knew any Roman poet, let alone Cicero. If she read at all, it was probably limited to the gossip columns and fashion magazines.

"Shouldn't you be on your way?" She didn't look at Ellis. "Do carry on. Perhaps find some farmgirl to seduce. Or a dairymaid." The duchess fussed with the plait of hair covering her right ear and most of her cheek.

If nothing else, the Duchess of Castlemare was incredibly predictable.

"Had I known it was you, Your Grace," Ellis replied, "I would have kept riding."

"And if I'd known my rescue was to be at your hands," the duchess replied in a chilly tone, glaring at him from beneath the brim of her hat, "I would have jumped off my animal, willingly seeking a broken neck to avoid you."

Ellis had to stifle the growl bubbling up his throat. His arousal had become that fierce. He'd forgotten the twin sensations of wanting to strangle and tup her at the same time.

The last time he'd seen Her Grace had been at a house party, one at which she had been expecting a proposal from the Duke of Granby but had not. Granby had tossed this jewel of the *ton* over for Andromeda Barrington. It was the only amusing thing that had happened at that bloody house party. Ellis had laughed when he'd heard. He'd seen her only twice after Granby's but had kept his distance. She had wed Castlemare, and Ellis had left for the Continent.

"Why are you still here?" Her snide tone met his ears.

Why, indeed.

"Good day, Your Grace." Ellis made a short, mocking bow, wondering briefly if Castlemare had an estate outside of Chiddon. It was the only explanation for the duchess's appearance in this formerly lovely meadow. He was surprised the wildflowers weren't curling up at her presence or the birds falling out of the sky.

I don't bloody care.

The duchess took the reins of her horse, walking away without another word, her back as stiff as a pike. The woman's bearing was as regal as any queen.

Ellis wondered how she'd get back on her horse without his help but found he didn't bloody care about that either.

He watched as the morning mist swirled around the duchess, swallowing her before she disappeared into the thick line of trees.

"Beatrice Howard," he said to Dante, "is *still* a bitch."

The Duchess of Castlemare, formerly Lady Beatrice Howard, led Cicero along the edge of the woods, the trembling of her fingers slowing the farther she got from the Earl of Blythe. Her thoughts and heart raced at the sudden, near violent collision of her past and present. Hands unsteady on the reins, she tugged Cicero between two ancient yew trees at the edge of the forest.

An unexpected meeting with anyone who had once known Lady Beatrice Howard would be distressing enough, but it was doubly so because it was Blythe.

He still found her wanting. Distasteful. That much was clear.

A bubble of bitter laughter clawed up her throat.

Well, you did set your sights on his best friend and then destroy a woman's reputation when you felt slighted.

Once hidden in the thick woods, Beatrice stopped, pressing her fingertips into the bark of a tree, and waited for her pulse to settle. She drew in several deep breaths, steadying herself.

Riding alone in the early morning was the way Beatrice

started each of her days. No one was ever about in this barely inhabited part of Hampshire, a place no one visited deliberately. Or even accidentally. Chiddon, the nearest village, was so far off the main road that it was rare to see a stranger, let alone Lord Blythe.

Was Blythe mocking her by mentioning Castlemare? Surely, he knew the duke had been dead for over two years. Not that it mattered. Even had he been alive, Beatrice's late husband would *never* have accompanied her on a morning ride. Castlemare had found Beatrice's company lacking in nearly every regard; it was fortunate their marriage had been so brief, though their separation had come *before* his death, not because of it.

Castlemare had banished his unwanted wife to a forgotten estate outside Chiddon as soon as he'd realized he had no use for her.

I valued your beauty, Beatrice. As I would a finely cut diamond. Now, I fear, there is nothing whatsoever to recommend you.

Ignoring the throb of her right hip, Beatrice took careful steps lest she slip on the damp leaves beneath her feet. She'd fallen harder than she'd thought. Any other woman would have asked Blythe for assistance in remounting. Not Beatrice. Having him close would have been problematic.

Beatrice lifted a hand to touch her hair, pressing the thick plait closer to her right cheek. The pins were still in place. Nothing had shifted or been exposed. If Blythe had noticed anything strange, she would have seen his handsome features shine, first with shock, then with pity. He might have even mentioned the irony of the situation, for surely, if anyone could appreciate Beatrice getting what she deserved, it would be Blythe.

But the only emotion reflected in Blythe's spectacular bone structure had been disdain.

For her.

She hadn't seen him since before her marriage to Castlemare, or if she had, Beatrice didn't recall. Consumed with being a duchess, Beatrice had no longer sought out his golden form at every opportunity, preferring to follow Castlemare's lead and lord over the rest of society. Then . . . well, life had become somewhat difficult, and Beatrice hadn't given thought to Blythe for some time.

A small frown tugged at her mouth.

Why would he be in Chiddon? An obscure locale, at best. The magnificent Earl of Blythe was a creature found most often at a gentleman's club or being followed about by a host of adoring nitwits, not riding about the countryside rescuing women from bolting horses. Honestly, Beatrice had trouble imagining Blythe outside of a ballroom. Did he have a hunting lodge nearby?

Or perhaps he was visiting a lover. Blythe must have dozens.

In either case, it was unlikely Blythe could go unnoticed for long—not here. Which led Beatrice to believe his visit to the area was of a more recent nature. Melinda, Vicar Farthing's wife and Beatrice's dearest friend, would have mentioned Blythe was flitting about had he been in the area for any significant duration. The good vicar was ambitious and eager to make connections—ones he hoped would lead him to a more prestigious position elsewhere. Farthing went out of his way to curry favor with anyone he thought might be of assistance. He'd given up on Beatrice. But an earl falling in his lap?

Vicar Farthing would be beside himself.

Blythe was a beautiful man, even if Beatrice hated to admit to it. He would likely shock Farthing speechless with his magnificence. He was exactly as she remembered. Broad shoulders atop a confident swagger, dripping with charm. A winning grin on his lips. Charming. Always assured of his welcome. The only difference Beatrice had noted was that the burnished gold of his hair was a trifle longer than it had once been, with a curl or two dipping over his ears. He'd once worn it cropped much shorter.

The longer length gave him a romantic appeal.

Beatrice tugged at her own hair once more, reassured by the thick weight along her neck. It was a habit she'd formed since coming to Chiddon. No one in the village ever questioned why the Duchess of Castlemare didn't wear her hair up in an elaborately styled coiffure more suited to her station.

Or if they did, they were far too wise to ask.

Nor were there inquiries as to why a duchess had taken up residence in the backwater of Chiddon, a place devoid of amusements, in the first place. Castlemare's estate here was little more than a cottage. The staff was small. Beatrice didn't even have a butler.

"A butler is unnecessary," she muttered to herself. "No one visits. I receive little to no correspondence. I doubt anyone remembers my existence."

As it should be. Chiddon was Beatrice's refuge.

But now Blythe was here, spoiling her continued isolation. Reminding her of things she'd rather forget. The ease with which she had donned the mask of Lady Beatrice Howard, snob supreme, had frightened her, but it had been necessary. Someone had to drive Blythe away, otherwise, far too many questions might be asked.

If she were anything but unkind, Blythe might persist in learning more about her circumstances—her reasons for being sequestered away. He hadn't always disliked her. He might—

Beatrice paused. *Yes, he had* always disliked her.

Strange, considering that at one time, she and Blythe had been two of the most attractive people in London. She might have anticipated being drawn together by their mutual vanity, having hushed conversations comparing the number of admirers they each had, but just the opposite had been true. Blythe, after assessing her, had found Beatrice . . . *distasteful*. He was the only gentleman who had *never once* paid her any attention. Instead, he'd taken great pains to avoid her.

Every title in London had tried to woo her. She'd never lacked for dance partners, had never been more than a word away from a fresh glass of lemonade, and had received a flurry of proposals, all of which her father had refused.

But none of that attention had ever come from Blythe. No, he'd avoided Beatrice as if she were covered in pox sores.

After a time, his inattention had annoyed her. Honestly, how dare he? No gentleman worth his salt ignored the great Lady Beatrice Howard. She was the *jewel* of London. Frustrated by his lack of interest, Beatrice had taken to mocking Blythe. Sneering at the young ladies who sought his favor. Poking fun at his intelligence. Anything to get him to notice her.

What a self-serving twit she'd been.

Beatrice halted, bending her right leg several times to stretch the muscle. A hot bath was in order the moment she returned home.

Horrible wasn't a strong enough word to describe the creature she'd once been. Beatrice had a host of regrets. So many, she'd taken to writing them down lest she forget.

Andromeda, Duchess of Granby was on that list.

There were others, of course. The poor younger son of a marquess who had a very pronounced overbite. He'd reminded her of a rabbit. She'd mocked him, in front of his friends, at a ball, and he'd tried to harm himself after. Or Miss Elkins, a slightly plump young girl who had only ever wanted to be Beatrice's friend and been treated unkindly for her efforts. The lady's maid, Mattie May, who'd burned the side of Beatrice's neck with curling tongs because she was new and terrified of Beatrice's mother, Lady Foxwood. She'd been sacked without a reference.

"The list of my sins is never ending, Cicero."

Unexpected accidents have a way of putting things into perspective. Pinned beneath Castlemare's second best carriage, half-drowned, her blood flowing into the river from lacerations on her face and neck, Beatrice had had quite a lot of time to think. Mostly about how she'd ended up as the Duchess of Castlemare because she'd been unable to admit defeat gracefully after being tossed over by the Duke of Granby for Andromeda Barrington.

Andromeda, the woman whom Beatrice had tried to destroy with gossip and vile innuendo. Whose reputation she'd gleefully shredded between her fingertips because Beatrice had felt *slighted*. Andromeda, who, if *she* were pinned beneath a bloody carriage, would have her entire family searching for her.

No one had looked for Beatrice.

Andromeda had been the first name Beatrice put in her ledger.

The small book, bound in green leather, sat in her parlor even now, careful notes in Beatrice's hand, written within the margins. It was how the Chiddon's lone church had been repaired, as well as the vicarage. Both had been to atone for Miss Elkins, who had married shortly after Beatrice and subsequently died in childbirth. She hadn't even attended the wedding, though Miss Elkins had invited her.

Beatrice sucked in her breath as a cramp struck her leg, tightening the muscles of her thigh. She bit her lip, waiting for it to fade. Since her accident, riding usually made her right leg ache, as did walking a long distance. But she refused to give either activity up. She had to get around somehow, and Beatrice no longer cared to ride in a carriage.

"Ah, there we are, Cicero. I thought I missed it."

The fallen tree, the one Beatrice had been looking for, finally came into view. The large maple had toppled against an outcropping of rock but at an angle which raised the trunk high enough that she could scale up the length and mount Cicero without assistance. Better to ride the remainder of the distance than attempt to walk. If she didn't return home soon, Mrs. Lovington, Beatrice's overly protective house-keeper, was likely to send out half of Chiddon to find her.

Admonishing Cicero to stay put, Beatrice placed her horse on one side of the tree trunk. Lifting her skirts with one hand, she forced herself up the trunk, groaning out loud at the stretch of her leg. But once upright, Beatrice easily climbed into the saddle. She settled and took the reins.

Branches snapped to her left, causing her to twist in the saddle. She scanned the trees and heavy brush but saw no one on the path.

"Only a fox." She patted Cicero. "We saw one just the other day; do you recall? Or possibly a deer. Either way, no more running off. You should be braver than that."

Giving Cicero a nudge, she pointed him in the direction of Beresford Cottage, dreaming of her warm bath and the welcome solitude of her own company.

❧ 3 ❧

Ellis watched Beatrice from behind the thick bramble. She'd been following the same path for the last half hour, which called into focus her obvious familiarity with the area. Beatrice had not been limping when she'd dismissed him in the meadow, but she was now. Every so often, she stopped and stretched or rubbed a hand up and down her thigh. The fall from her horse must have strained her muscles.

When Ellis had turned Dante away from Beatrice, he'd resolved that if he had the misfortune of seeing her again, he would merely ignore Her Ducal Snottiness and ride on. But not a moment later, Ellis found himself turning back to follow Beatrice. He told himself it was out of concern for her safety because she was riding without a groom or her husband. Anything could happen to a lone woman in the woods of Hampshire, and he wasn't about to desert a lady who might need his help, even if she *was* Beatrice Howard.

When she finally stopped before the trunk of a large tree lying on its side, Ellis moved Dante behind a thick over-

24

growth of what appeared to be blackberry bushes. He could see her purpose; she meant to get back on her horse.

Why didn't she merely ask me?

She grunted as she scaled the trunk, then vaulted into the saddle with a low sound of pain. Beatrice clutched the saddle, bent over the neck of her horse, her body moving as she breathed, before finally straightening.

Injured and too stubborn to admit she needed help.

Dante moved a fraction of an inch, snapping a thick branch beneath his hoof.

Beatrice paused, looking over her shoulder to search the thick forest, but she didn't see Ellis. After another moment, she nudged her mount down the path. The sun had climbed higher, dappling the trees and forest floor with circles of light.

Ellis hesitated only a moment before following.

He had nothing better to do that morning than follow Beatrice, and he was curious. And the least he could do, though she wouldn't appreciate his thoughtfulness, was to ensure she didn't fall off her horse.

He thought back to what he knew of Castlemare and whether the duke had property nearby. Or Lord and Lady Foxwood, Beatrice's parents. Sadly, he couldn't recall. Castlemare was a gentleman with whom Ellis had never been personally acquainted, nor had he ever wished to be. The man was the very *epitome* of ducal entitlement—so superior he rarely spoke to anyone he considered beneath him, which was nearly all of London. Ellis supposed that made him a perfect match for Beatrice Howard, who'd always thought so highly of herself.

Turning her tiny nose up at him. Disparaging Ellis at every turn. Coldly decrying him as some sort of mindless peacock.

A tingle, arousal again, shot along his thighs.

A succubus. *That* was Beatrice Howard. Inflaming any male, particularly Ellis, with an overwhelming lust which could only be expunged by an excess of sexual pleasure. There could be no other reason for this unnatural desire he had for her.

After another half hour of following Beatrice, the trees thinned out, and Ellis could see the roof and chimney of a house. It was nothing one would expect a duke and duchess to reside in, no matter how temporary. The cozy two story stone cottage looked of decent size, larger than Ellis's own residence, with a well-tended gravel drive and a path that probably led to the stables. Wisteria grew up the side of the house, purpled blooms dripping down to cover one window. The overall effect was one of welcome and comfort. Inviting.

Unlike either Beatrice or her duke. It had to belong to an acquaintance.

Ellis took Dante around the other side of the house where he could spy on Beatrice from the safety of the trees.

She rode right up to the front door, smiling as a groom or footman, though he wasn't wearing livery, came forward to help her from Cicero. He carefully placed her on her feet, looking down at her with concern, far more than a servant would usually express.

Beatrice shook her head and tapped the young man lightly on the arm with a smile. Limping up the steps, a gasp of relief left her when the door was thrown open to reveal a tall, big-boned woman wearing a lace cap. She took Beatrice's arm and led her inside, admonishing her the entire time. The door shut behind with a kick of the older woman's foot.

Familiarity with servants. Even if she hadn't been a duchess, the Beatrice Ellis had known would have never allowed such behavior. But here, there was no ducal livery. No butler. No sign of a duke at all. Just an imposing housekeeper in a lace cap who looked as if she could pull a plow across a field without oxen.

Ellis had never known Beatrice to acknowledge a servant, let alone touch their arm or allow them to put their hands on her. Lord and Lady Foxwood had always had a low opinion of their staff, which they'd passed on to their daughter—something Ellis had easily observed back in London. And Castlemare—well, he certainly wouldn't allow such familiarity if he were around to witness it.

Ellis walked his horse around the back of the house, taking in the well-tended kitchen garden. A bench sat a short distance away beneath a spray of wisteria, bordered by manicured beds filled with roses. Everything else was rather wild and not at all extravagant.

Which didn't suit Beatrice at all.

The click of a pistol had Ellis coming to a halt. He immediately put up his hands but didn't turn.

"Don't move," a grouchy rasp came from behind him. "Unless you want a hole blown clean through that expensive coat."

❧ 4 ❧

Beatrice sat back in her bath, nearly crying out at the sensation of the hot water against her aching muscles. "Oh, that feels lovely."

Peg, her lady's maid, bustled forward, sprinkling another handful of herbs into the water as more steam rose in the air. "There, there, Your Grace. Just close your eyes and relax. I've warmed the ointment —"

"I'll smell like one of the horses when they sprain a leg." Beatrice closed her eyes. "Can Jasper not make the salve a bit less . . . bitter smelling?"

"I don't think so, Your Grace. While you might mind the scent of comfrey, it doesn't seem to bother the horses." Peg started to unravel the plait holding Beatrice's hair, efficiently pinning the mass of curls to the top of Beatrice's head. "Get some of the water against your shoulder and neck. It will help."

Beatrice kept her eyes closed, not wanting to see the maid's reaction to the line of scars decorating the right side of her body. Not that it mattered. Peg had seen the damage any number of times, had even massaged the muscles of Beatrice's

28

hip and thigh. The rock lining a riverbed was surprisingly sharp. Pebbles, if one lays on them long enough, could embed in one's skin.

Had Beatrice been a soldier, she could have claimed the right side of her body had been hit with grapeshot. But it had been nothing so dramatic, only the shifting of the carriage along the riverbed with Beatrice trapped beneath, dragging her painfully along the rough edges of rock. After a time, her side had gone numb, and she'd floated, half in and half out of the water. Swaying with her mouth tipped up, no longer caring if she drowned.

Hideous. Like a lizard or another equally foul creature.

THE PADS OF BEATRICE'S FINGERS PRESSED INTO THE SIDES of the copper tub as she recalled her husband's bland assessment of the tragedy that had befallen her. The worst sort of catastrophe for a woman whose only value was in her stunning looks.

Castlemare, blunt to a fault, hadn't shied away from expressing his opinion of Beatrice's appearance. No sympathy had been offered. Not an ounce of worry. His main concern had been his own distaste that he was now saddled with a ruined, hideous wife, viewing her with the same sneer as he would a fallen souffle. He'd given no thought to the fact Beatrice had been pinned beneath his second-best carriage at the edge of a riverbed for the better part of two days. No alarm at her disappearance had even been raised from the ducal estate.

Two days. Two days until Thomas, the poor driver, had been found, finally alerting someone to the fact that an accident had occurred. His broken body had floated downstream, dislodged after a day by the rushing water, along with some of Beatrice's garments and her valise. Poor Thomas, bruised and bloodied, had been discovered with one of her best petticoats covering his face.

That reminded her. It was time to check on Thomas's elderly parents. His father liked to read. She would surprise him with another box of books from London. Anonymously, of course. It was the least Beatrice could do in addition to the monthly sum her solicitor sent.

Beatrice shivered; though the water was warm and a fire crackled merrily in the grate, she instructed Peg to add another log to the blaze.

The scars, most rounded, others jagged streaks, marred the right side of Beatrice's face beginning at the corner of her eye, then skirting along the edge of her hairline, cheek, and ear before twisting along the nape of her neck to her shoulder and ribs.

Beatrice would no longer draw the admiration of every male in the room. No gentleman wanted a woman whose skin resembled a gnarled tree.

Or a lizard, as Castlemare had so charmingly put it.

Beatrice had once delighted in gowns specifically designed to showcase her bosom. She'd practiced for hours under her mother's careful tutelage, perfecting the art of bending, just so, to draw the male eye to the deep valley between her breasts. Her necklines were much higher now, nearly up to her chin. There would *never* again be a baring of her shoulders, let alone her neck. She didn't even have her right earlobe any longer. No more sapphires would be dangling from her ears.

She inhaled steam and herbs.

Things were much worse the farther you went down the right side of her body, a jagged trail which led to even greater misery. A piece of the carriage's axle had stabbed her upper thigh, and though it wasn't deep, it was long. The axle had left a stream of splinters as it sliced open her skirts and skin.

It had taken the physician summoned by Castlemare's butler several days to dig out the bits of wood and rock from her body—an excruciating ordeal no matter the amount of laudanum pushed down her throat.

A knock sounded.

Peg wiped her hands before cracking the door. Stepping into the hall, the maid shut the door firmly behind her. A whispered discussion followed between Peg and what sounded like Mrs. Lovington, but Beatrice couldn't make it out. It was probably something to do with the dinner menu. Her entire staff seemed overly concerned with what was served at a duchess's table.

Beatrice didn't care. She'd said so several times. In addition to Mrs. Lovington and Peg, there was Mr. Lovington, her housekeeper's husband, who kept the grounds as her man-of-all-work, Jasper, the lone groom, and a girl named Susan, who assisted Mrs. Lovington in the kitchen and helped keep the cottage smelling of beeswax. They all liked lamb, and Beatrice didn't mind it on occasion. But still, her small staff took pains to ensure her comfort, and for that, she was grateful. They had become her family. Loyal and protective to a fault. Far kinder than Beatrice deserved.

Lady Foxwood had instructed Beatrice from an early age to *never* thank a servant, though it was acceptable for her to acknowledge their efforts from time to time. She'd cautioned against being too grateful, though, as a servant should not be congratulated for merely fulfilling their purpose. They would eventually overstep. Take advantage.

Her mother often gave the very worst advice.

The door shut, and Peg returned to the fire where she was warming a towel for Beatrice.

"I'll survive if she's set on making lamb tonight. Honestly, I will, Peg. It isn't my favorite, but I don't actively dislike lamb. I know *you* like it. As does Jasper. And Mr. Lovington.

There was little formality here because Beatrice didn't demand it. She'd been too ill when first arriving at Beresford Cottage, and now, well, it seemed ridiculous when she considered the staff to be more her family than she did Lord and Lady Foxwood. At times, she joined them in the kitchen to eat, but only rarely. It was awkward for all involved to have a duchess at the table no matter how informal.

"I need to review my ledger. I can do so while dining." She often did, making her notes with a glass of wine or brandy at her elbow.

Mattie May, the maid Beatrice had sacked—unfairly—so long ago had finally been located. She had employed a solicitor specifically to seek out Mattie and others she'd wronged. The work confused the Honorable Mr. Bush, but Beatrice paid him well to not ask too many questions. When he did inquire, Beatrice need only remind him she was a duchess.

The title came in handy at times.

At any rate, she still hadn't updated her ledger regarding this new information about Mattie. She would be happy to do so over her meal.

"That wasn't about dinner, Your Grace, though on behalf of the staff, we all appreciate your willingness to allow lamb when it isn't among your favorites."

"I don't dislike lamb, Peg. I only prefer lighter fare. Chicken. Pheasant. Capon. What was it about, then, if not the meal?"

Peg shifted her weight from one foot to the other. "Mrs. Lovington came to relay a message from Mr. Lovington. Something about a gentleman on horseback, lurking around the back gardens. He says he's a villain of some sort."

"A villain?"

"Well, who else would be sneaking about the gardens of a

duchess, Your Grace?" Peg puffed up to her full height. "Mr. Lovington fetched his pistol promptly."

How intriguing. There had never been an intruder at Beresford Cottage. Nor a guest save Melinda Farthing, but that was beside the point. Beatrice did keep a fine stable, though it wasn't large. Silver and fine bone china filled the house. A few marble busts of . . . well, *someone*. Those might be worth a pound or two. But the tiny village of Chiddon was so far off the main road and her home so remote, she couldn't imagine anyone intentionally coming here—

Beatrice's eyes popped open. She sat straight up in the tub, water splashing all over the floor. "Dressed like a gentleman?" *Dressed like an earl.*

"Wearing an expensive coat, according to Mr. Lovington, and sitting atop a fine horse. Probably stolen."

"Undoubtedly."

"Mr. Lovington escorted the villain to the stables."

"To do what, exactly?" Beatrice raised a brow. "Chiddon has no constable."

"Well, he's nefar—" A wrinkle appeared between Peg's brows. "Netfar—"

"Nefarious," Beatrice finished, vastly amused by this entire affair.

"Exactly, Your Grace. What sort of man lurks at the back of a house with no intention of knocking on the door? Peeking in the windows and such? I'm sure he meant to sneak into the kitchens and rob Mrs. Lovington."

"Doubtful." Mrs. Lovington was built like a prize fighter and would probably have brained him with a cast iron kettle. The nefarious intruder couldn't be anyone other than the Earl of Blythe. He'd probably charmed Mr. Lovington out of shooting him. She'd let him stew for a bit in the stables. A little horse dung would do Blythe good.

Beatrice drew her hand through the water.

Was it only curiosity that had drawn Blythe to her door? Interesting that her scathing manner toward the earl hadn't dissuaded him at all. She was well-versed in the malice of society, how dealing in secrets and innuendo could help destroy a person. Beatrice was guilty of having done so herself.

A bead of water rolled off her finger and onto the floor.

Blythe had no right to invade her sanctuary or pry into her affairs no matter how splendid he looked in a pair of riding breeches. The last thing she wanted was for Blythe to return to London with tales of the reclusive scarred duchess he'd come across in Chiddon. Could he really not know Castlemare was dead? Or that Beatrice no longer flitted about London?

"Perhaps our intruder is merely confused and bears no ill intent. Far more likely he's an acquaintance of Castlemare's who assumes I'll put him up for the night out of courtesy or invite him to dine at my table."

"Looking to take advantage of a widow? For shame," Peg said with a mutinous look. "All for a bit of lamb?"

Ah, Peg. I wouldn't trade you for the world.

"Please inform Mr. Lovington to put this unknown gentleman back on his horse and escort him to the road. Make sure it is impressed upon him not to return as he is not welcome."

Blythe would be incredibly annoyed at being tossed out. Served him right. Hopefully Beatrice wouldn't have to do so again.

"Yes, Your Grace." Peg bobbed before racing off to do her bidding. "We'll make sure he doesn't trouble you further."

5

Ellis whistled a merry tune as he strolled to Chiddon's only tavern. He'd grown bored with his own company, rambling about his father's old hunting lodge where he'd taken up residence. A tavern was sure to boast at least a tankard of ale and a conversation— likely the only sort of amusement to be found in Chiddon. Though he had seen a pamphlet nailed to a tree announcing an upcoming festival of sorts in the main square, but otherwise, the tiny village was devoid of entertainment. There were certainly no ducal estates nearby. No gentry to speak of. Only endless farms dotting the horizon interspersed with swaths of thick forest.

Indeed, there was nothing in Chiddon that should interest Beatrice Howard.

The gruff older gentleman who'd prodded him into an empty stall in Beatrice's stable hadn't cared when Ellis had protested and claimed he was an acquaintance of the Duchess of Castlemare. Nor had the grizzled mastiff been impressed when Ellis had informed him of his title. After Ellis had been pacing about in the straw for an hour, the man had returned, still waving a bloody pistol, and escorted Ellis and Dante back to the road where he instructed Ellis not to return.

The entire incident was annoying.

He'd gone directly back to the hunting lodge, or rather merely the *lodge*, since there was no hunting being done. Fishing for trout was more what Ellis enjoyed, though he hadn't been doing much of that lately either. Settling himself in a comfortable chair with a glass of brandy, he'd contemplated the mystery that was the Duchess of Castlemare.

The duke wasn't in Chiddon, that much was clear. Castlemare's name had been bandied about during Ellis's brief stay in London, but he'd paid little attention. Beatrice hadn't been mentioned at all.

He really shouldn't care one way or another.

Yes, Beatrice held an unnatural fascination for him, all of it entirely of a sexual nature. But he didn't *like* her. Never had. But liking a woman wasn't necessary to bed her. If that was a requirement, half the titles in London wouldn't have heirs. Whether she and Castlemare lived apart wasn't Ellis's concern.

It did, however, present an opportunity.

Ellis had yet to meet an estranged or unhappy wife who hadn't succumbed to his charms. Beatrice presented a unique challenge.

Still, her disdain for him had been palpable. Perversely, that only made Ellis desire her more.

At any rate, the possibility of seducing Beatrice Howard was far more enjoyable to contemplate than a future with Lady Anabeth Swift. He couldn't even remember what the chit looked like, just a fleeting vision of vaguely pretty features.

Mother's letter, demanding Ellis's return to London, still sat discarded on the table back at the lodge. Lady Blythe was beside herself. Anabeth was so sought after as a bride, she was being pursued by a host of suitors and would soon be forced to make a choice, though Anabeth and her mother, Lady Pierce, preferred Lord Blythe.

Ellis had flicked the letter aside as soon as he'd read it and poured himself another brandy. Mother made such dramatic threats.

Walking into the dim ale-soaked interior of the tavern, Ellis was greeted by a broad-faced man with a fringe of hair circling a nearly bald pate. "Welcome to The Pickled Duck," the man said with a flourish, directing him toward a scarred and battered length of wood where Ellis settled on a stool. "I am Gates, proprietor of The Pickled Duck, and a finer establishment you won't find in all of Chiddon."

The Pickled Duck was the only such establishment in Chiddon, but Ellis decided not to point this out to the exceptionally cheery Gates.

"Blythe," Ellis said simply.

Gates nodded, a question in his eyes.

"I'm visiting the area for a time. My father kept an old hunting lodge just on the other side of Chiddon."

"Ah. The previous earl." Gates nodded politely. "Met him once tromping about the woods. He wasn't much of an outdoorsman, begging your pardon, my lord. Liked to fish a bit, as I recall."

"As do I. Stabbing a worm at the end of a hook is the most savage I'll become, Gates. The wild game around Chiddon have no need to worry. I prefer a good roast to venison, at any rate."

"Very good, milord," Gates replied. "Not much good at hunting myself. The despair of my father. I'm much better at ale. Will you have a tankard?"

"I will." The Pickled Duck could rival the finest gentleman's club in London. A game of cards was taking place in a far corner, along with a heated discussion between two young men who appeared to be arm wrestling. "What is that delicious aroma floating toward me, Gates?" Ellis's stomach rumbled.

A tankard was placed before Ellis, the foam thick and delicious. "Rabbit stew, milord. My wife sets the snares least you think I've misled you about my skill." Gates gave him a toothy grin. "Of which I have none. Shall I bring you a bowl?" At Ellis's nod, Gates bustled away, returning with a steaming bowl and a hunk of bread. "Mrs. Gates is a marvel with rabbit, among other things." He wiggled a pair of bushy brows at Ellis. "The stew is a favorite of our duchess."

Ellis picked up his spoon, dipping it into the thick gravy steaming from his bowl. Hard not to miss how Gates referred to Beatrice as *our* duchess. There was a reverence in his tone usually reserved for martyrs and saints.

"The Duchess of Castlemare?"

"The very one," Gates assured him. "What other duchess is there in Chiddon?"

That was probably true. "Her Grace enjoys rabbit stew at The Pickled Duck?"

"And the occasional meat pie. Doesn't care for lamb." Gates frowned. "Not sure why." He shrugged. "When the duchess comes to check on the brewing, she often stays to sup," Gates said with little modesty before lowering his voice. "We're partners in a business venture, me and Her Grace."

"I see." The idea was as ridiculous as the thought of Beatrice tucking into a bowl of rabbit stew.

"The brewing of ale and cider, my lord. Her Grace is most interested in the process. I brew the best ale to be found in the entire county. Everyone says so. The duchess agrees and is making inquiries to sell my ale outside Chiddon. Discreetly, of course. It would hardly do for word to get out a duchess was dirtying her hands at The Pickled Duck." Gates looked chagrined. "I may have spoken out of turn."

"Not to worry, Gates. I won't say a word. I would never disparage a duchess." Ellis raised his tankard. "Nor you, for that matter." The ale was quite good. And if Gates hadn't been nearing sixty, bald and with a paunch, Ellis might have assumed Beatrice had taken him as a lover, because he could think of no other reason why she would ever be involved in a brewing enterprise. "And the duke? Does he approve of Her Grace's hobby?"

The furrow between Gates's eyes deepened. "There is no duke about, milord. Only the duchess. Her Grace is a widow, milord."

Impossible. He'd heard Castlemare's name in London, and he'd sounded very much alive.

Gates frowned, giving him the appearance of an annoyed pug. "Perhaps you've confused our duchess with another?"

What a thought. Two Beatrices terrorizing England would signal the end of days.

According to Gates, the Castlemare who had wed Beatrice Howard was dead. It had never occurred to Ellis that the Castlemare he had heard mentioned in town was not Beatrice's husband but his *heir*. He'd never inquired because . . . well, Ellis tried not to think overmuch about Beatrice Howard, and he'd been somewhat preoccupied with escaping the machinations of Lady Blythe.

"My mistake, Gates. The dowager duchess—"

"Her Grace don't like to be referred to as a dowager. Best not to use that term around her." Gates tilted his chin in warning.

"I see. I meant no disrespect. I only hadn't realized. I've been gone from England for a time and only returned a month or so ago." Ellis had an odd compulsion to explain himself to Gates, something no proper earl would have done. "An honest mistake."

Lady Blythe would reach for the smelling salts if she knew.

Gates appeared mollified and poured out another ale for Ellis.

Beatrice's reaction to the mention of Castlemare now made much more sense. She'd assumed, incorrectly, that Ellis had been taunting her. Or that he was merely a nitwit. She didn't seem to think him especially intelligent.

"I confess, your ale is wonderful. I can see why Her Grace would be interested. And the stew." Ellis gave a pat to his stomach. "My compliments to Mrs. Gates."

Gates beamed. "Thank you, milord. I'm rather proud of my ale." A discussion commenced with Gates which consisted of the aspects of malting, barley, and the like, all of which Ellis found mildly interesting.

"And though there's plenty of wheat and barley grown in Chiddon," Gates continued, "if you want your flours and such ground, you have to go to Overton."

"Overton?" That was a distance away from Chiddon. "Why?" Ellis took another sip of his ale. Gates really was on to something. Ellis had rarely tasted an ale so crisp. "Truly, Gates. This is finer than any I've tasted in London."

"Half and half, milord." Gates nodded to Ellis's tankard. "It's a mix of bitter ale and porter. But I can't give away the specifics."

"I would be distressed if you did," Ellis agreed.

Gates poured out a mug for himself before launching into another discussion of ales, stouts, and porters before pausing. "Oh, but you asked why we must go to Overton. Completely forgot. I lose my head while talking about my ale."

Ellis was enjoying himself immensely. This was far better than tramping about the cobwebs in his father's hunting lodge and carving unrecognizable animals.

"All Chiddon's wheat must go to Overton to be ground

because there's no mill. Not here. Or rather there is," he whispered. "But it is not in use."

Odd. Having grown up in the country, Ellis was well aware of the importance of a mill to a community. His father had often taken Ellis to the mill near Larchmont to watch the steady turn of the wheel as it ground the wheat.

"Because of the *murders*." Gates dared a peek at the table in the corner as if he didn't want to be overheard. "Terrible thing. The Mandrell family. A lover's quarrel is how it started. Mandrell killed his wife's lover beneath the grist stone of the mill. Lots of folks left Chiddon after that. Who wants their wheat ground on the same stone that..." His words trailed off.

"Understandable," Ellis agreed.

"Years went by, and Chiddon became quite deserted, milord. My wife and I nearly had to close The Pickled Duck. But then Her Grace came to Chiddon. Grieving her husband and the like. Terrible thing. She wanted privacy, and we gave it to her." He poked a thumb at his chest. "Vicar Farthing followed her about, helping her mourn, you see, and Her Grace fixed the church for his kindness. And the vicarage. Both had fallen into ruin after the last vicar got himself killed."

Chiddon. Hotbed of intrigue. Ellis never would have guessed. "How did the previous vicar perish, if I may ask?"

"The grist stone. He was Mrs. Mandrell's lover." The thick eyebrows above Gates's eyes raised into the line of his nonexistent hair. "Mandrell drowned the missus in the mill pond after grinding up the vicar. Her body stuck on the wheel, turning round and round. I suppose Mandrell was sorry after murdering them both, for he hung himself after, at the mill."

Intrigue and *murder*. Chiddon was no sleepy hamlet.

"I can see why the mill would have become abandoned after such tragedy. But surely—"

"Been nearly ten years. No one will take it up. The mill, I

mean. When Farthing arrived and saw the state of the church and vicarage, we all thought he'd go back the way he'd come. Had to give sermons in the square." Gates jerked his chin to an unseen location outside The Pickled Duck. "Because the church wasn't safe. Pews rotted. Roof falling in. The vicarage had rats the size of dogs living in it."

Ellis tried not to grin at the exaggeration.

"But the duchess fixed it all. Hired the stonemasons herself. One of the stone masons tried to cheat her, and she fired him on the spot. Snapped her riding crop at him after he threatened her."

Now that *did* sound like Beatrice, but nothing else. Saving a church? Restoring a vicarage? Brewing with Mr. Gates?

"She's had four of the abandoned shops down the street fixed up nice, and now Chiddon has an apothecary, a proper butcher, a cheesemonger, and a grocer."

"Her Grace is quite busy."

"Have you heard about the festival, milord? Last year was our first, but it won't be our last. Held right outside The Pickled Duck. Her Grace said we must draw folks back to Chiddon. I provide the ale and cider. There's meat cooked on giant spits. Peddlers and their wagons. Had a fiddler all the way from Babbington last year. Lots of dancing and trysting. There's a big feast set up on the lawn, free to all who wish to share a meal. Lots of pies. Courtesy of the Duchess of Castlemare."

"The dowager duchess," Ellis said absently, wondering how on earth he and Gates were both speaking of the same woman.

"I did tell you Her Grace don't care to be referred to as a dowager," Gates said with a pointed look.

"I'd forgotten." Lady Beatrice Howard had single-handedly become the patron saint of Chiddon, breathing life into a village struggling to survive. Perhaps doing so had kept her grief at bay after the death of Castlemare, but that reasoning didn't sit right with Ellis. Castlemare had hardly been the sort to inspire such emotion in a woman. From what Ellis recalled, the duke had been a demanding, demeaning man. Coldly superior. Cruel. The woman Gates described with such reverence bore no resemblance to the spiteful, gossiping harpy Ellis had once known. When Gates mentioned that Beatrice and the vicar's wife were thick as thieves, Ellis nearly spit out his ale.

Thanking Gates for the conversation, the excellent ale, and the stew, Ellis tossed him several coins and headed outside to Dante. He wanted to see Beatrice's handiwork himself. The church and vicarage were an excellent place to start.

6

"More tea, Your Grace?"

"I wish you'd call me by name, Melinda." Beatrice pushed her teacup across the table. "Seems ridiculous to address me so properly." She barely recalled she was a duchess at times, which was strange given how long she'd sought to become one. From the time she was a child, Lord and Lady Foxwood had groomed Beatrice for nothing else.

A sigh left her at the thought of her parents.

"It isn't proper." Melinda Farthing shot Beatrice a scandalized look. "Vicar Farthing would have a fit of apoplexy if he overheard me address you so informally. I suppose that wouldn't be entirely unfortunate, but then who would lead the flock in Chiddon, hmm?"

Vicar Farthing was *always* about to have a fit of apoplexy. He was so staid, so washed of any sort of humor, Beatrice couldn't fathom how the droll, slightly brazen woman before her had wed him. She suspected it was quite a tale, but as close as they were, her friend had so far refused to reveal anything about what had brought her to Vicar Farthing and Chiddon.

Beatrice didn't push. Everyone was entitled to their secrets.

"Mrs. Farthing," Beatrice admonished, the amusement bubbling between her lips. "The good vicar would rally, I'm sure. He wouldn't dare disappoint a duchess."

"No, indeed. The slightest distress from you lobbed in his direction, and the good vicar finds himself quite despondent."

The vicar was a fawning sycophant who had pleaded with his superiors to be sent *anywhere* besides Chiddon, but to no avail. Farthing had been here some time before Beatrice's arrival, whining at the fact he must give his sermons in the grass and not a proper church. He'd been sent to Chiddon by Castlemare, banished by the duke just as Beatrice had been. Probably for some minor infraction, such as not bowing low enough. Or daring to offer an opinion. God forbid, Farthing may have made eye contact with Castlemare.

I once found such things of utter importance.

"You frowned during church last week, Your Grace, and he spent the entire evening recounting each interaction you might have had which would account for your grievous mood toward him." Melinda giggled. "I didn't have the heart to tell him it was merely a headache brought on by sampling too much of Gates's ale the previous day."

"I am Gates's patron," Beatrice said primly, trying not to laugh. "If I am to offer my good name to his cause, I must sample the wares."

"I quite agree." Melinda lifted her teacup to her lips, eyes dancing with delight before glancing at the vicarage. "The vicar is working on his sermon inside, which I'm sure will be full of fire and brimstone with references to enjoying oneself too fully while having tea."

Melinda spoke of her husband with practiced tolerance

but loathed his attempts to curry favor with Beatrice. Thin chest puffed out like a rooster, Farthing would spot Beatrice in the village and fawn over her until she wanted to slap at him. He hoped Beatrice would use her influence to find him another post. One with prestige, unlike Chiddon.

Little did Farthing know, Beatrice possessed no power or influence outside of Chiddon. Castlemare's family and his younger brother, who had inherited the title upon her husband's death, had never liked her. Their joy at having Beatrice gone from their midst had not gone unnoticed. The Foxwoods had likewise abandoned her shortly after Castlemare's banishment. Her place in society, once assured, had faded away. She was not missed. Not inquired after. Her friends, more hangers-on, had deserted Beatrice in an instant once they'd realized she was no longer of any use.

Poor Farthing.

Melinda sat back and picked up another biscuit, biting into it with relish. "Please thank Mrs. Lovington. I fear my baking skills are sorely lacking, which I realize nearly every time you bring me a proper tin of biscuits."

"Melinda." Beatrice traced the pattern of lace on the cloth covering the small table between them. "Are you familiar with the Earl of Blythe?" She'd been meaning to ask her friend all during tea. If there was an earl in Chiddon, a powerful one, it seemed impossible Vicar Farthing wouldn't know of it.

"The Earl of Blythe?" Melinda frowned. "Sounds rather pompous. Not at all the sort of lord a poor vicar's wife would associate with unless, of course, the earl was handsome and insisted on becoming acquainted." She winked at Beatrice. "It wouldn't hurt if he possessed a full head of hair matched with a striking pair of cheekbones."

Vicar Farthing possessed neither.

Melinda, at times, reminded Beatrice quite a bit of Andromeda Barrington. An uncommon observation given that Andromeda would never have been Beatrice's friend. But both women spoke their mind. Expressed opinions, unpopular or not. Possessed a bold wit and a bravado Beatrice often wished was hers.

She had admired Andromeda *and* been jealous of her.

I was quite terrible.

The first *true* friend Beatrice had ever had was Melinda. The young ladies she'd known before had merely wished to be in her orbit, like tiny planets revolving around the sun Beatrice had once arrogantly imagined herself to be. They repeated her every thought. Agreed with her opinions. Were more than happy to turn on each other if Beatrice encouraged it. Rebecca, Lady Carstairs, was a perfect example.

"Melinda, you are a married woman. A vicar's wife. You should be above such musings."

"The good Lord gave me eyes and expects me to use them." Melinda sipped her tea.

Beatrice laughed gaily. "You are terrible."

"Terrible I may be, Your Grace. But without me, you'd be reduced to sipping tea with Mrs. Tidwell and her herd of boys. Seven, at last count. You'd leave every visit with crumbs in your hair or a frog hiding in your skirts. Besides, there is nothing wrong with admiring the beauty around me. Even yours."

Beatrice's lips hovered over the edge of her teacup. "I am no longer beautiful."

"That is a matter of opinion."

Melinda was the only person in Chiddon, save Peg and Mrs. Lovington, who had seen what lay beneath Beatrice's thick golden hair, tied tightly with ribbon and pinned to the right side of her head. After sharing a nip of brandy one cold day—more than one—and feeling full of pity for herself, Beatrice had—rather *dramatically*, according to Melinda—exposed her damaged cheek and neck. Closing her eyes, she'd waited, hands trembling, for Melinda to shriek in horror as Lady Foxwood had done upon seeing her daughter's injuries.

Melinda had put down her brandy on a side table in Beatrice's parlor. She'd peered closely at Beatrice's cheek and shoulder, tracing one nail over a jagged scar. After asking if the skin stiffened or pained Beatrice overmuch, Melinda had suggested a combination of herbs for the bath and the use of the same ointment Jasper used on Cicero.

Then Melinda had calmly gone back to her brandy.

"Buy an assortment of ribbons, Your Grace. Wear your hair as you like. No one will question a duchess." She'd taken Beatrice's shaking fingers in her own. *"It may not seem so, but Castlemare did you a great service in sending you to Chiddon. I do not believe it to be punishment but providence. A second chance of sorts."*

The memory fell away as the sunlight of the garden warmed the tip of Beatrice's nose. Whatever would she have done without Melinda?

"I'm assuming you are acquainted with this Lord Blythe?" Melinda questioned, waving away a fly who was invading their tea tray.

"Years ago. Before." Beatrice trailed her fingers along her cheek. "We are barely acquainted. We rarely, if ever, spoke. But Blythe and I revolved in the same circles. Were invited to the same events. I saw him often at balls and the like."

And at a disastrous house party where Blythe had borne witness to her humiliation.

"He admired you." Melinda bit into another biscuit. It was likely she'd eat the entire tin.

"No, definitely not. If anything, he found me—" Beatrice searched for the right word. "Loathsome. Blythe is quite handsome. Golden, if you will. His manner is that of an overindulged Labrador whom everyone adores. Young ladies, upon spying him, would wave their fans in a furious way to keep themselves from fainting at the sight of such magnificence."

"Hmm." Melinda's brows drew together.

"Not me, mind you," Beatrice assured her. "But plenty of others."

"I'm surprised you noticed, surrounded, as you were, by your own throng of admirers, Your Grace. At least from what you've told me of your time in London. Did it matter that Lord Blythe paid you little attention?"

It had. *It did.*

"You must remember, Melinda. I was a stunning *jewel* of a woman. A diamond."

Melinda rolled her eyes. "Diamonds are rather common. I often think of you as topaz."

"Common or not, Blythe didn't so much as glance in my direction. I was *incredibly* spoiled. Very sure of my place in the world. Blythe ignoring me brought out the worst of my character because I felt it unjustified. He was only an earl."

A magnificent one.

"To salvage my wounded pride, I whispered unkind things about him, always when he was certain to overhear. That he was a preening peacock. An unintelligent rake who spouted poetry or other romantic drivel. His dislike for me could be felt across a room, all while Blythe treated everyone else he met with kindness."

"How dare he." Melinda's teeth snapped on a biscuit.

"Finally, after months of such behavior, our mutual animosity erupted in a rather spectacular way at a house party."

"A house party?" Melinda leaned forward. "You must describe every detail to me. The dresses. The delightful games." She gave a sigh. "Scavenger hunts where a gentleman partners you merely so he can steal a kiss. What?" She grabbed another biscuit. "I am fond of romantic novels."

"A house party isn't nearly as much fun as you imagine; at least, this one was not. My parents shadowed my every move, dictating to whom I might speak and how I might behave. The other young women present found me dislikable, which, I must assure you, I was. I had to be perfect no matter the cost."

"That does sound awful."

The house party at The Barrow had been a lifetime ago. Truly, Beatrice felt like the events had happened to someone else. "I failed to bring a gentleman up to scratch." She tilted her head. "He'd expressed a great deal of interest in me, and a marriage proposal was thought to be forthcoming." The unending disappointment of Lord and Lady Foxwood, stabbing Beatrice when Granby had failed to propose at the end of the house party, had only been made worse when Granby had chosen Andromeda Barrington instead. Her mother had shaken Beatrice like a rag doll. Father had refused to look at her, wondering out loud if he would be mocked upon their return to London.

I could not be more ashamed of you. What an utter and complete failure.

"Your Grace?" Melinda gently touched Beatrice's knee.

Through it all, Blythe's disdain had glittered at Beatrice from across Granby's ballroom. Her emotions high, shaken from the displeasure hurled at her by Lord and Lady Foxwood, Beatrice had behaved badly.

"An unpleasant memory, that house party." She waved away her friend's concern. "I may have at one point referred to Blythe as an overindulged rake with poor taste in dance partners. Loudly enough so the entire ballroom could hear. He retaliated by calling me a vapid creature with all the depth of a thimbleful of water."

"Quick-witted." Melinda nodded.

"You see, the gentleman I nearly wed was Blythe's closest friend. The Duke of Granby."

"*Another* duke? Goodness. Aren't you the lucky one."

Beatrice rolled her eyes. "There is no need for sarcasm, Melinda. Granby was in love with another woman. I was quite terrible to her. Spread gossip which harmed her reputation and caused her much pain. A great deal of ugliness for which I am truly sorry, though I doubt I'll ever have the opportunity to apologize. Lord and Lady Foxwood applauded my questionable behavior, whispering to me that it was justified, under the circumstances. You wouldn't have liked me very much, I'm afraid."

"You would never have deigned to speak to me, Your Grace. Now, get back to Blythe."

Beatrice shrugged. "That is all there is to tell. A history of loathing and insults cast behind each other's backs. Well, and the fact that he happens to be in Chiddon. Cicero was frightened by a flock of birds during our usual ride, and Blythe found me, to my great shock. I thought the vicar might know—"

"What sort of birds?"

"The birds are not relevant. I toppled to the ground. Fell and bruised my hip, which aches nearly all the time as it is."

"He flustered you, Your Grace. I hadn't thought anything could."

"I wasn't flustered. I was terrified that he would see." Her finger tapped the right side of her face. "I should have been kinder, but we insulted each other. He called me a harpy and said if he'd known it was me, he would not have bothered with a rescue."

Melinda's eyes widened. "And what did you say?"

"I called him a prancing dandy and said that if I'd have known he was my rescuer, I would have gladly broken my neck."

"How *interesting.*" Melinda put a bit more honey in her tea. "Such sparks."

"Sparks?" Beatrice's mouth opened, aghast at the very suggestion. "Are you mad? There are *no* sparks, just loads of mutual dislike."

Not entirely true. She had always found Blythe to be —*splendid.* Like a prince in a fairy tale.

"I disagree," Melinda said.

"Blythe had the audacity to follow me home after our reacquaintance, and I had Mr. Lovington escort him back to the road at the end of a pistol," Beatrice said.

"Dramatic. Definitely sparks." Melinda shot Beatrice a knowing look as she chewed on yet another biscuit. "Good lord, I'm going to eat this entire tin."

"Don't be *smug.* It doesn't suit a vicar's wife. Stop this instant. At any rate, I don't know why Blythe is in Chiddon. This isn't the sort of place a man like him *should* be." Beatrice worried her bottom lip with her teeth. "Granted, he might be visiting an acquaintance, but Chiddon is surprisingly devoid of titles or families of any renown."

"Farthing sniffs out a nobleman faster than a hound scenting a defenseless rabbit. Perhaps Blythe has a lover nearby?" She tapped her chin. "A young lady from Overton? He followed you home which tells me Blythe had concerns for your welfare despite his dislike. Speaks well of his character though mutual dislike in no way precludes the spark—"

"Stop it, Melinda. I mean it. There was absolutely, *positively* no sparking. We don't care at all for each other. Blythe struts about, constantly demanding everyone's affection. Off-putting to say the least." Beatrice turned toward the line of trees to her right, a rambling stone fence the only obstruction to the beauty of the forest. The air was still and quiet with only the sound of insects buzzing about. All was peaceful in a way London had never been.

"You cannot remain hidden forever, Your Grace. Not from Blythe or anyone else. I don't mind, of course, as long as you keep bringing biscuits."

"Blythe would find my accident justified. A just recompense for past behavior. Pity would follow along with the snide remarks of nearly everyone in London. And I include my parents in that number. I know you think it absurd that I insist on remaining in Chiddon, but you've no idea how vicious society can be. They will tear me to shreds with a great amount of glee."

Beatrice's stomach pitched just thinking of what she could expect if she set foot in London once more. "I'm not brave enough, nor do I have good reason to return."

"Beatrice." Melinda's tone was gentle as she reached for Beatrice's hand. "You would not be alone, I promise. I would not abandon you to them."

She squeezed Melinda's fingers, smiling that her friend had slipped and called her by name. "I don't deserve such a dear friend."

Melinda gave Beatrice's hand one last pat and returned to her tea. "Probably not, but you have me all the same."

7

F eminine laughter floated on the air, carried on the breeze riffling Ellis's hair as he approached the vicarage. The residence stood before him, ancient and magnificent, the recently replaced stones a sign of the repairs Beatrice had made.

Ellis dismounted and wandered over to inspect the stonework. He knew a thing or two about masonry and fitting stone together. Beatrice's tradesmen had done decent work. A short distance away, a neatly tended graveyard stood, stark white markers bearing the names of generations of Chiddon villagers. Just on the other side, there was a small church.

Both the vicarage and the church boasted a new roof. Not a shingle out of place.

Ellis knew a bit about roof repair as well.

The low hum of conversation came again, along with more giggles. Pausing at the front door of the vicarage, Ellis thought to knock but decided to investigate the source of such amusement first. Stepping over a large tabby sunning himself on the stone, Ellis made his way around the sturdy residence. A small kitchen garden came into view. Beans and snap peas. Cabbages. Careful not to step on what looked like beets, Ellis peered around a large blackberry bush.

Two women sat on opposite sides of a small table covered with a scrap of lace. A pot of tea graced the table along with an enormous tin of what appeared to be biscuits.

The woman facing Ellis was unfamiliar. She must be the vicar's wife, Mrs. Farthing. The soft luster of her walnut hair dulled in comparison to that of her companion. A thick mass of sparkling gold, neatly tied with a ribbon, cascaded over her right shoulder.

Music lit the air at something the vicar's wife imparted to Beatrice.

Not the cackle of a harpy, or the false, patronizing sound Ellis had heard her make while lording over everyone else, but genuine happiness. It did strange things to his insides.

The first time he'd glimpsed Beatrice had been across a crowded ballroom, hair glittering under the chandeliers. Glowing like the beacon of a lighthouse. She'd shone so brightly that Ellis had seen no one *but* Beatrice. It had been impossible. Though he'd already suspected her identity from the color of her hair, Lady Foxwood's presence beside her had confirmed it for him.

Lady Foxwood, greedy, ambitious, and perfectly coiffed with jewels dripping from her ears. A fan had covered her mouth while she'd whispered to Beatrice before tapping her roughly on the wrist.

A shadow had crossed Beatrice's beautifully sculpted features before she'd nodded, throwing back her shoulders to face the crowd as if instructed to go to war.

Lady Blythe could be intolerable at times, but she couldn't hold a candle to Lady Foxwood.

Ellis had made his way casually across the ballroom, careful not to reveal either his quarry or his destination. A slightly plump young lady, an awkward thing, had cast an adoring gaze at Beatrice while Ellis looked on.

Beatrice had stared down her perfect nose at the girl, lips curling in mockery.

The girl had blushed and stammered, clearly hurt by such an unwarranted attack. She'd looked down at her slippers, bottom lip trembling, while Beatrice had continued to snipe at her.

Ellis had had no idea what was being said, but it hadn't mattered. He had a low tolerance for cruelty, though at times he practiced it himself. He'd asked for an introduction to both young ladies and received one.

Miss Elkins was the name of the graceless girl. It was she whom Ellis had asked to dance while he'd completely ignored the stunning jewel that was Lady Beatrice Howard.

Beatrice had glared at him, outraged he'd chosen Miss Elkins over her.

A lesson had needed to be taught. Certainly Lady Foxwood hadn't been going to school Beatrice.

The discord between Ellis and Beatrice had sprung from that lone incident and only intensified over time.

The lesson Ellis served to Beatrice that night had not compelled her to modesty or even introspection. Instead, she'd begun a war, wielding insults in Ellis's direction with amazingly good aim. Beatrice would find Ellis at a ball and murmur along the shoulder of his formal wear just how *ridiculous* she found him. His favorite slight from Beatrice had been that he preened like a pathetic rooster seeking the attention of hens.

In turn, Ellis would whisper loudly that every woman in London, even Miss Elkins, held some measure of appeal for him, except for Lady Beatrice Howard. He'd taken delight in toying with her. Approaching Beatrice for a dance, Ellis would pretend not to notice the refusal forming on her lips, then abruptly change direction and ask a young lady inside Beatrice's circle instead.

It had been immensely satisfying to watch Beatrice fume and curl her hands into fists while they battled. Of course, he'd spent some of that time imagining her naked, preferably on her knees before Ellis, panting and begging for the release only he could give her.

Ellis had a vivid imagination.

But he hadn't liked her. Not only had Beatrice accepted the part of fishing lure her parents had so adeptly cast out to any duke or marquess wandering about, but she'd seemed to enjoy, when their back was turned, torturing others with gossip and innuendo.

As she had Miss Elkins.

"Melinda," Ellis heard Beatrice say. "You are a terrible vicar's wife." There was no bite in her words. No scorn. Only an abundance of affection.

A soft pulse rippled over Ellis. Beatrice had a lovely voice. Maybe that was what had caused him to intervene when Granby had rejected Beatrice and she'd begun to wage a campaign to destroy Andromeda Barrington. Ellis had told himself it was for Andromeda, but . . . well, it hadn't been. The knowledge that Beatrice was hurt, justified or not, had pained him greatly. He hadn't been able to stop thinking about the way Lady Foxwood had swatted her daughter with a fan at that long-ago ball.

I am overly sentimental.

Living in Rome had made Ellis entirely too soft. Beatrice didn't deserve a shred of sympathy from him. Seducing her would relieve the worst of this . . . obsession he had for her, then Ellis could leave her in Chiddon. Return to London and the waiting arms of Lady Anabeth, someone who didn't find him at all loathsome.

"I *am* terrible, aren't I?" Mrs. Farthing agreed before the smile froze on her lips. She leaned discreetly to the side, eyes roaming over Ellis. "This magnificent Blythe, Your Grace. Does he possess a head of tarnished gold, like an old coin? Arrogantly attractive? Looks as though he sits a horse well?"

Ellis winked at her.

All things considered, he appreciated the thoughtful assessment of his person, though Ellis didn't completely agree with *arrogantly attractive*. In truth, he cared little about his appearance. It was merely a fact of his existence. Like being an earl or his inability to write a poem. Society put far too much value on his looks. He'd rather be known for his talent at fixing a watch for instance, something he did regularly but didn't bandy about.

"Well, yes," Beatrice answered. "Though I think magnificent is a bit of a stretch. He's incredibly vain. I'm sure his home is covered in mirrors so he can admire himself from every angle."

Ellis winced. He had once said the same of her.

"Wait." Beatrice set down her teacup with a rattle. "I thought you said you hadn't seen him." She jerked to her feet, the line of her shoulders taut. "Bollocks."

What a delightful vulgarity from Beatrice. He'd never known her to utter a curse until finding her in Chiddon. Castlemare must have taught her.

Beatrice spun to face Ellis, her lovely features so coldly furious, she seemed sculpted from the marble he adored. One hand immediately patted at the pile of golden hair gathered at her shoulder, smoothing the thick mass close to her cheek.

"Good day," he greeted both women, doffing his hat as he walked toward them.

Mrs. Farthing came to her feet, a cautious gaze darting between him and Beatrice. "Good day to you, my lord."

The tin of biscuits was well within Beatrice's reach. She glanced in that direction, possibly contemplating tossing what remained at Ellis's head. He waited patiently for her opening salvo. Anticipation, like a lightning rod striking his skin, coursed through Ellis, though he knew he was about to be insulted.

"My God, are you so starved for female attention you must invade a vicar's garden?"

"Your Grace." Ellis bowed, hiding his grin. "Goodness, but you make me sound quite desperate for your attention. You are not the only lovely woman taking tea in the vicar's garden, are you? A pleasure, Mrs. Farthing. I am Lord Blythe. Apologies for the intrusion, but Mr. Gates spoke in such glowing terms of the newly repaired vicarage and church, I thought to see them for myself." He took her hand.

Mrs. Farthing blushed prettily. "My lord. It is a pleasure to make your acquaintance."

Beatrice gave them both a frosty glance.

"Oh, dear," Mrs. Farthing said, jerking her hand from his. "I've completely forgotten about the pie . . . I have baking. Yes, a pie. I should—well, I wouldn't want it to burn."

"Melinda," Beatrice warned.

"If you'll excuse me, my lord." Mrs. Farthing hurried off, skirts flying, in the direction of the vicarage before disappearing into a small door set into the stone.

"You," Beatrice said in a cool tone. Small, gold curls danced at the corners of her temples, begging Ellis for merely a touch.

"Yes, me." He tilted his head toward the vicarage. "Lovely woman. I haven't yet made the acquaintance of the vicar. But I'm told he gives a rather stirring sermon from the pulpit of his newly rebuilt church, courtesy of you, Your Grace. And you repaired the vicarage. Full of rats previously, according to Gates. That would explain the enormously fat tabby I found on the vicarage steps. He must have eaten every rodent for miles."

"It was Castlemare." She regarded him a bit defensively. "He decided the church required a new roof. I only did his bidding."

"Did he order you to do so from the grave?" Ellis replied casually, watching the color sweep across her cheeks. "Allow me to apologize, Your Grace. I had no idea the duke was dead."

"My lord, I'm uncertain why you are lingering about Chiddon inspecting roofs and flirting with the vicar's wife—"

"I merely took Mrs. Farthing's hand," he interrupted, "and greeted her properly. As to roofs and stonework, such things are interesting. Perhaps the country air has bored me."

"I suggest you find other ways to amuse yourself. I've advised Mrs. Farthing of your questionable charms. You won't find any welcome here. Go sniff about another set of skirts. You are shameless in your pursuits."

The low thrum of arousal slid down Ellis's legs.

"I'll take your opinion under advisement." Trading insults with Beatrice was akin to foreplay of sorts, tossing barbs far better than tepid conversation. It was part of his attraction to her, he supposed, which made Ellis worry for the state of his mind.

"Mrs. Farthing appeared to be very welcoming," he said with a hint of impropriety merely to see how Beatrice would react. "I'm sure she isn't baking a pie for you, Your Grace."

"She isn't baking a pie at all." The cobalt of her eyes glowed with disdain and a small flicker of . . . envy. Beatrice didn't like that he found Mrs. Farthing attractive. "Why aren't you in London?"

"Why aren't you?" Ellis countered. "Frivolous parties. Bland conversation. Dancing about in your newest gown while ruining the reputations of those you deem deserve it? A vicar's garden seems to pale in comparison. Are you deciding how to sour the milk of the cows of Chiddon? Seems a proper thing for a witch to do."

Her fingers tugged at her skirts, the only sign of her agitation. "What a pretty compliment. You recall me quite fondly, my lord. But I no longer care for London as creatures like yourself call it home."

Ellis grabbed his chest as if struck by a blow. "You wound me, Your Grace."

"As *delightful* as it has been to see you"—her words dripped with ice—"I have other matters to attend to. Enjoy the remainder of your stay in Chiddon." Beatrice spun on her heel and marched off in the direction of the heavy woods. Ellis could just see a path peeking around the stone wall of the vicar's garden.

Dismissal? That wouldn't do, especially since it wouldn't further his aim of seducing her, which became more crucial with each passing moment. The reaction of his body, humming like a bloody tuning fork in her presence, was not to be borne. He must exorcise the demon that was Beatrice Howard from his system, and Ellis couldn't do so if she kept stomping away.

The twitching of her skirts disappeared into the dappled light sifting through the big trees, urging him to follow. Unusual to see her in such clothing. The dress was high-necked. Buttons nearly up to her chin. Beatrice had always been proper, but her necklines had not.

Ellis took off after her, his longer legs eating up the distance between them with little effort.

Sensing him trailing behind, she stopped. "What *is* the point of your continued harassment?" She tugged at the length of hair cascading over her right shoulder.

His eyes followed the movement, wondering why she didn't wear her hair up, as she always had before. Not even while playing bowls at Granby's stupid house party had he seen the golden mass down around her ears. Usually, the sunshine-kissed curls were artfully piled atop her head so that one could admire the gentle slope of her neck. Or compliment the seashells of her ears. Or pine after the gentle swell of her bosom, which was so well hidden at the moment as to be non-existent.

"I'm not done speaking, Your Grace."

"Yes, but I am done *listening*, my lord." She waved one hand as if batting away a fly or some other annoying pest. "Rarely have I heard anything of interest come from your lips. I doubt I will do so now. Please excuse me."

The urge to toss Beatrice into the leaves covering the forest floor and take her roughly, savagely, had Ellis struggling for breath. Beatrice was the only woman to make Ellis feel so bloody . . . *primal*. As if his control might snap at any instant.

"You never bothered to listen," Ellis bit out. "You were too busy sharpening your knives on the likes of Miss Elkins."

Beatrice took a halting breath. Regret flitted across her flawless features, so brief it could have been a trick of the light. She touched the ribbon holding her hair once more. "I believe you named me the vilest creature you'd ever met at Granby's house party. I was listening then."

"I never called you vile."

Honestly, he *might* have. Ellis spent a great deal of Granby's house party slightly foxed, irritated, and out of sorts. Annoyed by the presence of Beatrice Howard.

"I believe I called you shallow and vapid. Your pursuit of Granby, with whom you had little in common and didn't even care for—"

"Was none of your affair. Even so, your dislike of me, my lord, was well entrenched before Granby." An ugly smile floated across her lips. "Is it because, unlike every other ridiculous woman in England, I never found you special? Poor

Blythe." She pouted in false pity. "Is your ego so fragile to be wounded by me?"

Anger rippled over him in a wave, followed by an indecent amount of humming around his cock.

"You offered me condolences for the dearly departed Castlemare. But what you really wish to do is offer me comfort, I think." She took a step closer. "As a widow, you wonder if I've lowered my expectations enough to permit you to seduce me."

Ellis took a shaky breath. "Alas, not seduction. Only curiosity. The mating season grows near in London, does it not? There's a duke and a marquess available. I can't fathom why you haven't set your snares for either one."

"I have had enough dukes for a lifetime." Beatrice lifted her chin. "Nor do I care for earls. *You*, in particular, not at all." Her delectable mouth, lips plump and full, parted with scorn.

Damn. "Harridan."

"Pathetic rogue."

As they glared at one another, Ellis's hand snaked forward with a jerk, taking Beatrice firmly around the waist and bending her smaller form to his. "Conceited chit," he snarled.

"Arrogant peacock," she snapped, not pulling away.

A painful sound, a growl, came from his chest only seconds before his mouth crashed and claimed hers.

❧ 8 ❧

Beatrice had considered many times what it would be like to kiss the Earl of Blythe. She'd pictured something . . . romantic. Gallant, perhaps. Not Angry. Near violent. Hostile.

Magnificent.

Blythe was a man who knew how to capture a woman's mouth. Torture it. Draw sensation from what had formerly only been a pair of lips used for talking and sipping tea.

Oh, this is quite marvelous.

He tasted of ale, probably from The Pickled Duck. The warm, clean scent of him fell over Beatrice in a wave, pulling her closer. Heat seared her mouth, the consequence of so much restrained aggression. Without truly thinking, she reached forward and grabbed at his coat with her fingers.

Blythe kissed her with such *ferocity,* he bent Beatrice nearly in half with his efforts to devour her. Licking and biting, he demanded Beatrice surrender to him.

And she *did* surrender.

She and Blythe tore into each other with passion she hadn't thought either had ever possessed. Her breath held, stolen by his attention to every inch of her mouth. The beat of Beatrice's heart, at first wild, now slowed, catching the rhythm of Blythe's until both organs beat together. It was akin to the sweet intoxication of exactly two brandies enjoyed before the fire. Or the languid feel of staying in a warm bed on a chilly morning.

Her breasts, trapped beneath the fabric of her dress, chafed with longing against Blythe's muscled chest. A swell of—

Fire. A flame. Something heated. Molten.

—spilled down the length of her body, sinking deep between her thighs. Blythe was drinking Beatrice in, swallowing up every last bit of her. And she *wanted* him to.

His free hand snaked up the back of her neck, toying with the high neck of her gown and the ribbon restraining her carefully tied and pinned hair. He was mere inches from the ear missing a lobe, from the scars along the edge of her cheek. A scream sounded inside Beatrice. A warning. Terror seeped over her skin, washing away all the desire rippling over her in waves. She placed both hands on his chest and shoved. Hard. Pushing him away.

He musn't see. He can't. The panicked words circled her mind in a litany.

A feral, nearly inhuman sound came from Blythe as he released her, his hands springing open as if to ward her off.

My God. He growled at me.

Blythe. The sunny earl. Always smiling. Annoyingly confident and self-assured. A man who could charm the birds out of the trees.

I do seem to have an unpleasant effect on people.

A measured, predatory gaze gleamed in his eyes as he circled Beatrice, eyeing her like a starving dog, one whose bone had been taken away before the meat had been properly chewed off. His broad chest rose and fell, his breath ragged and gasping before Blythe finally turned from her. Would he apologize?

Please no. That would be mortifying. She'd kissed him back.

His burnished curls caught against his collar and cheeks in a tumble. Far too long. Impolite. It all gave Blythe a rather menacing look in the quiet between the trees. There was no charming smile pulling at his lips. Certainly no apology to be found. The blue of his eyes, like the sky filtering through the trees above their heads, remained still and calm. There wasn't even any distaste in his gaze . . . just . . . nothing.

Her anger, laced with the pain of knowing what lay beneath the thick curls at her shoulder, flared and popped. Once again, Beatrice viewed Blythe from a series of balls, watching him dance with every other young lady in attendance *but* her. As if she were unworthy of Blythe, the great golden earl. Well, she was less worthy of his attention now.

"Go away, Blythe." Beatrice heard the hiss come from her mouth. "Just leave."

His features remained impassive, regarding her with unnerving silence.

"I've no need of your companionship or anything else you feel required to offer." His perusal had her touching the neatly tied tail of her hair once more, smoothing the strands along her cheek. A protection of sorts.

Something stirred between them, wanting to rise out of the scatter of leaves covering her half-boots. The panicked flutter of her heart started up once more. Blythe was dangerous to the life Beatrice had so painstakingly pieced together from the remnants of her past. He would ferret out her secrets and spill them.

"The next time you show up at my home," Beatrice warned as he watched her, big and still, "I'll have my man put a hole through your lovely coat."

She turned and headed in the direction of Beresford Cottage, blindly stumbling down the path, touching her lips, which still throbbed from his kiss.

TEA WITH A HINT OF HONEY.

A tiny bit of sweetness in a woman who had little. A great deal of obstinance, the sense that she would never capitulate. Ellis tasted all those things along with something surprisingly carnal. That had surprised him. Yes, Ellis had often likened her to a succubus, determined to prey upon any gentleman foolish enough to get too close, but he hadn't considered that Beatrice actually possessed passion. Or that if she did, the emotion would need to be drawn out of her. Forced.

She was a spoiled chit. A harpy. A snob.

Surprising to find what was trapped beneath all those starched, frilly petticoats. More so to have all that sensuality come rushing unexpectedly out to *him*. There was a thin line separating love and hate, especially between him and Beatrice. It felt as though the dam holding such powerful emotions had cracked, then erupted completely, nearly drowning them both.

That's what it had been like to kiss Beatrice.

I don't even like her.

Ellis ground his teeth. That was a half-truth. It would be more correct to say he didn't *want* to like her let alone find her so bloody desirable. His actions had startled him. Ellis, as a rule, didn't *pounce* on women; he *seduced* them. But he'd wanted to rip the clothing from Beatrice's body, bite and suck every inch of her—

"Damn it," he said out loud, frightening a group of wrens from a nearby shrub.

This wasn't at all how he'd meant to start the overdue

conquest of Beatrice Howard, an idea which now seemed naïve in the extreme. A tupping would not expunge the harpy from his system. Kissing her had made his . . . *obsession* that much worse. My God, he'd practically—

Beatrice could bloody well enjoy Chiddon on her own. Ellis decided he didn't care why she was helping Gates brew ale or rebuilding churches. Seducing her wasn't worth the effort. Not if it made him an animal. Not if he lost his soul.

"She *is* a succubus," he muttered to himself. Perhaps that was how Castlemare had died; that harpy had inhaled his soul, leaving nothing but a withered husk. The idea would make a splendid poem, if only Ellis had an ounce of talent with which to write one.

He followed the trail until he saw the stone fence surrounding the garden of the vicarage. Mrs. Farthing was once more seated outside, the nearly empty tin of biscuits before her. She looked up at his approach.

"Tea, my lord?" she inquired. Her gaze lingered over Ellis a moment. "Are you wounded? Bleeding? Her Grace has been known to draw blood."

Mrs. Farthing was quite sassy for a vicar's wife. "No blood, Mrs. Farthing. I hope that isn't disappointing. I have an aversion to it."

Her eyes, a deep brown, twinkled back at him. "As do I." She cast a glance toward the path disappearing into the woods.

"I promise only insults were used as weapons, madam. Do I look like the sort of man who would strangle a duchess?"

"I suppose not." She gnawed on another biscuit. Ellis had never seen anyone eat so many biscuits at one sitting—except Haven. "But I'm of the opinion that a person's appearance does not necessarily reflect their character."

"Indeed." He sat across from her and snatched up a

biscuit, ignoring the look she gave him. "I could be a villain of sorts, couldn't I?"

"You could," she agreed with a sigh. "Though I don't think that the case. You're much too shiny. Like a newly minted guinea. If you don't mind my saying, my lord."

"Not at all." Ellis smiled at her cheeky description. "And if you don't mind me asking, shouldn't a vicar's wife be out ministering to her husband's flock instead of giggling with a duchess over biscuits and tea?" He took a bite, nodding in appreciation. "Delicious."

"Her Grace provides the best biscuits. It is the only reason I invite her to tea. She is the vicar's patron, after all. Thus, my concern over her welfare. Vicar Farthing would be most distraught to lose the support of a duchess."

"Hmm." Ellis doubted that was the case. He'd observed the affection between the two women. They were close friends.

He stood, finishing off the biscuit. "I bid you good day, madam. Thank you for the biscuit." He strode over to Dante, taking hold of the reins.

"My lord, will we see you on Sunday? Vicar Farthing noted your presence in the garden earlier, and he is most anxious to make your acquaintance. He might be disposed to arrive when you least expect it. A vicar can never have too many patrons." Her eyes twinkled with mischief. "Probably best to become acquainted at church, don't you think? At least, that is what I suggested. An earl of your reputation would wish to hear the vicar's sermon before committing himself."

The good vicar would seek him out if Ellis didn't appear Sunday, that much was clear. He imagined an entire afternoon listening to Vicar Farthing's ambitions.

"I should like to hear the vicar speak."

"I assure you the sermon will be marvelous. The subject is the wages of sin on our eternal soul."

"Splendid." Ellis hoped he didn't nod off.

"Her Grace sits in the front pew. A place of honor," Mrs. Farthing continued. "Due to her station, she often sits alone." A sad nod of her head. "There is a dearth of titles in Chiddon, as I'm sure you've noticed."

There was a dearth of *everything* in Chiddon.

"But now you have arrived. How wonderful that you can provide proper escort for Her Grace with only a bit of coaxing."

Ellis paused, one foot in the stirrup. He wasn't blind to Mrs. Farthing's machinations; it was only that he had no idea what her reason could possibly be for wanting him to escort Beatrice. He wasn't even sure he wished to see her again, let alone endure a sermon on the wages of sin with Beatrice seated beside him.

"And what makes you think, Mrs. Farthing, that I could convince the Duchess of Castlemare to do anything?"

Mrs. Farthing drew her fingers through the air. "Because of the sparks, my lord," she said in a solemn tone. "Surely you can see them."

9

Beatrice brushed a tendril of hair from her eyes before bending slightly until her back made a satisfying snap.

"Much better."

She and Mr. Gates had spent the better part of the day at The Pickled Duck discussing adjustments to the new batch of ale he was brewing. Gates, bless him, always asked for Beatrice's opinion on the amount of barley. The color. The taste. Honestly, she didn't care how he brewed the ale, only that he did. But occupying her mind with business matters was the first step in keeping thoughts of Blythe—thoughts which had grown *erotic* in nature—at bay. Hard work was the only cure for the disease of Blythe.

A tiny snort left her. He would hate being compared to a dreaded affliction or blight on crops. But it served him right, after the way he had invaded Beatrice's peaceful existence. An existence that *wasn't* hiding, as Melinda claimed. Chiddon was Beatrice's sanctuary. A serene bubble. Balm to her soul. She was not hiding.

"I think we're nearly done for today, Mr. Gates," Beatrice announced.

"But you haven't tasted the last batch." The top of his bald head appeared behind a large vat.

"I trust it to be as wonderful as all the others I've tasted," Beatrice assured him. Gates and his determination to brew the best ale in Hampshire—indeed, all of England—was laudable, though it was amusing he assumed Beatrice to be a connoisseur of ales and ciders. She'd never even tasted ale before coming to Chiddon.

But a duchess was assumed to know everything.

Gates came forward, disappointment that she was taking her leave apparent on his reddened features. "Are you certain, Your Grace?"

"Quite. I trust your palate implicitly."

His brows drew together.

"Your taste for ale," she clarified. "Remember, I am only your patron, nothing more."

Gates nodded. "Can't have a duchess getting her hands dirty."

"No, indeed." It was a useless request. Gates treated Beatrice as if she'd come down from the heavens to help him brew the ale. And honestly, did she give a fig what Lord and Lady Foxwood or Castlemare's brother thought? She *was* a duchess. A tattered, scarred one, but a duchess, nonetheless. Even if all of London found out, Beatrice would do as she saw fit, which was to help Arnold Gates achieve greatness by selling Chiddon ale.

Atonement for Martin Dilworth.

Dilworth, lips trembling, sweating far more than any human being should, had been one of Beatrice's many hopeful admirers. He'd been handsome, outside of the sweating. Wealthy. But not titled. Dilworth had always been kind to Beatrice, though she'd treated him as if he were no more than a trifle. A flea that had infested her clothing. He'd professed his love, and Beatrice had laughed. Determined to win her, Martin had left for France on a business opportunity he hoped would elevate his status. Make him more *worthy* of her. He'd asked Beatrice to see him off, and instead, she'd taken a nap.

Dilworth's ship had broken apart during the crossing to Calais. A sudden storm. All aboard were lost.

Beatrice pressed a hand over her heart. Gates and his ale were for Martin Dilworth.

When the first cask of Chiddon ale was delivered to several establishments in Overton, Beatrice would cross Dilworth's name from her ledger. The Dilworth family's wealth had come from the importing of wine and other spirits. The ale wasn't wine, but she thought Martin would appreciate the sentiment all the same.

She said her goodbyes to Gates and headed to the building she was having renovated. Next to the apothecary, the space of weathered wood and stone wasn't large and required a new floor and roof. Dilapidated, as had been nearly everything in Chiddon before her arrival. But the building did boast living quarters on the second floor.

Perfect for a dressmaker or draper.

Castlemare was likely pitching about his grave at knowing his widow was performing such acts of charity. He'd found Chiddon to be the worst sort of backwater. A dreary village filled with uninteresting common folk who weren't worth his attention. He'd hoped Beatrice would wither here, among the thick trees.

Instead, Beatrice had found purpose.

Chiddon was in dire need of care, as Beatrice had been herself when she'd first arrived. The village had embraced her, thrilled to have a duchess take up residence in their midst.

Beatrice might never dance at a ball again or visit the

grand establishments on Bond Street. Nor change who she'd once been.

But Beatrice *could* help Chiddon.

When Castlemare's coach had first deposited Beatrice at Beresford Cottage, she'd barely been conscious enough to see her surroundings. A great deal of laudanum had been required to force Beatrice into a closed box pulled by horses. Bandaged. Alone. Wounds seeping and painful. Not even her maid, a girl who'd been tupping Castlemare behind Beatrice's back, had cared to make the journey. Lord and Lady Foxwood had sent a note. They'd been hosting a house party and couldn't be bothered to see their daughter off.

A puff left her at the thought of her parents. It was hard to still desire the love of two people who hadn't the capacity to give it.

Mrs. Lovington had taken one look at Beatrice and proceeded to castigate the Duke of Castlemare's two footmen and driver. Tucking her beneath one muscular arm, Mrs. Lovington had gotten Beatrice upstairs and settled, clucking over the blood seeping through the bandages, cursing Castlemare under her breath. The stoic housekeeper hadn't left Beatrice's side for months, nursing her with far more care than Lady Foxwood ever had.

Beresford Cottage came into view, and Beatrice nudged Cicero in the direction of the stables, shouting for Jasper, her groom. She peered into the dark interior of the stable. "Jasper."

"Apologies, Your Grace." There was a half-eaten carrot in Jasper's hand, a treat usually reserved for her mount, Cicero. A gelding was tied to the post nearby, chewing on the portion of carrot her groom had given him. A familiar horse.

Jasper bowed, guilty and clutching the carrot like a shield. His throat bobbed. "You have a visitor, Your Grace."

"Hmm. Give Cicero an apple instead of his usual carrot."

"Yes, Your Grace." Jasper helped her dismount Cicero.

Beatrice stormed up to the front door, cursing Blythe the entire time. The staff had been instructed to turn him away if he appeared. Knowing Blythe, he'd managed to charm her entire household long enough for them to forget all about tossing him out. Her fingers smoothed the thick tail of hair along her shoulder, making sure the length was firmly secured.

Assaulting her in the woods—unexpectedly and without permission—did not give Blythe leave to call on Beatrice.

Her mouth tingled at the remembered touch of his lips. The warm, male scent of him.

Very well. Less an assault than a mutual taking of liberties.

Mrs. Lovington swung open the door at her approach, cheeks flushed, stern features softened enough to almost make her attractive. "You've a guest, Your Grace. Lord Blythe. I've put him in the parlor."

"So I've been informed." Beatrice stepped inside. It would do no good to chastise her housekeeper. Faced with an onslaught of Blythe's sunny manner and well-timed flirtation, Mrs. Lovington hadn't stood a chance.

"I was just about to bring in tea." Mrs. Lovington dipped her chin. "And some of those small cakes you like. Just out of the oven." A worried crease took up residence between the housekeeper's brows. "I've used the pink icing," she said hopefully.

"Don't bother with tea. Lord Blythe won't be staying."

Beatrice marched to her cozy parlor and flung open the door, unsurprised to see the burnished gold of Blythe's head hovering above the edge of the chair where he'd settled himself—*her* favorite chair—a glass of brandy at his elbow.

"Good day, my lord. Did I invite you to enjoy my fire or my brandy?" Beatrice snapped at him from the doorway.

"Oh, you didn't." Blythe peeked around the side of the

chair as if they were the closest of friends and his appearance was welcome. Spectacular, as usual. Hair, wind tossed by the gods. The merest scruff of beard lining his beautifully chiseled jaw. Though Beatrice couldn't see the rest of him, she assumed Blythe's riding breeches were expertly tailored, tight in all the right places so the masculine length of leg would draw the eye.

A flirtatious half-smile tugged at Blythe's mouth.

The sight of those lips caused a slide of warmth along Beatrice's mid-section. She winced at the sensation, willing it to stop. She was close to becoming yet another ninny undone by the Earl of Blythe.

"I grew concerned, Your Grace, as I waited for your arrival. The hour grows late."

"My welfare is none of your affair. But as you can see, I'm well. Good day, Blythe."

He didn't move, damn him.

"While I waited, I entertained myself by looking through your books." He nodded to a crate on the floor. "Quite an assortment of topics." Another grin. "The fire is warm, your parlor exceptionally cozy, and there's a chill in the air."

A chill in the air. He compared her to a blast of ice.

Beatrice glared at Blythe. She strode into the parlor, taking off her gloves. "Why are you here, my lord?"

"I required a brandy." He lifted the glass and took a sip.

Always so bloody sure of his welcome. And why wouldn't he be? Blythe *was* magnificent. Attractive without a hint of the snarling dominance of say . . . Castlemare. His appeal was nothing like the brooding handsomeness of the Duke of Granby. Or Haven, the only other friend of Blythe's Beatrice had met. Haven was all coarse edges and seemed moments from engaging in fisticuffs. Instead, Blythe's presence was akin to walking into a patch of sunlight.

Beatrice *wanted* to bask in Blythe's presence. Roll about in all that warmth.

"Surely, my lord, you have brandy at your own residence . . . or wherever it is you are staying. I leave you to seek out your second glass there." She crossed her arms, tapping one foot, impatient for him to leave.

Blythe stood, regarding her with another charming smile.

She'd been correct about the breeches. They stretched taut across his thighs, clasping at the muscles and skin beneath. Indecently so.

Beatrice jerked her chin to gaze at the fire.

"You think I have a lover. In Chiddon." The blue of his eyes flashed from beneath impossibly thick lashes. "Put aside your jealousy. It is unbecoming in a duchess. I've a hunting lodge just on the other side of Chiddon, though I don't hunt. I rarely fish. But I do like nature."

"I don't care what you do with your time," Beatrice bit out, imagining him tromping about the woods, charming the animals. "Only that you are intent on infringing on mine." His unexpected appearance had unsettled Beatrice greatly.

Like hyacinth in the spring. That was the exact color of Blythe's eyes. Blue with just a hint of violet. She'd never bothered to take note before. Or admire the dimple in his cheek.

Another spool of warmth curled up inside her.

"Your Grace." The rich tenor was soft. Coaxing. It had undoubtedly lured many a female into bed. "Shall I pour you a brandy?"

"I bid you good day, my lord." Beatrice pointed at the door.

"I don't think so." Blythe roamed over to the sideboard. "Let's not argue, Your Grace. How is Mr. Gates today?"

He didn't think so?

"If you are concerned with Mr. Gates, visit him yourself." She smoothed down her hair, ensuring her neck and cheek were covered. "The audacity of coming here, where you are not welcome. Seducing my poor housekeeper—"

"I did no such thing, Your Grace." Blythe held out a snifter of brandy. "I merely told Mrs. Lovington I wanted to ensure you were well after your tumble the other day." He rolled his shoulders. "I may have mentioned my heroic rescue."

Of course he had. Mrs. Lovington had probably swooned.

"I thought your interruption of my tea with Mrs. Farthing was to make that assurance."

"Yes, but I didn't get around to doing so. You became agitated. And other matters"—Blythe's gaze fell to her mouth—"took precedence." His own lips grew tight, uncertain. Perhaps he was as unsettled as Beatrice from that kiss.

The sparks Melinda kept blathering about made themselves known, skittering along the skin of Beatrice's arms. Her pulse throbbed gently, responding to Blythe's nearness. His appeal, she finally acknowledged, had less to do with his looks and more to do with his manner, which was at turns respectful, improper, and oddly comforting.

"I must insist you leave." Blythe made Beatrice *feel* things, emotions barely allowed to bloom in her past life where an excess of affection had been frowned upon.

"Are we going to come to physical blows, Your Grace?" He dipped his chin in the direction of her hands. "Possibly . . . tussle?"

Another wave prickled the skin of her arms at the thought of rolling about with Blythe. "No need," she shot back. "I've become quite good with a riding crop."

"Have you? How intriguing." Blythe took a sip of his brandy, eyes darkening, shrugging off the mask of the pleasing, charming rake with little effort. There was nothing careless about Blythe now. Not with his innate sensuality curling about his larger form like a snake. This was the Blythe who'd nearly swallowed her whole in the forest.

"I find I'm not entirely opposed to the crop." The words rumbled from his chest, a hungry look crossing his handsome features.

She took the glass of amber liquid he held out, refusing to consider the feel of his mouth on hers any further. Or the arousal fluttering between her thighs.

Beatrice took a shaky swallow of brandy. He *really* must leave.

"What is your purpose, Blythe?" she managed to get out. "Other than torturing me with your company, which I never asked for and do not want."

"I made the acquaintance of Vicar Farthing quite by accident this morning."

Blythe had been in Chiddon. Probably looking for her.

"Don't frown, Your Grace. I behaved appropriately. Though I must say that if Vicar Farthing were a young lady in her first season, he would have given you a great deal of competition." The predatory look left him. "Such ambition for a vicar."

Beatrice's grip on the snifter tightened. "How lovely to know the vicar and I have something in common."

"I cannot wait to hear his sermon on Sunday. He was delighted I'd be in attendance and overjoyed I'd be escorting you."

"Absolutely not," Beatrice choked out. "I require no escort. Let us speak plainly, my lord, because it is becoming clear that you did not take note of my words earlier. If you are bored and longing to give comfort, seek out a bored housewife in Overton. Or better yet, return to London, where a herd of impressionable young ladies no doubt awaits your return."

Blythe raised a brow. "No herd of young ladies, unfortunately, only an overbearing mother and two sisters who wish to visit Gunter's every day. I don't particularly care for ices. I do like widows, however."

Heat flew up Beatrice's cheeks. "Yes, but shouldn't they like you in return?" Blythe had never liked her. What had happened between them was merely physical desire between two attractive people. Or at least Blythe was still attractive. But she—

"Challenge accepted, Your Grace. Let us enjoy our brandy. I'll tell you tales of my adventures in Rome while your charming housekeeper brings us refreshments. That's where I've been these last few years. Rome."

"I don't believe I asked. Nor even wondered at your absence."

"Far too busy being Castlemare's duchess, weren't you?" A bit of disdain bled into his words. "I'll admit, I hadn't thought you'd consider Castlemare."

Beatrice sat down in one of the chairs facing the fire. Blythe would always assume the worst of her. He considered Beatrice to be nothing more than an unprincipled mercenary, incapable of anything other than marrying well. Driven by ambition and little else. It was best Blythe continue to hold that opinion of her else he might wish to delve deeper. Few in London knew of her accident or that it had been Castlemare, and not grief at his death, which had forced her to Chiddon.

"I had already lost one duke, my lord, to a Barrington, no less. I wasn't about to allow another to slip through my fingers."

❧ 10 ❧

Ellis regarded Beatrice, wondering what sort of madness had possessed him that he'd sought her out a second time. He hadn't meant to. After that tenuous, tortured kiss, Ellis had returned home so unsettled, he'd started making plans to return to London. But longing for Beatrice had struck him in the chest just after dinner. At first, he'd thought the wine sauce too rich. Hoped it was merely indigestion.

No, it was Beatrice.

Ellis had *always* wanted her. That was the hard truth. Even when filled with disdain at the way she treated others, he had still felt the pull of Beatrice reaching out to him across ballrooms and parties. He should return to the life waiting for him, but Ellis couldn't seem to summon the energy to make arrangements. So, he'd gone looking for her today in Chiddon, against his better judgement.

After listening to Farthing pontificate for the better part of an hour—*the man was a complete windbag*—on his role in assisting the duchess through her grief, Ellis had to call on Beatrice. Farthing alternatively worshipped Beatrice for being a duchess, while passively voicing his dislike for a woman he thought should have long ago written to her contacts in London to find Farthing another position.

Ellis agreed.

"I liken Granby's defection to more an escape," he said, settling in the chair next to her.

A sound came from Beatrice. "How eloquent of you."

Assisting Farthing wouldn't have been difficult for Beatrice, especially since it would have kicked the annoying gnat of a vicar out of Chiddon. There was at least one bishop in Lord Foxwood's family. Castlemare had numerous estates. Her reluctance to contact anyone in London struck Ellis as odd. He also believed the excessive mourning over Castlemare, which nearly everyone in Chiddon had mentioned, to be non-existent.

Beatrice gripped the brandy in her hands so tightly, her knuckles whitened.

"I find Farthing's claims of your grief to be exaggerated," Ellis finally said, watching her reaction.

"Why? Because you find me heartless?" she retorted, not bothering to look in his direction.

"No, because of Castlemare. I knew him by reputation." Castlemare wouldn't have inspired an ounce of grief in anyone, especially the woman he'd wed. It should have pleased Ellis that Beatrice had ended up with the sort of man Castlemare had been. But he wasn't. "I'm not sure he would have liked what you've done with Chiddon."

Beatrice's lips twitched. "I'm very sure he would not."

When Ellis had first arrived at the very lovely Beresford Cottage and charmed his way past Mrs. Lovington, he'd been certain that Beatrice's reason for being in Chiddon couldn't possibly be grief over Castlemare. It had to be revenge of sorts. That seemed more suited to Beatrice.

Her response at least assured him he was on the right

track, but he still couldn't make sense of her continued seclusion.

"My anecdotes about Rome are fascinating," he said, changing the subject deftly. "And I want the pleasure of annoying you with my presence. Now drink your brandy."

"I don't wish to be fascinated," she whispered, looking into the fire, but she obediently sipped.

"But you *are* open to being annoyed by my presence. Wonderful. We'll sit here and enjoy our brandy, shall we? We can practice not antagonizing each other."

Beatrice turned to him. "Why?" Something flickered across her beautiful features.

He didn't bloody know why. Seduction was the obvious answer, but—well it wasn't entirely true—or rather, he did want to seduce her—but his reasoning had become murky after that kiss.

Ellis shrugged. "The brandy you keep is excellent, Your Grace. And perhaps I want to see how long it will take you to summon Jasper or Mr. Lovington and have me escorted from your presence."

Beatrice glanced at the clock ticking away on the mantel. "A quarter hour, I wager. No more."

A smile hovered at his lips. "Challenge accepted."

His gaze fell on the stack of books strewn haphazardly over a side table. *The Works of Cicero*, *The Voyage of the Beagle*, and *The Adventures of Lord Thurston*. An unusual collection for a woman like Beatrice Howard.

There was a slim volume clad in green leather with nothing written along the spine. A ledger of sorts. Ellis had hovered over it, wanting to open and peruse the contents, but he had not.

"I went to Rome to learn how to sculpt properly," he started. "Needless to say, my talents lie elsewhere." He launched into a somewhat ribald tale of having finally secured a nude model, only dismayed to find that the model in question was a somewhat elderly gentleman.

The tension left Beatrice's slender form as he related the tale, her lips turning up at the corners as he related how Signore Bentato had needed the sum promised to model as his wife had cut off his allowance due to his love of wine. Ellis had paid him off, of course, not wanting to hurt the man's feelings nor wishing to see his naked body every day while first sketching out the man's form then transferring it to marble.

"It was a wasted effort, at any rate. I've little of the artistic genius required to complete such a project. No skill whatsoever with marble or stone unless I'm building a wall." Ellis had tried, becoming more frustrated with every attempt. Finally, bottle of wine in hand, he'd walked along the Tiber, resigned that he'd only ever be an earl and not a poet or a great artist.

"Then why attempt it?" There was genuine curiosity in her tone and no mockery for his pathetic attempts at sculpture.

"I admire artists. Musicians. Poets. I longed to be counted in their number. Create something that would survive the ages. Move the emotions of others," he found himself admitting.

"You're a romantic." The flames bathed the edges of her profile with a soft golden light. Beatrice's features should have been committed to canvas or marble by a great master.

"Somewhat." His friends often poked fun at that side of Ellis. Granby found umbrage with Ellis's attempts at poetry. Haven insisted Ellis's love of Keats was due to him being a spoiled twit who had the luxury of contemplating verse. Haven was often bitter.

"Is that why you were so enamored of Theodosia Barrington?"

The question took him aback. Ellis hadn't thought Beatrice ever paid him a great deal of attention other than lobbing slurs in his direction. "I was never enamored of Theodosia, Your Grace. I was aware of Haven's attachment to her, apparent from the moment she spilled ratafia on him at the house party. Had you not been so intent on shackling Granby at the time, you would have noticed."

Beatrice turned her chin back to the fire, the line of her jaw mutinous.

"Theodosia's affection for me was pure infatuation. *Not* love. I have five sisters and recognized the signs. But I have a great deal of admiration for her as an artist. As a gift to Haven, she painted the drawing room at Greenbriar." At her questioning look, he said, "Haven's country estate. The walls now mimic the night sky, complete with constellations. Nestled in one corner is a young boy, Haven, and his father, studying the stars." The painting spoke volumes about Theodosia's love for Haven, apparent in every brushstroke.

That artistry invoked a great deal of envy in Ellis. Not because of any excess of feeling for Theodosia, or jealousy that he couldn't paint with such talent, but because Ellis wondered if he would ever be worthy of such love. He couldn't imagine Lady Anabeth even embroidering him a handkerchief.

"Sounds impressive. I can't paint either." Beatrice sipped at her brandy, her tone wistful. "Or sketch."

Ellis glanced at her, gaze running along the delicate line of her profile, surprised at the admission. "All I have left is carving wood. A skill I picked up from my father, who also wasn't possessed of any talent." He pointed to the buttons on his coat. "See the bird."

Beatrice sat up a little in her chair and peered at the buttons of his coat. "I have always been curious."

"I knew you were discreetly ogling me."

"Never." She rolled her eyes and made a sound of disgust before sitting back.

"My father set out to create a raven."

Beatrice took in the buttons once more and snorted in derision. "A raven."

"But this looks more like some sort of waterfowl, doesn't it? Perhaps an egret. Or a stork. The legs are clearly wrong for a raven. The design decorates everything belonging to the earldom. Buttons. Tablecloths. The silver. My mother even has a cameo with this bird."

"To what end?" Beatrice finally tilted her head to him, the brandy making her eyes sparkle in the firelight.

Ellis wanted to kiss her again. As much as he was aroused by barbed, scathing Beatrice, he also liked this softer version of her. The longing for her knocked about his heart.

Stop that.

"My grandsire expressed joy at the design, asking if it was an egret. And my own sire, perhaps embarrassed to admit he'd been trying for a raven, agreed. Grandfather was pleased, because unbeknownst to my father, he adored egrets. And before you ask, I've no idea why. Once he saw the design, Grandfather wanted the bird on *everything*. Now my family is stuck with this symbol for eternity. The product of two generations, both lacking in creativity."

Beatrice nibbled thoughtfully at her bottom lip, drawing his gaze. Incredibly erotic of her, though Ellis didn't think that her intent. He considered just going down on his hands and knees before her. Lifting her skirts. Pressing his mouth to—

"But you like to create, do you not?" she asked, interrupting his lustful thoughts. "You shouldn't stop doing so merely because you aren't Donatello or Michelangelo."

Another sigh came from his heart. Most young ladies couldn't name one sculptor of the Renaissance, let alone two.

Or find Charles Darwin fascinating enough to read the book he'd published of his travels.

Arousal, sharp and nearly painful in its intensity, shot between his legs. His riding breeches tightened uncomfortably.

"You should see what I make from a block of wood, Your Grace. A squirrel looks more like a confused dog. A wren looks . . . well, like an egret. I've already scoured the woods around Chiddon for the perfect chunks of oak, pine, and the like. Anything I can use to make a hideous rabbit or fox."

"Hideous or not, it brings you pleasure, does it not?" Her head tilted just slightly as she took another sip of her brandy. "I—have never been artistic. My talents lie more in—"

"Decoration? Restoration? Dare I say it, construction? Hardly what I would have expected, Your Grace. A duchess doesn't often toil at such things."

Beatrice's lovely mouth parted, and Ellis thought again of kissing her. She didn't answer immediately, as if she were trying to decide if he mocked her. "I enjoy putting things to rights, I suppose." She looked about to say more, but the clock above the mantel chimed, stopping her.

"I survived an entire hour, Your Grace." Ellis stood without preamble, giving one last glance at the stack of books. When he'd first entered the parlor, he'd expected London papers, all open to the gossip columns. Or tomes on fashion. It occurred to Ellis he might not really know Beatrice at all.

"So, you did," Beatrice murmured, oddly subdued. Her hand absently went to the thick mass of hair pulled over her right shoulder. "I'm sure you can see yourself out."

Ellis resisted the urge to fold her smaller body into his, pull Beatrice in his lap and hold her until the sudden sadness lingering about her faded.

Instead, he merely bowed. "Good day, Your Grace."

Beatrice stepped out of her room, hoping a cup of tea, a bit of toast, and a brisk walk to the church for services would set her to rights. She'd tossed and turned in bed last night, unable to settle after sharing a brandy with Blythe. Other than Melinda, Blythe was the only person to have ever paid a call upon her since coming to Chiddon. Observing social niceties reminded Beatrice far too much of London. Castlemare.

A carriage bobbing at the edges of a riverbank.

She tugged at the twist of hair pulled tightly against her right cheek.

Castlemare had invaded her dreams last night, among other unpleasant memories, and he was still here, haunting the landing where she now stood. The duke had approached Beatrice during a ball while she'd still been reeling in disbelief from Granby's rejection. Lord and Lady Foxwood had fixed the blame for the debacle of Granby's deception firmly on Beatrice. She'd embarrassed the family. Shaken the standing of the Foxwoods. Her *sole* purpose in life, Lady Foxwood had declared, was to secure a duke. At the very least a marquess. And to be routed by the likes of Andromeda Barrington?

Inexcusable.

Beatrice had been suffocating, unable to breathe without Lady Foxwood criticizing her every move. Castlemare had made no secret of his admiration for Beatrice, likening her to crown jewels. She had run right into the duke's arms, not pausing to consider what sort of man Castlemare might be. It hadn't mattered that he bore her not a whit of affection nor she him. Their marriage was for status. Wealth. Power was within Beatrice's grasp. The culmination of the ambition of the Foxwoods. Finally, Beatrice had gained her parents' approval. Lord Foxwood had boasted of the connection to Castlemare. Lady Foxwood had accepted dozens of new invitations as the mother of a new duchess. Beatrice had been fawned over. Showered with invitations, gifts, offers of friendship. Castlemare had treated her kindly.

Now, Lady Foxwood had insisted, Beatrice need only to secure her future by giving Castlemare an heir.

Disappointment had returned in droves when she'd failed at her appointed task.

Castlemare had ceased being kind.

The aroma of bacon hit her nostrils as Beatrice made her way down the hall. She'd eaten little last night, preoccupied and too unsettled by Blythe's visit. She'd poured another brandy after his departure, fingers trailing over the green, leatherbound ledger, still buried beneath the stack of books on her table. Blythe had been in the parlor for only a short time before her arrival, according to Mrs. Lovington. It was doubtful he'd done more than glance at the table. Even if he had, Blythe wouldn't have known what to make of the list of names and notations. Not even Beatrice truly understood what she was trying to accomplish. Some of those listed were dead and beyond caring. But the ledger gave Beatrice a sense of purpose. A duty, of sorts, though no one had asked her to brew Chiddon ale on Martin Dilworth's behalf.

This duty was about atoning for the horrid creature Beatrice had once been.

Her fingers tightened on the banister as she made her way down the stairs. The desire gleaming in Blythe's eyes would become moot once he realized there was no possibility of nibbling on her right ear lobe. Or if Blythe caught sight of the gashes decorating her right breast and shoulder. Possibly the holes in the skin of her neck and cheek.

She'd woken up just as dawn streaked across the sky, a scream lodged in her throat. She'd once more been trapped. The stream. The rocks. The absolute blackness of the riverbed where she'd lain for two days. Thomas's bloodied face, neck hanging at an odd angle before floating away while she'd sobbed for help.

Blythe's presence brought the past back to her. This was his fault. All of it.

Admittedly, Beatrice had enjoyed his company the previous night, but she would not, under any circumstances, receive him again. A fingertip touched her lips.

No matter how marvelously he kissed.

Resolved, Beatrice continued down the stairs, almost toppling down the remainder as a masculine rumble drifted up from the breakfast room.

"Mrs. Lovington, you are a treasure."

Damn him.

Blythe had, *unbelievably,* once more invaded her sanctuary. Why could he not leave her alone? Hadn't she politely listened to his tales of Rome?

Lifting her chin, Beatrice steeled her shoulders and made her way down to the bottom of the stairs. She stood at the entrance of the breakfast room, lip curled in dislike as she viewed the scene before her.

Mrs. Lovington, likely thrilled to be able to wait on the *magnificent* Lord Blythe—*oh, and he was quite splendid in a coat the color of burnt toast*—bustled about his golden form, presenting Beatrice's unwelcome guest with what appeared to be an omelet sprinkled with herbs while asking if his lordship would like more bacon. Two tiny pink dots stood out on Mrs. Lovington's cheeks as she fussed about him like a mother hen, smothering him with attention. When Mrs. Lovington, normally the most uncompromising of women, *giggled* like a schoolgirl, Beatrice burst into the room.

This was intolerable.

"Lord Blythe," Beatrice greeted him curtly. "How unexpected to find you at my breakfast table."

"Delightful is the word you're looking for, Your Grace." Blythe sat back in his chair, eyes alight as she came into the room, daring her with a wink to be tossed out. He had never more resembled her description of him as an affable, slightly annoying dog. She hoped he hadn't tracked in any mud.

"Perhaps your definition is different from mine, my lord. Tea, Mrs. Lovington, if you please." Beatrice took a chair at the opposite end of the table, eyeing Blythe with annoyance.

Blythe had taken Beatrice's place at the head of the table. As if sharing one brandy, telling her stories about a naked man in Rome, and *not* being escorted out at the point of a pistol entitled him to do so.

Wretch.

He raised a brow and chewed his omelet, a bit more seductively than Beatrice thought necessary. The way he drew his lips over his fork, lips dragging over each tine, had a flare of heat inching up her spine.

"Do you often appear, my lord, uninvited for breakfast?" Beatrice kept her voice chilly.

"Not often, Your Grace. But I did promise to escort you to church today. The vicar has a wonderful sermon planned."

He rubbed his hands together as if the idea of Vicar Farthing and his sermon excited him. "Don't tell me you forgot, Your Grace?"

Overindulged peacock.

If she could stab him with her fork, she would.

He'd anticipated her reluctance at his escort to the church, arriving at her home far earlier than merited. She'd hoped to gulp down her tea and hurry along the path behind her home which led to the vicarage. Beatrice had even mapped out several spots to hide among the trees should Blythe attempt to seek her out. It was rather terrifying that he'd guessed she might avoid him and outsmarted her. What was his purpose in doing so?

He wishes to torment me.

"Your services are not required, my lord. I'm perfectly capable of making my own way to the vicarage. I have been doing so without your assistance for some time."

"Your Grace," he chastised. "What sort of . . . *friend* would I be if I didn't go with you?"

"We are not friends, my lord." At least, they hadn't been when he'd found her riding Cicero. Not after years of . . . armed hostility. When had a truce been called?

When he kissed me.

The memory of that kiss came roaring back once more. In truth, it rarely left her thoughts, instead becoming a catalyst for other, more improper imaginings.

"I disagree." Blythe chewed thoughtfully. "I am friendly toward you. Though our relationship needs a great deal of work."

Beatrice took a sip of the tea Mrs. Lovington hurriedly poured for her. "We are barely acquainted."

"We can discuss our differences on the ride to the church." Blythe stabbed at the omelet, eyes closing in rapture. "Perfection, Mrs. Lovington. If only you weren't already wed."

Oh, for goodness' sake.

"I prefer to walk," Beatrice stated. "Unescorted."

"Nonsense. My carriage sits just outside."

Carriage. The very word invoked an entire well of panic in Beatrice. Silly, really. But she could almost smell the rotting vegetation. See the blood in the water. Thomas's broken body.

"No, thank you."

Beatrice didn't take carriages, gigs, barouches, landaus, or any other type of conveyance pulled by a horse. Nothing with axles that could break. Or doors that could jam shut. Yet another reason why she would never return to London, because part of the journey would require sitting in a coach. Even if she could feasibly make it back to London without an excess of panic, then what? No. Better to stay in Chiddon.

"I don't often get to drive myself or anyone else." Blythe waved his fork gracefully about as he spoke. "I bought the vehicle especially for the country." His gaze dropped to her hair, gathered by a ribbon to the right side of her face. "And it is a lovely day." Blythe took one last bite and smiled at Mrs. Lovington before coming to his feet, intent on helping Beatrice up.

"I—"

Blythe's hands fell to her shoulders before he pulled back her chair, and she was enveloped in his warm, clean scent. Beatrice had the urge to turn her chin and bury her nose in his chest.

"Come, Your Grace. Don't you want to be the envy of every woman in Chiddon, walking into the church with me on your arm?" He took her elbow.

"You are such a strutting peacock." There was a slight

quiver in her voice, the result of knowing she was going to be trussed into a carriage and could do nothing about it.

"In truth, I am."

Beatrice's heart thumped heavy in her chest. She consoled herself with the knowledge that the ride to the church would take little time. If her eyes remained closed, Beatrice could imagine other, more pleasurable things, like how to strangle a splendid earl with his own cravat.

A worried look came from Mrs. Lovington. "Your Grace—"

Beatrice gave a small shake of her head. There could be no fuss, or Blythe would wonder at it. She need only wait him out and tolerate his presence and this carriage ride. Blythe was merely bored. After today, he would tire of annoying her and find some other way to amuse himself. Or he would return to London.

"My hat, Mrs. Lovington. Will you instruct Peg to fetch it?"

"Yes, Your Grace." The housekeeper bobbed and hurried off.

"A pity you don't have a butler, Your Grace." Blythe stood far too close, his thigh brushing the outside of her skirts.

"Unnecessary. I prefer to live simply."

Peg came down the stairs, pausing, eyes wide at the sight of Blythe standing just outside the breakfast room. "Your Grace." She held Beatrice's hat, veil dangling from the brim, in her hands.

"Thank you, Peg." Beatrice nodded at Blythe. "This is Lord Blythe. Should you see him again, slam the door in his face. If he's lurking about the grounds, have Jasper or Mr. Lovington shoot him."

"Yes, Your Grace." Peg nodded.

"She doesn't mean that, Peg," Blythe said in a loud whisper. "The duchess is only a bit put out this morning. Or possibly every morning."

Beatrice snatched the hat from Peg, along with a handful of pins, and stood before the mirror hanging in the foyer. Carefully, she placed the hat on her head, securing it so that the veil dipped lower on the right side of her face. She didn't really need the veil, not with her hair secured, but it still felt like a small, necessary shield against Blythe. "Shall we, my lord?"

He didn't take her arm. Instead, the light press of his fingers trailed over her spine, sending a tingle below her waist as he led her out.

Beatrice was scared nearly out of her wits. Once outside, she stumbled at seeing the smart little gig parked on the gravel drive.

Blythe deftly caught her elbow.

"Your Grace?"

"A pebble rolled beneath my foot." She tried to jerk her arm away, but he wouldn't allow it. Was he being cruel on purpose? Did he know of her aversion to carriages? Did he know what had happened?

No. No, she assured herself. *He's just being Blythe.*

The gig appeared impossibly small and fragile, but at least the top was rolled back. Should an accident occur, Beatrice would be thrown clear and not crushed. Her neck would break instantly. A much better fate.

Her fingers trembled, and Beatrice hid them in her skirts.

Broad hands lingered over her waist, longer than was proper, digging pleasurably into her skin as Blythe helped her up. The blue of his eyes remained smooth. Unrippled. Like a broad expanse of the sky at dawn.

Once settled on the leather seat, her fingers found the lacquered edge of the carriage and clung for dear life.

Looking up from beneath the brim of her hat, Beatrice caught sight of her staff, watching from the front door.

Mrs. Lovington and Peg knew well of Beatrice's fear. The two women stood mute and still, powerless to help her. They would take the path through the woods to the vicarage, the same she trod with them nearly every Sunday, along with Jasper and Mr. Lovington. The safest, quickest way with no bloody wheels beneath her or—

Beatrice pressed a hand to her chest, pushing down the panic threatening to choke her. She took several deep, calming breaths. Good lord, a nip of brandy would be quite welcome, if only she'd thought to bring some.

Blythe climbed in beside her, and the gig rocked gently with his weight.

Her fingers dug into the wood. *Nothing* would happen. There wasn't even so much as a puddle of mud on the way to the church. No streams to cross.

Blythe leaned into her, and warmth pressed into her thigh, comforting Beatrice through the thick folds of her skirt.

I don't want his bloody comfort.

At a snap of the reins, the carriage moved forward, and Beatrice had to press a hand to her lips to keep from shrieking. Sucking in a lungful of air, she tried to focus on the sound of the birds in the trees.

The carriage jerked to the side as Blythe deftly missed a small rut.

Beatrice's grip tightened. Her entire body grew stiff with terror.

"What is it, Your Grace?" Blythe said in a soothing tone. "We are barely moving. At this rate it will take days to reach Vicar Farthing and his church."

"I don't know what you mean."

Breathe in, breathe out.

A low terrified sound came from her though she tried to

stop it. She shut her eyes against the miniscule sway of the vehicle.

"Beatrice," Blythe said, gently forcing her stiff fingers away from where she gripped the seat. He threaded her fingers carefully between his, thumb moving back and forth across the top of her hand in a soothing motion.

"It is only that I am prone to a touch of sickness when I ride in a carriage," she lied, opening her eyes once more. "Your carriage isn't at all well-sprung. At the very least, you should have a driver."

"You should have told me, Your Grace." The gentle caress of his thumb along her hand calmed her. She tightened her fingers, clinging to him, unable to speak.

"My heart aches, and a drowsy numbness pains.
My sense, as though of hemlock I had drunk,
Or emptied some dull opiate to the drains.
One minute past, and Lethe-wards had sunk:
'Tis not enough envy of thy happy lot."

The rich tenor wrapped firmly around Beatrice, soothing the fear so that it didn't erupt.

"But being too happy in thine happiness,
That thou, light-winged Dryad of the trees
In some melodious plot
Of beechen green, and shadows numberless,
Singest of summer in full-throated ease."

He had a lovely voice for reciting poetry. No wonder those dithering chits in society flocked about him. Any young lady faced with a shimmering Blythe reading a poem would surely swoon.

"Keats," Beatrice said, drawing in a long, shaky breath. Her pulse still raced but no longer skipped about in fear. The poem was one of her favorites, though Blythe couldn't possibly know.

"We've arrived, Your Grace."

A breeze ruffled the veil on her hat, teasing at her nose until she opened her eyes and pushed it away.

Vicar Farthing and Melinda stood just outside the tiny church, welcoming in the crowd of parishioners and waving them to their pews. Her friend looked up, not surprised at all to see Beatrice with Blythe.

Beatrice pulled her fingers from his. "Let go of me." The embarrassment over her fear had begun to sink in. She felt ridiculous. Exposed before Blythe. "Did you think a small bit of poetry would result in my allowing you to take liberties?"

"I'll choose something longer next time." Blythe laughed. "Maybe Byron."

Beatrice's heart thumped loudly in her ears. Blythe was breathtaking when he laughed. *Or* walked. *Or* ate an omelet. Glorious sitting a horse. Magnificent quoting Keats.

Things were far easier when we snarled at each other.

He helped her down, the pads of his fingers sinking into her waist. Without giving her time to pull away, Blythe tucked Beatrice's hand into the crook of his elbow and led her to the entrance where Melinda stood, ignoring her repeated attempts to separate from him.

"Don't cause a scene, Your Grace," he whispered into her ear, leaving a maddening tingle behind. "You don't want to cause gossip, do you?"

Vicar Farthing sputtered and stammered at the appearance of Blythe and Beatrice. His dark eyes gleamed with avarice as he greeted them far too effusively for Beatrice's liking. He could barely take his eyes from Blythe, gazing at him like an adoring lover.

Melinda turned away from her husband. "Sparks, Your Grace. I see them floating about your shoulders like glowworms," she murmured. "Lord, but he's rather spectacular up close, isn't he? Blinding, almost."

"You should know. Didn't he visit the vicarage? Have tea?" Beatrice lowered her voice. "You could have warned me."

"I had no idea Lord Blythe was capable of coaxing you into a carriage. One wonders what else he might induce you to do."

"I'm not amused," Beatrice whispered back. "I shall never forgive you. You are a terrible vicar's wife."

Melinda bit her lip and attempted to appear contrite. "I didn't know he'd insist on a carriage," she whispered back, before turning to greet Mrs. Tidwell.

Chiddon's church remained small, even after Beatrice had made vast improvements to the structure. A larger building had been suggested but ultimately deemed unnecessary for the village, given the current population, though Beatrice thought her other improvements might bring more families to Chiddon.

Farthing, illustrious vicar that he was, deemed the church too small, quaint, and the vicarage far too humble. He had tried, unsuccessfully, to appeal to Beatrice for something grander, once he'd given up that she might recommend him to another post. Farthing probably viewed Blythe as a godsend, a golden earl who might finally take him from Chiddon.

A soft hum filled the church as Beatrice walked to her pew, Blythe gleaming at her arm like a newly minted coin. Women of every age, most old enough to know better, stared as if an angel had descended down to their humble church. There were plenty of gentlemen in England who were as handsome as Blythe but none, perhaps, who had his presence.

Four of the Tidwell boys, dressed in their Sunday best, waved at Beatrice, and she waved back. When Beatrice had last visited the Tidwells, she'd brought them three roasted hens, courtesy of Mrs. Lovington. Mr. Tidwell had been away on business in Overton and Mrs. Tidwell had just given birth to their last child. Another boy.

"Aren't you a bit long in the tooth for them?" Blythe led her to their seats. "Do they even know what an exalted personage you are?"

"Like most males, their affections can be bought with a pat on the head and a leg of chicken." She discreetly jerked her elbow out of his hand as she sat.

"I think you're referring to a dog, Your Grace. And you've yet to pet me . . . anywhere."

Beatrice kept her eyes forward, refusing to encourage such impropriety, especially in a church, but she bit back a smile. It was pleasing to have a handsome gentleman, even if it was Blythe, flirt with her. Vicar Farthing didn't flirt, only fawned. Castlemare had never tried to charm Beatrice because being a duke was all the charm he'd needed.

She cast Blythe a sideways glance. Would it truly be so terrible to engage in an indiscretion with him? Beatrice had told him she was in no need of comfort, and she wasn't. But— she was lonely. Rebuilding Chiddon and atoning didn't fill every empty space inside her.

The length of Blythe's muscled leg once more pressed into her thigh as he shifted on the pew.

Blythe was fit. A male in his prime. Unlike Castlemare, who'd worn a male corset of sorts to fit into his formal wear and possessed spindly legs.

"Are you warm, Your Grace? There is a flush to your cheeks," Blythe murmured, shifting once more so that his shoulder brushed hers.

"I'm quite well, thank you."

The problem with giving into Blythe, if he meant to seduce and not merely annoy her, was twofold. He *was* a rake by reputation, and she had little desire to have her name added to his list of conquests. Secondly, nakedness would be required in any sort of affair they engaged in.

Beatrice's fingers fluttered over the right side of her body.

Blythe would certainly be unclothed, which would be spectacular. But he would surely insist she be naked as well.

I simply cannot allow that.

That she was even considering allowing Blythe in her bed was . . . unsettling. Beatrice tried to summon up all the things she found distasteful about him while listening to Vicar Farthing drone on and on. Instead, she found herself recalling the warmth of his hand as he'd tried to comfort her in the carriage. The sound of his voice reciting Keats.

Good God.

This was intolerable.

When at last the service ended, Blythe stood beside her as she greeted an endless stream of villagers, looming a bit too protectively over her the entire time. He didn't stand stiff and unyielding; instead, Blythe greeted every soul as if they were old friends.

"Shall we walk back to Beresford Cottage, Your Grace?" he said, gently leading her across the grass toward the vicar's garden. "All that sitting. I need to shake off Vicar Farthing's brimstone and stretch my legs."

"What about your carriage?"

"Mr. Lovington will drive it back. I think Peg and Jasper can squeeze between him and Mrs. Lovington, don't you?"

Blythe was being kind to her. *Again.* If he kept being so lovely, it would be difficult to keep him at arm's length. Which she supposed was the point.

Yes, but I'll have to be unclothed.

"I hope you don't have any aspirations to take liberties in the woods, as you did before," she asserted in a crisp tone.

"I would *never*, Your Grace." But his tone was deceptively silky, moving over Beatrice's skin like warm bath water. "I just don't think you're overly fond of my driving. I'll spare you having to tolerate the ride once more."

He'd noticed her discomfort but would not address it directly. Nor did Beatrice have any inclination to tell him. "But I must still tolerate your company? A poor bargain."

The blue of his eyes twinkled down at her. "A sacrifice you must make, I fear. I'm going to have you search for appropriate tree limbs which might be lying about. Ones I may carve into something atrocious and unrecognizable. Perhaps I'll make you something."

They passed through the vicar's garden. Bees buzzed in a lazy manner over a patch of salvia, ignoring the hydrangeas. Beatrice stopped, watching them land on the flowers.

"I liken you to a bee," Blythe said. The breeze caught his hair, moving the thick, honey -colored strands about his temples.

"Because I possess a stinger?"

"That isn't what I was thinking, although it certainly fits." An amused sound came from him. "No, I think it because there is one queen surrounded by scores of male drones, all waiting to serve her. An entire hive. I recall watching every gentleman worth his salt swirling about you, fetching a lemonade or stooping to pick up your fan."

"That was long ago, Blythe." She plucked a daisy, twirling it between her fingers. A strange bit of tranquility had settled between her and Blythe since he'd forced himself into her house and dictated they share a brandy. Beatrice was loathe to dislodge it.

"Not so long. Only a few years," he answered, plucking at a hydrangea bloom. "I used to think your eyes were this color." Blythe held up the flower to her cheek, twisting the petals along her skin. "But yours are a far deeper hue."

A quaking sensation started low in Beatrice's belly, caused by the mere press of the flower. Their attraction buzzed in the air, louder than the group of bees. Had it always been present? Just buried beneath a layer of scorn and scathing remarks?

"I quite like Chiddon," he murmured. "I have always preferred the country."

What an odd comment from a gentleman whom Beatrice had always thought of as the epitome of a London lord. "It is easier to avoid your mother in the country, I suspect."

Blythe gave her a half-smile. "Clever duchess. Lady Blythe is quite fierce. Determined. I often liken her to a general. It is not always a compliment."

"You have a deep affection for her." Beatrice could tell that he did, though it was clear Lady Blythe annoyed him. Blythe could have simply forced his mother to the country-side and dictated the rest of her days. It would make his existence simpler, but he'd chosen not to.

"I do. I care very much for my family." There was a serious cast to his handsome face. "Their happiness is my responsibility and has been for a very long time."

Beatrice looked up at the man she'd so often assumed to be a careless rogue, one who survived on his vanity and connections. Blythe was unfailingly kind. His manner in the church had proven it. Self-deprecating about his lack of talent as well as his good looks, which she honestly didn't think he gave a whit about. A bit of a romantic. Many lords would see their overbearing mother and herd of sisters as a burden, but not Blythe.

"Lady Blythe is only anxious because she wishes me to wed." He shrugged. "Mother worries that should I perish, she would be subjected to another man's whims. Become little more than a visitor in her own home."

"Is that why you became a rake?" Beatrice said lightly. "To avoid her determination?"

"Partially, though I was never as bad as rumors would have

you believe. I adore women. How could I not? My entire household consists of them. You can't imagine how thrilled I was to receive a nephew." A lopsided grin pulled at his lips. "I admit only to making improper remarks mostly because I love the way a woman blushes, and I think I possess a unique wit. Reciting poetry when the moment calls for it takes exquisite timing. Oh, and appearing dashing at every turn, though as far as my looks and title, I had nothing to do with either, so I refuse to take credit for those."

"No wonder you attracted such a flock of admirers," Beatrice mused.

"Do I possess a herd or a flock?" He gave her an outraged look. "Perhaps a murder. That's what they call a group of crows. I've always found that incredibly interesting, to refer to a flock of crows as a murder."

"Parliament of owls," Beatrice said, "is another interesting term. When I was younger, I would imagine an entire group of owls in long robes deciding the fate of England."

"Clever duchess." Blythe nudged her gently with his shoulder. "I didn't imagine you would ever find such things interesting. But I should have guessed, given your reading. *The Voyage of the Beagle* isn't a book I'd ever considered you curling up before the fire to study."

He had looked at her books. "I suppose not. Vain, shallow creature that I am."

"Can we agree that our past dealings have little to do with our present, Your Grace?" He nudged her once more. He was smiling, the creases spreading out from his eyes making him that much more attractive.

A dangerous proposition. She hadn't yet decided how to deal with Blythe.

"Agreed. If you will admit that you seek to involve me in an indiscretion due to your boredom in the country and the fact that I am a widow."

"I am not bored, Your Grace. Far from it."

Beatrice could hear the truth in his words. It made her stomach pitch in the most pleasant way.

"But I do not deny that I seek to engage you in an indiscretion."

He stopped, angling his body closer to hers. Reaching out, Blythe gently swept his finger along her bottom lip, stroking to life a gentle hum along her skin. "After all," he said in a matter-of-fact tone, the blue of his eyes darkening to near violet in the late morning light. "Who better? I've disliked you. Been annoyed by you. Found your behavior, at times, abhorrent."

She parted her mouth to issue a retort, but Blythe shook his head, cupping her chin in his large hand.

"But still," he whispered against her mouth. "I am drawn to you like those bees are to the flowers. I have always been."

His mouth descended gently over hers, with none of the pent-up fury of their previous kiss. His palm ran down the length of her spine, sending flames down her back until he cupped her bottom. Pulling Beatrice more firmly into his arms, Blythe slanted his mouth over hers, tongue licking against her lips, coaxing her to open.

A sigh left her, one full of longing. No one had ever kissed her as Blythe did, with such fiercely restrained passion, as though they would both combust if great care weren't taken.

"Beatrice," he murmured against her lips.

She sagged against Blythe, lifting her chin just a fraction to take more of his mouth in hers, loving the sound that came from him as she did so. His palm trailed up her stomach to cup one breast, his thumb brushing along the curve, but going no farther.

Beatrice's fingers slid up his chest to the base of his skull, threading through the thick gold of his hair, tugging at the ends to pull him closer. Blythe ignited a maelstrom inside her, a mix of physical longing and a delicate pinching of her heart. She'd never thought to be capable of any depth of emotion. It had been deemed unnecessary given the future her parents had laid out for her. But this—she was *feeling*. Deeply. Intensely.

Just as every coherent thought in her head started to ebb away, Blythe ended the kiss, nipping softly at her bottom lip.

Beatrice drew away from him with reluctance, feeling foolish and more than a little desperate. There wasn't any instance when involvement with Blythe didn't end badly for her. She twisted from him, embarrassed.

He took her hand and pressed an open-mouthed kiss to her wrist before lacing their fingers together once more.

Beatrice tried to pry their hands apart, but Blythe wouldn't allow it. After a time, she ceased struggling, accepting his presence. When Beresford Cottage came into sight, he came to a halt and pressed her hand to his chest.

"I want you, Beatrice Howard. I have from the moment I set eyes on you. That's what all those insults and slurs were. Desire. A terrible way to go about flirtation when I'm usually so bloody good at it. Just not with you." His eyes fluttered shut for a moment before opening once more. "I don't know *why* I want you so desperately. I can't explain it. I definitely don't like it. But that is how I feel."

Blythe dropped her hand abruptly, leaving Beatrice open-mouthed and speechless. He sauntered in the direction of his gig, which Mr. Lovington had indeed driven back for him. Climbing inside, he snapped the reins, and gave her one last look, before disappearing down the drive.

Beatrice made her way to the steps leading to her door and sat down, not caring if she dirtied her dress, staring after him.

"Damn you, Blythe," she whispered. "Why couldn't you have just stayed in London?"

❧ 13 ❧

As amusing as it was to see Beatrice struck dumb by his little speech, one he hadn't meant to give and thought he might regret, if he stayed, there wasn't any telling what other sort of madness might take him. Questions might be lobbed at him, ones that Ellis surely couldn't answer. The entire confession had sounded ridiculous given their history. If he'd had the least talent, he could have put those words into a poem instead of inelegantly spewing them out.

There is a fine line between love and hate.

Ellis was wise enough to know that the opposite of love was apathy. Indifference.

He had never once been indifferent to Beatrice.

The seduction of her would not be conducted with the intent of vanquishing an obsession that haunted him. Not any longer. Ellis had a good idea that no matter how often he bedded Beatrice, she would linger in his bones.

"So bloody complicated." He snapped the reins.

She's afraid of carriages.

The look on Beatrice's lovely countenance as he'd

escorted her out to his waiting gig flashed through his mind. Ellis had first assumed it was merely a continuation of the general annoyance she felt toward him, but the concern evidenced by Beatrice's housekeeper and lady's maid said differently. There was genuine worry stamped clearly on their features—worry for Beatrice. Ellis had to nearly drag her to the waiting vehicle. Once inside, Beatrice had gripped the edge of the gig so tightly it was amazing the wood hadn't shattered. She'd paled at every sway, turning the color of spoiled cream. A tiny shriek of panic had erupted when Ellis had hit a small rut in the road.

A wave of protectiveness had prompted Ellis to take her hand and recite Keats, comforting Beatrice as he would one of his sisters. He'd nearly stopped the gig to take her into his arms, but her body was so stiff, so tight, Ellis had worried she'd shatter. She hadn't relaxed until they'd arrived at the church.

Another mysterious revelation had awaited Ellis. Not the sermon of Vicar Farthing, a sanctimonious windbag who'd done everything but toss himself at Ellis like a young lady in her first season, but the reaction of Chiddon at having Beatrice in their midst.

Beatrice Howard, snobby, superior, *destroyed-reputations-for-sport* Beatrice Howard, was *beloved* in Chiddon. Adored. Worshipped. Close to legendary. Gates hadn't exaggerated in the least when he'd referred to Beatrice as *our* duchess.

Could Ellis seduce and discard a bloody saint? The villagers of Chiddon would chase him back to London with pitchforks if he hurt their beloved duchess. He'd marveled at the children who waved at Beatrice. The smiles sent in her direction. An older woman had thrust a pie at her.

Desiring the horrible Beatrice Howard, wanting to bed her until she cried for mercy, had been one thing. Distasteful, but acceptable. Lust and nothing more.

But liking her—wanting to protect her. *Comfort* her.

God help him, based on what Ellis had seen today, Beatrice had become admirable.

Admirable.

The apocalypse must be very near.

Ellis jumped out of his carriage with a growl, caught up in his own emotions, and nodded to one of the grooms before jogging up the steps. The hunting lodge was much smaller than Beresford Cottage and needed some updating, but Ellis had only visited the place twice in the last ten years. His home was primarily in London these days. Or at least it had been. Before Rome.

The lodge's butler and caretaker, a dour elderly man named Sykes, opened the door at his arrival.

"My lord."

"Good day, Sykes. I prayed for your soul, in case you were wondering." Ellis doubted his butler ever grew overly concerned for the whereabouts of his master. He'd been in residence at the hunting lodge, along with Cook, for years. Ellis was probably interrupting their routine with his presence.

"Very good, my lord." The expression Sykes wore, always that of an exhausted bloodhound, never changed. If Ellis's butler was ever happy, sad, frightened, or anything else, one would never know. "Mr. Estwood has arrived."

"Estwood?" Ellis stopped short. He'd completely forgotten about Estwood's visit. Finding Beatrice Howard in Chiddon had him thinking of little else but her.

Another sound of aggravation left him.

Sykes raised a brow. "He awaits you in the front room, my lord. Shall I tell him you are indisposed?"

"Do I look indisposed?" Ellis breezed past the butler. "Bring a tray of . . . something." He waved a hand. "Set another place at the table. And prepare a guestroom."

If Sykes had been capable of rolling his eyes, Ellis thought he would have. "Yes, my lord."

The hunting lodge wasn't grand enough for a drawing room. Or a parlor. The largest room at the front of the house was a toss between both. There was an ample sideboard. A mounted deer's head that Ellis hung his hats on, much to the dislike of Sykes. Some rusty weaponry displayed along one wall. And a collection of overstuffed, comfortable chairs all clustered around a massive fireplace.

Estwood sat sprawled in one, a thick packet of papers at his side.

"I was wondering when you would arrive home, my lord." His friend didn't bother to stand. Estwood wasn't well-born and discarded manners as quickly as he assumed them. "Your unbelievably dismal butler told me you were at church. Do you suppose Sykes is taking nips of the sherry?"

"I don't keep sherry. And I *was* at church." Ellis strode over to Estwood who finally stood. He wrapped his friend in a warm embrace. "There is a roast on the menu for tonight, and I'll have the dust blown off the guestroom bed for you."

It was Estwood who had overseen his affairs while Ellis had been in Rome attempting to bring forth his nonexistent artistic talent. His friend had taken on, without complaint, the daunting task of managing Lady Blythe in Ellis's absence. Lady Blythe, bastion of decorum and breeding, had initially balked at having a man such as Estwood looking out for her, but she'd come around. Estwood was self-made, the fortune at his command not the result of numerous generations but carefully curated through intelligence and his own ambition.

Ellis had a great deal of respect for Estwood.

Estwood had helped Haven dig his estate out of poverty by wisely investing Theodosia Barrington's dowry in a mix of property, railways, and shares of the East India Company. Haven would never be poor again.

"Has all the machinery arrived for the textile mills in Lancashire?" Ellis asked, walking to the sideboard. A great deal of factories decorated the portfolio of the Earl of Blythe, and Ellis was determined to modernize every one of them. Not only was it a profitable practice, but Ellis liked machinery. All those lovely gears spinning about. A curious habit for an earl, to admire axles, pistons, and the like. Poetry and art seemed much more colorful.

"Yes," Estwood answered. "Installation begins next week. Productivity should more than double within the next few months."

"I hope so." Ellis spilled some brandy into a glass. "And the ironworks?"

Estwood nodded to the thick leather packet. "It's all there. Including the importing of bat guano for fertilizer. You've a head for business, my lord. If you weren't an earl, I think you would have become wealthy on your own merits. Your idea to turn one of the mills from manufacturing textiles to producing rope was quite astute."

"Everyone needs rope."

Estwood nodded in agreement. "Even so, I'll admit I hadn't considered rope. Or twine. Given my origins, rope should have been the first thing that came to mind."

Estwood was the son of a village blacksmith, a man who had struggled at times to provide for his family. Days had been spent attempting to bring forth crops from the tiny plot of land Estwood's family home sat upon. Estwood's mother had kept chickens and sold the eggs. His sisters had grown vegetables to take to market. It had been an existence of never having enough. Of always being hungry. Some wondered at Estwood's ruthless determination. Not Ellis.

"You've grown soft living in London," Ellis replied. "To forget the importance of a good length of rope. Besides, it is wise to never depend too entirely on the rents of your tenants for your wealth." Ellis's father had taught him that. One year of poor crops or disease wiping out an entire herd of sheep and a lord could find himself near destitute.

"You've a keen instinct for such things." Estwood regarded him with eyes like two slivers of pale moonlight. "You're a fine engineer with your love of industry and machinery. But not a painter. Definitely not a sculptor." Estwood picked up one of Ellis's carvings which had been discarded on a table beside him. "What is this supposed to be?"

Ellis sighed in resignation. No one saw his vision. "I was trying for a trout."

"Looks like a rock with eyes. It's an honest mistake. There is weathering across the side." His friend swallowed the remainder of his brandy before leaning toward Ellis, waving his glass in a plea for it to be refilled.

"Those are scales, you idiot. And I hope your manners are better when dealing with Lady Blythe." Ellis splashed more liquid in Estwood's glass.

"Lady Blythe has made the decision to ignore my humble beginnings. Now she merely corrects me on the proper fork while instructing me to retrieve you from the country. Lady Anabeth awaits."

He smiled at Estwood. "She'll be waiting a little longer." A vision of Beatrice, strolling through the garden of the vicarage, profile lit against the morning sun, lingered before his eyes. The thick twist of golden hair snugged up to her right cheek, tied with a ribbon to match her eyes.

Why doesn't she wear her hair up?

"Lady Blythe will be displeased. At any rate, I can only stay two nights. A business matter has arisen, one I must see to personally. Waterstone." The name echoed with dislike.

Mr. Waterstone, related to an earl and a consummate self-important gentleman, had been forced to deal with Estwood on occasion because Estwood had powerful friends, the Duke of Granby among them. "Waterstone? Don't tell me you're helping him."

"I'm not assisting him out of the kindness of my heart but at the request of Granby." Estwood's already pale eyes took on the sheen of ice, a thoughtful look crossing over his harsh features. "Every courtesy Waterstone has afforded me I plan to return. It is the very least I can do."

Ellis would not wish to be Waterstone in this circumstance.

"So, you attended services in that little village over the hill. Chilton?" Estwood asked.

"Chiddon. Vicar Farthing hopes I'll become his patron. He wishes to leave the country and preside over a more prestigious post."

"Doesn't he already have a patron? Someone must have sent him here."

"The Duke of Castlemare, I suspect. Farthing must have done something awful to have been sent to Chiddon, though I find the village and its inhabitants lovely. Castlemare's duchess seems lax in offering him support, so he has focused his efforts on me."

Another image of Beatrice, chin lifted, mouth greedily devouring his, sent a tendril of arousal curling around his thighs.

"Castlemare's duchess. Impossible. I just saw her in London at the theater and—" Estwood stopped. "Oh, you mean *Beatrice Howard*. I'd nearly forgotten about her, as has most of London. There was quite a game for a while, guessing where Castlemare had sent her before he died. I wouldn't have thought a remote part of Hampshire. I was hoping for Russia. She'd be indistinguishable from all the other bits of ice and snow."

Ellis's fingers tightened on the glass he held. "Castlemare sent her to Chiddon *before* he died?"

"You can't possibly think she's here of her own accord." Estwood sent him a curious look. "Chiddon must be a particular form of hell for a woman like Beatrice."

"Vicar Farthing claims she came to mourn Castlemare's death in private and decided not to return to London." And Beatrice had never said otherwise. Ellis had known that couldn't possibly be the truth, or at least, not all of it.

"Mourn Castlemare? No one misses that prick. He and Beatrice detested each other and lived apart. I forgot how much you missed while you were in Rome sculpting babies—"

"Cherubs," Ellis corrected, though to be fair, most of his cherubs had looked like chubby birds. He could never get the legs right. "Lady Blythe didn't mention anything about Castlemare to me. I confess, I didn't even know he was dead until I arrived in Chiddon."

"Foxwood claimed his daughter was prostrate with grief over Castlemare's death, which everyone knew wasn't the case because she left London well before her husband died. Castlemare made no bones about his disappointment in Beatrice's failure to produce an heir. He sent her to his country estate, but later, rumors swirled that Beatrice was not in residence. The Foxwoods stayed tight lipped, as did Castlemare's brother who inherited after he died. But Castlemare's mistress wasn't so discreet. Apparently, there was some sort of accident."

"An accident?"

"One in which Beatrice was horribly disfigured." Estwood sat back. "That was why Castlemare really sent her away. Why no one has seen her in years. I must say, if that is the case, there is no one more deserving of tragedy than Beatrice Howard. I've never met a more malicious creature in all my life."

"Then you haven't spent enough time in society," Ellis replied.

"Her attempts to make Andromeda Barrington a pariah speak for themselves. You'll find no one in London who has a kind word for Beatrice. Nor is her presence longed for. The Foxwoods behave as if they no longer have a daughter."

"I never cared overmuch for Lord and Lady Foxwood," Ellis said. He cared less for them now.

"But you were always drawn to Beatrice. Not sure why. She is a collection of things you find abhorrent. Granted, she is beautiful, or at least she was." Estwood looked at Ellis for confirmation.

"I hate to disappoint you, but the Duchess of Castlemare is still stunning. I've never seen a more beautiful woman." Ellis sipped his drink and thought about the kiss he'd shared with Beatrice. The way she'd angled her body so that her right side was protected. The hair gathered along one shoulder with a ribbon. Her fear of carriages, which he'd witnessed first-hand. "I see no evidence of any accident."

"Something about a carriage overturning, but that was according to Castlemare's mistress. Foxwood denies any such thing ever occurred, though no one asks after Beatrice any longer." Estwood paused. "But if you say she is still lovely—"

"She is." He cut Estwood off.

"Then the words of Castlemare's mistress were only out of spite. You wouldn't consider bedding Beatrice otherwise. Don't bother denying it."

"I won't." Ellis strolled to the sideboard and refilled his glass. "As you say, I've always been drawn to her. I find seducing a widow to be a pleasant diversion while I'm in the country. There is a lack of amusement in Chiddon. I must make my own."

"Castlemare used to crow that tupping Beatrice was like bedding a block of ice." Estwood shrugged. "We met over a card table once. I can't say I liked him. Sloppy when he became foxed. Lots of spit when he regaled us all with his ducal personality."

"She may not be worth the trouble," Ellis said smoothly. "I do find her a bit chilly, but there is challenge in that. Even so, I'll be returning to London soon." The words hurt because none of them were true. But he sensed Beatrice wanted to stay hidden behind her walls of Chiddon villagers, high neck-lines and an appealing if unusual hairstyle. She would not thank him for drawing any attention in her direction. Beatrice may not have asked for his protection, but she had it all the same.

"Yes, Lady Anabeth awaits." Estwood laughed, showing a line of even, white teeth. "Shall we have a look at the packet I brought you? There is an interesting opportunity for an exporting company. I'm starving by the way."

"Sykes is on the way with refreshments of some sort," Ellis said, his thoughts not on his friend, an exporting busi-ness, or whether Sykes would bring anything decent for them to eat. He wanted to question Estwood further about Beat-rice but didn't dare. Estwood was bound to mention to Lady Blythe that Beatrice was in Chiddon, and though Ellis's mother had never liked Beatrice, she was well acquainted with the Foxwoods. Everyone was. She might be curious.

"There is a piece of property nearby I'd like to purchase," he informed Estwood, resigning himself to a shift in the conversation. "There is a tavern in Chiddon, the only one, as it happens." He told Estwood about Gates and his ale, leaving out Beatrice's involvement. Soon, the brandy was put aside for two very expensive bottles of French wine. The tiny sand-wiches brought by Sykes wouldn't have satisfied anyone. Thankfully, the dinner roast was much better. Still, throughout the entire evening, Ellis's enjoyment was dimmed as his mind wandered to Beatrice and the life she'd led before he'd found her in Chiddon. He was only certain of one thing. The horrible creature he'd once known no longer existed, or at least, not all of her.

After retiring, Ellis stared at the ceiling above him, remembering the feel of Beatrice's mouth beneath his own.

He wished Estwood was returning to London tomorrow.

❧ 14 ❧

"What do you think, Your Grace?"

Beatrice cast her gaze over the pond before her, thick with some sort of sludge, before taking in the abandoned mill. She had no idea why Blythe had brought her here today. Morbid curiosity, perhaps, over the gruesome history of the place.

"I think it is a mill falling to rubble and a pond with dead fish." She put a finger to her nose. "At least it smells like something dead." There were rumors of ghosts about. "And I believe the area is haunted."

"Hmm."

Beatrice hadn't seen Blythe for nearly a week, not since the odd, painful confession he'd thrown at her after church. She'd gone about her business, mildly bereft at his absence. But this morning, Blythe was once more at her breakfast table, happily tucked into a rasher of bacon and flirting outrageously with the previously dour Mrs. Lovington.

"I thought you might have returned to London," she'd announced. Her pulse had throbbed gently at seeing him; she was unaccountably pleased he was once more sitting in her chair, even if she didn't want to be.

Blythe had looked up from his bacon. "Nonsense, Your Grace. I've something to show you."

Hustling her outside before Beatrice could properly finish her tea, she'd found Cicero already saddled beside Blythe's horse, Dante. They'd ridden for the better part of a half-hour. Blythe had gestured to various points of interest as they traveled, though there wasn't truly anything of note—just trees and grass. Now they were here, at the abandoned Mandrell mill.

The mill's importance to the tiny village of Chiddon couldn't be underestimated, but no one wanted their wheat ground on the same stone where Mrs. Mandrell's lover met his fate. After drowning his wife, Mandrell had hung himself. Farthing's predecessor, Vicar Kent, had been Mrs. Mandrell's lover, his death leaving Chiddon without spiritual guidance. Efforts to induce another villager to take on the mill had proven futile which meant all the wheat in the surrounding area had to be taken to Overton. Cursed, was what some said of Chiddon after such a tragedy, and many villagers had left for greener pastures.

"Grim scenery for a morning ride," Beatrice announced. The entire tale left goosebumps covering her arms.

Blythe grinned. "Mr. Gates gave me the lurid details, Your Grace. Imagine, a lecherous vicar ground to death. Still, it isn't enough reason to leave a perfectly good mill standing abandoned for over ten years when Chiddon is so obviously starved for one. Overton is some distance away. You won't be able to keep your cheese monger or anyone else if the mill continues to stand idle."

Beatrice narrowed her eyes. "Are you mocking the need for a proper cheddar?"

The breadth of his shoulders rolled carelessly as a bit of wind teased at his hair.

He was so bloody handsome, Beatrice's heart flitted about in her chest before settling. "The wheel doesn't even turn."

"Clogged with debris which can be easily remedied. That's why the pond is stagnant. Well, that and the dam which is also overgrown." He tilted his head to the left. "But I've seen much worse." Blythe gracefully slid from Dante's back.

Indecently tight breeches. The leather pulled exquisitely in all the improper places.

Beatrice looked down, afraid he'd catch her ogling him.

"Besides, Your Grace, don't you need a new project, or do you still believe you can lure a baker to Chiddon without a mill?"

Beatrice did want a proper bakery, but the problem of the mill had stopped her. The bakery was for Rosalind, the Barrington cousin who created pastries which were regarded as works of art. Beatrice had used Rosalind in her campaign to destroy Andromeda.

"I was thinking more a dressmaker," she replied.

The dressmaker was to be penance for Andromeda.

"Hmm. A mill would be far more useful to Chiddon."

"But who do you suppose will operate the mill?" she asked. "No one in Chiddon will volunteer. I've tried." She gestured to the crumbling building. "There isn't a soul who would buy the mill either. I posted a notice in Overton but received no offers."

"You've such little faith, Lady Beatrice, Patron Saint of Chiddon." A dazzling, heartbreaking smile broke over his lips, sending warmth along her limbs as if Beatrice had just walked into a patch of sunlight.

"Make sure to say that with the proper respect." She cocked her chin, pretending to be annoyed. "I cannot do much about the mill at present, so I've turned my attention to other matters. Sugar beets."

"Ah, yes. Sugar beets. Just the other day, after that rousing sermon from Vicar Farthing, Mr. Tidwell and I engaged in a lively discussion on sugar beets," Blythe said. "Your plan is to allow his son to work those fields at the edge of your property. I quite agree with the assessment. You aren't doing anything with the land."

"Sugar beets are a profitable crop, and Mr. Tidwell is a renowned expert on the vegetable, though I fail to see why he felt the need to discuss my affairs with you." Duchess or not, Beatrice was still a woman, which meant her opinions were often questioned. There was a reason she'd threatened that stonemason working on the vicarage with a riding crop. It was the only way he would listen.

"Prickly, aren't you?" Blythe stood, looking at the mill, moving from the stream emptying into the pond to the wheel and back, likely envisioning the movement of the water in his head.

A softness for him took root in her chest—a gentle ache which had her looking away from him once more.

"This could be a more profitable project than your sugar beets," he said with certainty. "And more useful than a dressmaker or a baker, Saint Beatrice."

"Every woman deserves to eat a proper scone while dressed in an elegant gown."

Blythe snorted. "Chiddon *needs* a mill. The assumption that the place is haunted by anything other than mice, spiders, and other vermin is ridiculous and not enough reason to allow it to remain empty."

"My lord, not one person within a hundred miles will set foot in that mill. Even now, no one in Chiddon dares to mention Mandrell. The entire incident was quite gruesome. A man of the cloth was murdered." She glanced once more at the rubble of the mill covered in weeds. "I'm told his blood still stains the stone floor."

Blythe rolled his eyes. "Good lord, madam. I'd not thought *you* to be taken in by tales of ghosts and specters. Thankfully, I don't believe in such things. Which is why I had Estwood purchase the property for me," he said, still studying the pond and the wheel. "Come, let us take a look."

"You bought *this* mill?" Beatrice said in disbelief.

"Estwood did on my behalf. Do you recall him? You may have met at Granby's house party."

Disquiet settled over Beatrice at the mention of the stupid house party. She recalled a striking man with eyes like silver, one of low birth who Lord and Lady Foxwood had instructed Beatrice to keep her distance from. "Vaguely. But I don't understand why you would have him buy the mill. It's a poor investment. You've no ties to Chiddon."

"Estwood handled my affairs in London while I was absent. And he's a friend." Blythe's eyes caught hers. "And as to the mill? I cannot stand the thought of you being more adored than myself in any instance. It goes against the grain, Your Grace."

Beatrice's fingers tightened on Cicero's reins. "If you are bored, Blythe, you should return to London."

"Never said I was bored." He studied her intently. "At present, I am quite entertained."

Her heart, already unsure how to beat properly with Blythe so near, once more lost its steady rhythm.

She drew in a breath and turned her attention to the mill. The pond. The stream. A great deal of water. If Beatrice listened *too* long, the stream would become *the* riverbed. A vision of poor Thomas would float before her. The scream inside Beatrice, the same one she'd made for two long days trapped beneath a carriage, might erupt. "If we are done here, my lord—"

"The flume is blocked," Blythe said. "But the pitwheel is still in fine condition. Come, take a look with me." He raised his arms to help her down.

"What on earth is a pitwheel?" Blythe's palms spread over her waist, and a tiny shiver shot along the base of her spine. The idea that they could be lovers for a time struck Beatrice once more. It was impossible, of course. But—

"Come." Blythe took her hand, lacing their fingers together with a great deal of familiarity.

Beatrice did not pull away.

He led her into the cobwebbed, spider-infested interior of what must once have been a fine mill. Not that Beatrice knew a great deal about such things; she didn't. But she had an eye for buildings, especially after all the renovations she'd overseen in Chiddon. The masonry was solid. The roof, still mostly intact. And the air smelled of nothing more than wet earth and dust, not decades-old blood. Solid stone walls covered with the slightest condensation greeted her as they stepped down a set of stairs curling down to the base of the building.

"The Mandrells came to a bad end," she reminded him in a hushed tone, looking around and batting at a cobweb stuck to the brim of her hat. A pile of what looked to be rodent droppings sat in one corner where an ancient bag of grain had been torn open.

"Why are you whispering?" Blythe leaned over her shoulder, allowing his nose to drift along her neck. The light touch sent a spray of sensation across her shoulders and between her breasts. Her nipples grew taut, peaking beneath the velvet of her riding habit.

Oh, good lord.

"Let's go look at the pitwheel," Blythe said with undisguised enthusiasm, dragging her behind him. The pitwheel, as it turned out, was a large axle to which a toothed gear was affixed. The water came through the flume, which was indeed clogged with vegetation, rocks, and other debris, and moved the water wheel, which then turned the pitwheel and forced the stones to grind.

Blythe explained everything to Beatrice, taking time to examine every inch of the pitwheel, much to her dismay. The mill was infested with all sorts of unpleasantness. She crushed a large spider beneath the heel of her boot and hopped about to avoid another. "Blythe."

"Hmm." He placed his hands on his hips, completely absorbed in a gear of some sort while Beatrice fought off a horde of arachnids.

"How on earth do you know so much about mills and the grinding of wheat?" she asked him. "Shouldn't such knowledge belong to your steward?" Beatrice ducked to avoid a web strewn across one corner. "Could we please move to another location? There is an exceptional number of spiders." She stomped on another, and it gave a satisfying crunch beneath her boot.

"My father was involved in the management of his estates, so much so that he knew each of our tenants by name. Took tea with them several times a year. He would roll up his sleeves and dive in if a plow broke or there were issues with the thresher." A wistfulness crossed Blythe's features as he related that long ago memory.

He missed his father. Had loved him. Beatrice thought of Lord and Lady Foxwood, for whom emotion was something foreign and repellent. "And what about mills?"

A boyish grin, devastating to any female, was leveled at her. "My father had a natural curiosity about what made things work. He liked using his hands. Probably where our paltry skill at carving came from. When I was a boy, I came upon him in his study, taking apart a clock which had stopped working. He explained how all the springs and gears worked together to move the clock's hands."

Beatrice tiptoed over a small pile of refuse. The end of a tail was sticking out. She didn't bother to examine further. "You shared his fascination."

"I did. Unfortunately, I was also blessed with a mother who didn't think an earl should know how to repair a harness or the mechanism in a thresher. Such pursuits were for common folk. But I've always thought such knowledge useful."

"Sounds rather contrary to your other pursuits of sculpting and poetry."

"Oh, it is. I think I'll always admire the written word and other creative pursuits simply because I lack the skill for any of them. It's possible I also possess an elder sister who might have advised me that young ladies would be more inclined in my direction if I enjoyed more romantic pursuits. Over time, I hoped to be counted among the number of poets or artists." He gave a self-deprecating shrug. "But the fates decided differently. I can only recite words written by another. Speak about brush strokes, but not make them myself. I realized in Rome that while I see only a flower, an artist like Theodosia Barrington sees a complex weaving of color and emotion which she can translate to a canvas. Keats or Byron could do so with words."

"I expect that reciting a poem to an adoring young lady has the same effect as if you penned the words yourself." Beatrice's tone was tart, thinking of all the women who'd been struck by Blythe as he read them poetry.

"Don't be jealous, Bea." The side of his mouth lifted. "I can't write you a poem, but I'll carve you something." He turned back to the pitwheel. "And fix your mill."

"I'm not—" Beatrice stared at the back of his golden head, hating that she *was* jealous. Of every bit of attention this glorious man she'd once thought she disliked had showered on any other woman. And Blythe knew it.

How had this happened? Two kisses, admittedly both magnificent, and Beatrice was mooning over Blythe.

Abruptly, she backed away, nearly tripping over an old piece of wood that had come lose from the floorboards above. She coughed, waving her hand before her nose. "There is a rather pungent pile of . . . something over there. Can we please leave?"

"Yes, duchess." Blythe once more took her hand, cautioning her to watch her step as he led her out into the bright morning sun. Walking back to Cicero and Dante, Blythe winked before reaching into his saddlebags. "You're prickly because you need to eat something. I should have allowed you to finish breakfast, but I wanted to talk to you about the mill."

"I'm not prickly."

Blythe produced a blanket, a bottle of wine, cheese, and a somewhat battered loaf of bread. He dug around a bit more and came back with one lone apple. "I thought I packed two."

"You are oddly prepared for our jaunt to view a potentially haunted mill," Beatrice murmured.

"It isn't the least haunted. And I *do* appreciate a good cheddar." He nodded at the cheese wrapped in cloth. "I'm afraid my larder isn't stocked nearly as well as yours. I hope this will suffice for a picnic."

Beatrice took the blanket from his hands and spread it across the grass. "I've never been on a picnic, at least, not without scores of footmen rushing about with trays and a small group gathered to observe something scenic."

"I'm not sure you are at a picnic now," Blythe laughed. "A paltry apple, some bread, and a bit of cheese on a blanket doesn't qualify. I should have asked Mrs. Lovington for a chicken leg or a pie. But at least we have wine."

Blythe took off his coat, uncaring at the impropriety of being in his shirtsleeves, and formed the garment into a pillow. Laying back, he patted the spot beside him and looked up at the sky. Pointing to a large cloud directly above them, he said, "Do you see that, Beatrice. Right there? A fish." He tugged at her skirts, insisting she lay beside him.

Beatrice stretched out, conscious of his hard, muscled body so close to hers. Blythe smelled of clean linen with a hint of citrus. Lime, possibly. The warm, delicious scent pulled her toward him, billowing over her senses.

"Can you make it out?" He tilted his head until the top touched hers. "Maybe not a fish. A snake, possibly." Blythe had made sure to position himself so that his lean form aligned with Beatrice's left side, not her right.

"I don't see anything." Trepidation shot through her, blotting out the pleasure of being mere inches from him. She thought back to his mention of Estwood, a gentleman who must inhabit London. A place where all sorts of rumors survived about Beatrice Howard.

"Relax, Bea."

The shortened form of her name, which no one but Blythe had ever used, flustered her as did the increasing intimacy between them. Had he told Estwood she was in Chiddon? And in return, what had Estwood told Blythe?

"Just look at the clouds," he said. "Stop behaving as if I'm about to pounce on you. You haven't eaten, and you could faint if I attempt ravishment."

The words he'd said to her the last time they were together pulsed through her mind.

I want you, Beatrice Howard. I have from the moment I set eyes on you.

"So that is still your intent?" It was the only thing she could say without asking directly if his friend had told him about Castlemare and her banishment to Chiddon. "Ravishment? As you informed me the other day?" She attempted to sound blasé.

"I confessed my desire." The low tenor of his voice washed over her skin. "Ravishment never came up in our discussion, though I see it has been on your mind, Your Grace. How improper."

Beatrice felt her cheeks color. "I see nothing but a white cloud, my lord."

He rolled to his side so that his nose barely touched her cheek. "So difficult. I meant every word, in case you think I was merely driven mad by Vicar Farthing's sermon. My intentions toward you have not changed. Does that put you at ease?"

Estwood had told Blythe . . . *something*. But he wouldn't question or force the truth from her. Nor had it deterred his pursuit of Beatrice. There was a small amount of comfort in the knowledge, though she still hadn't decided if engaging in an indiscretion was wise.

"Is this your attempt at seduction, my lord? A reputedly haunted mill?"

"Is it working?" Blythe gave her a cheeky grin before brushing his mouth over hers.

At the touch of his mouth, Beatrice's entire body melted into the blanket and the soft pad of grass beneath. "But the mill—"

Blythe's fingers toyed with her skirts before trailing up the edge of her leg to trail lazily between her thighs, which parted without protest at his touch.

"The mill will never be profitable," she choked out as his teeth nipped at the skin beneath her left ear and his hand pressed into her mound.

"Estwood agrees with you," he whispered against her neck. "He told me much the same."

Blythe's lips moved slowly over the line of her jaw, so gentle and teasing that Beatrice turned her face just to hurry him to her mouth. The tip of his tongue darted out, tracing her bottom lip. His fingers stroked idly at the juncture of her thighs, finding the slit in her underthings with little effort. A delicate ache settled over the lower half of her body.

Blythe claimed her mouth with gentle desperation, kissing her as if he might never do so again, all the while stroking her damp flesh. A slow roll of pleasure built inside Beatrice, one she'd sensed before but had never been able to reach. Castlemare hadn't cared whether she enjoyed the marital bed, and well, there hadn't been anyone else.

A delicious pleasure built inside her.

"I have you, Bea." Blythe nipped at her lower lip, the blue of his eyes glowing down at her as he very deliberately pressed two fingers inside her, all while his thumb tortured—

A gasp left Beatrice. Her hips arched against his hand. She writhed as the pleasure cascaded over her, like a brilliant shower of stars. Goodness, was *this* what she'd been missing?

Blythe's fingers never stopped their tender onslaught against her flesh while Beatrice panted and shifted on the blanket. When the last tremors left her, she opened her eyes to find Blythe regarding her with the intensity of a fire threatening to burst free of the grate. Awareness of him and the hard length pulsing against her thigh had Beatrice shutting her eyes once more.

"Don't look at me like that," she whispered.

"You're beautiful, Bea. More so when you climax. If I could paint you at this moment, I would."

She wasn't beautiful any longer. Blythe could only see the best, undamaged parts of her. Beatrice thought of London, of the life she would never have again. *Could* never have again.

No balls. No parties. Hiding beneath a veil. My God, she could never even get in a carriage to properly attend the theater. Pushing up on one elbow, she slapped away his fingers.

"Bea?" Blythe regarded her in puzzlement. He reached for her again, and she moved further across the blanket.

"*This* is a foolish venture," she said stiffly, glaring at him. "As Estwood claims." Beatrice wasn't speaking only of the mill but also of her and Blythe. Was this another amusement for him? Now that he knew she was disfigured and found himself curious? Perhaps he'd go back to London and brag of his exploits in Chiddon with the scarred Beatrice Howard.

"Whatever you are thinking, I insist you stop." Grim determination was etched on his handsome face.

"You should go back to London. Where you belong." They could never be lovers or anything else. Blythe was part of a world that would no longer welcome Beatrice into their midst. Even if she allowed further intimacies to take place, all of it was bound to blow up in a spectacular fashion.

Oh, Beatrice. You'll be regarded as one of those unfortunates in a circus, to be stared at and pitied. Would you bring such attention to our door?

Kind words from her mother, Lady Foxwood, when Beatrice had begged to be allowed to stay at their London home.

The only man who would take you as a lover, my dear wife, is one who seeks to use the tale for an invitation to sup.

Castlemare's not so gentle reminder that she no longer possessed any value to him.

"There is nothing for you in Chiddon. Not even this mill," she said in her chilliest tone, her body still throbbing from Blythe's touch. Beatrice wanted to be away from him and this wishful longing for what could never be hers. She jerked to her feet, smoothing down her skirts, and marched off in the direction of Cicero.

"Bea," Blythe snapped, following close behind.

"The sun has made my temples ache, my lord," she said, refusing to look at him. "Will you kindly assist me?"

Blythe stood there so long, watching her, Beatrice thought he would refuse. But he came forward, lifting her with such force into the saddle she thought she'd fly off Cicero's other side.

"You are being foolish," he bit out. "Estwood—"

"This has nothing to do with your friend or whatever gossip he brought with him to Chiddon." Her breath hitched. "But it has everything to do with me not wishing to be yet another conquest of the Earl of Blythe."

"Surprising you didn't stop me before I brought about your release," he drawled coldly. "If you were so averse."

"I merely wanted to see what all the fuss was about, my lord. Now that I have, I'll take my leave." She looked pointedly to Cicero's bridle, held in the grip of his hand. "Let go."

Blythe's hand fell away. "By all means, Your Grace."

Beatrice nudged Cicero into a gallop, away from the mill and the earl she'd once hated.

She felt far differently now.

15

E llis wandered down the main street of Chiddon, amazed at the preparations for the upcoming festival. Seemed out of proportion given the population of Chiddon, but Gates had said the idea was to draw people to the village with the hopes they would wish to stay. A peddler's wagon, complete with a dancing monkey and mountains of pots, pans, tools, and other household goods was set up at the end of the main street. Opposite sat a stall full of ribbons, lace, and other frippery. At another stall, a plump man, round like a ball of dough, manned a booth selling fresh-baked breads, tarts, and pastries.

Beatrice's baker. Well, at least he'd have a mill close by now, thanks to Ellis. The building she'd had renovated for the baker's use possessed fine glass windows at the front, perfect for the display of cakes and pies. Living quarters were above. The rent was minimal and set for two years.

Ellis nodded to the baker but continued on to the village green. The thought of the Duchess of Castlemare spoiled Ellis's mood, as it had for the past week. He'd returned from

KATHLEEN AYERS

their tour of the mill—and Beatrice coming apart for him—intending once more to return to London with all haste.

His trousers tightened immediately. Ellis couldn't get the erotic picture of Beatrice's pleasure at his hands from his mind. Her dismissal of him had done nothing but make Ellis want her more, if such a thing were possible.

What *was* he still doing in Chiddon? Buying mills for duchesses who would never—

She is only afraid.

Settling before the fire later that same day, with a tray brought to him by a morose Sykes, Blythe had finished the bottle of wine he'd meant to enjoy with Beatrice. It was the talk of London and Estwood which had altered her mood toward Ellis. They had only danced around the carriage accident when Ellis should have bluntly confronted her, told her that he knew. Untied the damnable ribbon holding her hair and forced Beatrice to confront that which terrified her. Coddling her had been a mistake as it had given her too much time to conjure up a host of absurd reasons for his pursuit.

I couldn't just find a nice farmer's wife to tup.

"Ho there, my lord."

Gates, red-faced in the late afternoon heat, waved from a long table. The owner of The Pickled Duck presided over a makeshift bar, handing out mugs of ale and cider. Several wooden casks were being taken to the village square by a pair of sturdy lads, muscles straining under the weight. Two young boys ran back and forth filling mugs, but there was no collection of coin. Refreshments, Ellis recalled Gates saying, were courtesy of the Duchess of Castlemare.

More of Beatrice's bloody benevolence. She had it in abundance for everyone but Blythe.

"I worried that your lordship had returned to London before the festival," Gates said. "Perhaps the good vicar's sermon had driven you off. Or perhaps the vicar in general."

Farthing's ambition was a poorly kept secret in Chiddon.

Ellis inclined his head. "And miss the most fun Chiddon is likely to have all year? Perish the thought, Mr. Gates. I merely had business which required my attention." In actuality, Ellis had pondered what to do with Beatrice while taking apart the large clock sitting at the top of the stairs at his hunting lodge. Sykes had been aghast at seeing the pieces strewn all over the rug with Ellis, a bottle of wine at his elbow.

A small stack of correspondence sat in his front room, awaiting a response, and the clock was an excellent way to avoid them—particularly the latest plea from Lady Blythe to return to London. Which he should have done by now.

Ellis determined he would respond. When the clock was put back together and he felt steadier, more in control of his emotions. Instead, he'd busied himself looking over plans for the mill. Estwood had already taken the liberty of sending a master stonemason to oversee rebuilding the crumbled walls. Laborers would soon arrive to dredge the pond and get the water flowing properly.

"The music starts at sundown, my lord," Gates said. "I've already got the pigs and birds on a spit." He jerked his head in the direction of The Pickled Duck where a plume of smoke rose behind the building along with the tantalizing aroma of roasted meat. "Mrs. Lovington is back there ordering around those that volunteered to help her."

"We are acquainted," Ellis said. "Lovely woman."

Gates gave him a dubious look. "Are we speaking of the same Mrs. Lovington, my lord? Tall. Looks like she could take down a sturdy man with one punch?"

"The very same," Ellis replied with a smile. "Makes a splendid omelet."

"Hmph." Gates grumbled and motioned for one of the young boys running about to bring Ellis a mug. "My best batch thus far, my lord. Her Grace is fond of it. I expect you are looking for her, my lord. The duchess."

"Am I?" Ellis accepted the mug. He *was* looking for Beatrice but discreetly. It would do no good to make a show of seeking her out, not when she was so bloody skittish. She was damaged, his lovely duchess. Inside and out.

A sheepish look crossed the coarse features of Mr. Gates. "You did escort the duchess to church, my lord. Chiddon is a tiny village. There's been talk."

"I liken Chiddon to more of a hamlet." Ellis took a sip of the ale. "Delicious."

"There's few secrets here, my lord. We'll all know who will sneak off into the dark tonight. There will be a spate of marriages and new babes born, and no one will question it."

"I'll take note, Mr. Gates." Ellis tipped his hat and meandered down the street, listening to various conversations and feeling a sense of contentment he hadn't even known while sculpting in Rome or attempting to become the next Keats. When Ellis had been younger, his parents had rarely gone to London, preferring to stay in the country with their six children. Lady Blythe hadn't been a matron of society. That had come later. After his father's death. He supposed she'd been bored.

Until he went off to school, Ellis had spent his days running through the woods, skipping rocks across the stream bordering Larchmont and carving blocks of wood. He'd known everyone in the small town of Larch, just outside his father's estate, and they had known him. It had been a simple, peaceful existence. He missed it.

Wandering in the direction of a patch of lawn that was the village green, Ellis spied a handful of burly young men unloading an assortment of benches and tables from a large wagon. He caught sight of Peg, Beatrice's maid, flirting outrageously with one of the workers who had paused in his labors to eat a slice of pie.

A flash of sunlight gleamed at the far edge of the green, tied firmly with ribbon and slung over one slender shoulder.

There's my duchess.

When he'd decided Beatrice belonged to him, Ellis wasn't sure. Probably after that first, violent kiss. Even after their last tumultuous meeting, he didn't care to relinquish her no matter what nonsense she spouted.

That had been what Ellis decided when he finished the clock.

Content to observe Beatrice directing the activity on the green, Ellis sipped his ale and didn't move closer. Hands on hips, she strode about, motioning for tables and benches to be set just so. The pale blue of her dress belled around her as she moved. A scarf one shade darker than her dress was wrapped around her neck and tucked firmly into the bodice. Not a bit of skin could be seen, nor her right cheek. Daisies sprouted from the hem of her dress, swirling about her ankles.

A pair of young boys, the same who had waved at her in the church, ran up to Beatrice, offering her a half-wilted bouquet of flowers. Daisies. To match her dress. The boys made identically awkward bows to her.

The musical notes of her thanks floated over to Ellis as she bent down to thank them.

Ellis exhaled softly. Something tugged at the muscles of his chest, as if a rope were tied to his heart and the other end, holding an anchor, had been tossed into the sea.

Beatrice wouldn't care to be compared to a ship's anchor.

She patted the tail of her hair, smoothing the thick strands, and adjusted the ever-present ribbon before standing. A smile, one never bestowed on Ellis, lit her features before she abruptly turned in his direction.

Relief softened her features, along with the same sort of longing Ellis held for her.

Beatrice didn't really want Ellis to leave Chiddon; he could see the truth of it in her face. Nor was the woman before him *truly* the Beatrice Howard who had once terrorized society. This was some other, better version of her.

She is damaged, Ellis. Proceed with caution.

"My lord." The daisies, poor crushed things, dangled from one of Beatrice's hands.

"Your Grace. I see your admirers are already plying you with gifts. Alas, I only come bearing ale. Do you require additional assistance?" He handed her his nearly empty cup.

"You don't have to. I wish to say——" She bit her lip. An apology flitted across her face, perhaps for the day at the mill, but she said nothing more. Beatrice rarely apologized. Ellis didn't think she knew how.

"I am more than happy to lend my back to such things." He doffed his coat. "Come now, Your Grace," he said, seeing her surprise. "You've seen me in my shirtsleeves." Ellis leaned in. "Well past time for offended modesty."

A hint of pink touched her cheeks at his reference to what had transpired at the mill. "You merely wish to show off for any young lady in the vicinity. Like some strutting rooster."

"No." Ellis breathed her scent. Honey. Lavender. "Only one."

16

Blythe paused, wiping the sweat from his brow, haloed by the sun. A perfect picture of masculine beauty set against the pastoral countryside. Muscles rippled beneath the fine lawn of his shirt, waistcoat unbuttoned and hanging from his shoulders. If he took off the waistcoat completely, as he had his coat, half the girls in Chiddon might faint.

His teeth flashed as he grinned at something Robert Tidwell related to him. Hair curling around his temples, Blythe bent over, giving Beatrice an enticing view of his backside, before straightening once more.

Ogling. He's made me into one of those nitwits in London.

It had been several days since she'd left him at the mill, and until Beatrice saw him strolling through Chiddon, ale in hand as if he hadn't a care in the world, she'd been afraid she might never see Blythe again.

"We're going for cider." Blythe picked up his coat laying across one of the tables. "Would you like a mug, Your Grace?"

You. I think it is you I want.

It seemed pointless, at least to herself, for Beatrice to

admit otherwise. Blythe had always gleamed, even when they were saying the worst about each other. A poor way to flirt.

"No, thank you, my lord."

"Come, Mister Tidwell." Blythe slapped young Robert on the back. "Let us avail ourselves of refreshments at The Pickled Duck."

Blythe sauntered off, nodding and greeting people as he passed.

Good lord, the entire village knew him already.

She turned, looking for Peg, unsurprised to find her maid missing. Peg was enamored of the eldest Tidwell boy, Martin, who, along with his brothers, had been helping with the tables earlier. Martin was a strapping young man in his early twenties and handsome to boot. In addition to the land his father meant to give him, Martin was the one who would be planting sugar beets and sharing in the profits. He'd been carefully courting Peg for some time, first asking for Beatrice's blessing. Which Beatrice had given immediately. Peg deserved happiness.

She tried not to be envious. It was only that Beatrice wanted a sliver of joy for herself. Her life here was peaceful. Content. Chiddon and its villagers formed a solid phalanx of support around Beatrice, protection that gave her solace, especially when she wallowed in self-pity. But the loneliness inside her refused to abate. It wasn't satisfied by brewing ale or atoning for her past sins.

Looking up, Beatrice caught sight of Blythe outside The Pickled Duck, shining like the brightest star in the sky. At a distance, Blythe might be mistaken for a wealthy merchant or a country squire; the air of privilege so many lords clung to wasn't noticeable on him. But converse with him, and there was no doubt he was titled—no farmer had ever commanded attention as he did. Still, Blythe was obviously as comfortable in Chiddon as he was speaking to an entitled bunch of snobs over cards at White's. He treated lords and tavern owners with the same degree of respect no matter their station.

Reaching up, Beatrice touched the rope of her hair, ensuring none of her cheek showed before walking back to the vicarage to find Melinda. She turned once to glance at Blythe again, that perverse urge to bury her nose in his chest nearly forcing her in the other direction.

He was laughing at something Mr. Gates said, a cup of ale held aloft in one hand, then he turned, catching sight of Beatrice. Pressing a hand over his chest, he gave a slight bow in her direction.

17

"Finally." Melinda set down her cup as the fiddle player started up at the far side of the green. The sun slanted over the village and would soon dip below the horizon. "I thought he merely meant to drink our ale and eat our food."

Beatrice gave her friend a wry smile. She'd paid for the fiddle player, the food, the ale, and nearly everything else. But not the peddler and his dancing monkey. He'd come purely for the roasted chicken and one of Mrs. Lovington's pies. "You're impatient."

Melinda's feet danced back and forth beneath the table. "I want to dance. Do you think Mr. Milhenny will be convinced to stay?"

Milhenny was the baker. A gregarious man from Overton who wished to get from under his uncle's thumb. "I believe he will. The building is more than suitable for his needs, especially the living quarters. I mentioned the renovations to the mill—"

"Did you mention that the owner of the mill is the Earl of Blythe?" Melinda asked innocently.

"I did." That *had* made a big difference to Milhenny, knowing there would be a working mill close by. "He sold all his breads and pastries in less than an hour. I think that is what convinced him more than anything else." Beatrice could return home tonight and cross Miss Rosalind Richardson, Andromeda Barrington's baking cousin, from her ledger.

"Good." Melinda drained the rest of her mug. "I am as terrible at bread as I am at biscuits. Can't make a proper stew. If it weren't for the kindness of Mrs. Lovington and Mrs. Gates, the good vicar would starve." There was a generous amount of dislike for Vicar Farthing in his wife's eyes, something Melinda rarely allowed to show, not even to Beatrice.

"You may have had too much ale."

"Or not enough." Melinda winked at her. Sadness hovered at her friend's shoulders, a sort of blighted frustration at marriage to Farthing. Beatrice was determined not to push her, but one day, she still hoped she'd hear Melinda's story.

Beatrice took in the flushed faces of her neighbors and the couples spinning about in the village green to the music of the fiddler, most feeling the effects of Mr. Gates's ale. It pleased her to know she'd brought this liveliness to Chiddon. Worth every pound Castlemare had been forced to leave her. Beatrice hoped Castlemare could see what she'd done, and she hoped it displeased him greatly. Consorting with farmers and bakers. Swilling ale from a mug. Allowing the two younger Tidwell boys to grab at her skirts with their sticky fingers. Nevermind Castlemare, Beatrice would give her best ribbons to see the faces of Lord and Lady Foxwood at seeing what had become of their daughter.

Beatrice snorted.

"Something amusing, Your Grace?" Melinda peered into her mug. "Empty."

"I was thinking of Lord and Lady Foxwood. How horrified they would be by this evening's festivities. My mother would die of thirst rather than drink from a mug. Or sample ale at all.

Melinda made a sound. "Your parents rival mine in who views their daughter with more disappointment, Your Grace. I often wonder if the Foxwoods will appear one day."

"Doubtful. Lady Foxwood is far too busy with her crowded social calendar and Lord Foxwood has his club, his mistress, and his ambitions."

"Lord Foxwood has a mistress?" Melinda regarded her wide-eyed. "I mean to say, Your Grace—"

"I've met her, Melinda. Accidentally. Lovely woman. I'm not sure how she tolerates Lord Foxwood. My parents have one of the most successful marriages in the *ton*, but success doesn't equate with emotion. They are partners and little else."

Lady Foxwood wrote twice a year. Pages filled with the balls, house parties, and other amusements she attended. Not once had she asked after Beatrice's welfare. Lord Foxwood had never written at all. At first, when she could still barely leave her bed after the accident, Beatrice had been shocked at their lack of concern. It had taken some time to acknowledge that the depth of Lord and Lady Foxwood's affection had always been contingent upon Beatrice's usefulness to them.

And I am no longer a tool for their ambition.

The stunning woman Beatrice had once been, was gone. She had not produced a ducal heir. Another match, one which would benefit Lord Foxwood, was not an option.

"Goodness." Melinda jumped from her seat, mug clasped tightly in one hand. "I've just been seared by a spark."

Beatrice frowned. "You *are* foxed. They haven't even yet lit the bonfire—" A warm, clean scent enveloped her along with a hint of citrus.

"Good evening, Your Grace. Mrs. Farthing." The sound of Blythe vibrated pleasurably along Beatrice's skin. He stood just behind her, so close his breath ruffled along the top of her head. For most of the evening, Blythe had kept his distance, his lean form flashing in and out of the crowd gathered near the bonfire.

"I believe I was promised a dance, Your Grace."

"Promised? Surely you are incorrect. Allow me to check my dance card." Beatrice didn't miss the significance of the moment. How often had she watched London's most eligible earl from across a crowded ballroom as he approached nearly every other young lady for a dance? But never Beatrice.

"Long overdue, I think, Your Grace." Blythe leaned close before she could refuse, the tip of his tongue touching just the edge of her left ear. "Don't be a coward, Bea."

Beatrice narrowed her eyes. She'd been considering her cowardice as of late, particularly in regard to Blythe. Taking the last mouthful of her ale, she swallowed it down, slamming the empty mug on the table before taking his hand. She turned to Melinda, half expecting a knowing look or at the very least a tart remark, but her friend's hand was already clasped in that of a large, heavyset man who in no way resembled Vicar Farthing.

Good for Melinda. Her friend's desolation worried Beatrice.

Blythe swung her into his arms, a smile tilting at his lips. He moved her effortlessly across the green as if he danced a country jig every day. He kept their hands tightly clasped, bending forward every so often to trail his nose along the left side of her neck, careful to avoid her right cheek.

"You smell of lavender and honey," he murmured in a teasing tone. "Unusual for a social-climbing harpy. You should smell of something acrid. The charred bodies of your enemies, for instance."

Beatrice giggled, somewhat intoxicated, whether from the excess of ale or being held in Blythe's arms. Impossible to determine, just now, with his breath edging along the rim of her ear and his hips brushing against hers, just why she had fled from him at the mill.

Oh, yes. London.

"Enjoying yourself, Bea?" The low rumble of his voice vibrated along her neck.

She did adore it when he called her Bea. It was so informal. Familiar. Intimate. As if she meant a great deal to him.

"I am. But don't imagine it has anything at all to do with you." Beatrice swatted his shoulder. "I don't wish to feed your vanity, my lord."

"But I bought you a bloody mill." He grinned back at her.

Not for Chiddon. But *her*. "You are only trying to encroach on my impending sainthood with the good people of Chiddon. You can't stand for someone else to be worshiped." She tilted up her chin. "I expect a statue of myself to be erected any day. Not sculpted by you, of course."

"No, indeed. You might take on the form of a bear or some other creature, not the harpy you are." He nosed along the top of her head, pulling her tight. "I didn't realize you liked ale so much, duchess."

There was little more than an inch separating them, something that, if Lady Foxwood were present, she would have harangued Beatrice over, insisting she never behave in such a shameless fashion, widow or not.

"Mr. Gates's influence," she answered. Beatrice's dress, while quite lovely with its pattern of daisies, was a poor shield against the charms of the Earl of Blythe.

"I enjoy dancing with you in the grass and dirt of Chiddon, Your Grace. I find I like doing so much more than any ball I've ever attended. The refreshments are better, I'm sure you will agree."

"You don't long for the taste of champagne?"

"I long for the taste of you." His lips brushed deliberately over hers and Beatrice felt herself arching in his direction. "It is not a recently acquired taste as I may have mentioned."

"You obviously haven't had any of Mrs. Lovington's apple pie."

"Mrs. Lovington makes an excellent pie, but I still prefer you." The hand on her waist moved to press along her ribs. "I liken you to a stale, hardened oat cake. One left out on its own for a while. A prettily decorated one."

"That isn't flattering in the least." But Beatrice was smiling. He did have a way with words. Not poetry, per se, but something she liked just as much.

"At first, you imagine the cake not worth the effort. You could break a tooth—"

"Because the exterior has gone hard?"

"Exactly." His cheek slid along hers, sending a ripple of pleasure down her neck. "But once you sink in your teeth—" Blythe nipped at her skin. "You find the interior soft. Delicious. You wish to bury yourself in it." He spun her once more, catching her deftly.

Beatrice closed her eyes, welcoming the dizzy intoxication of her senses.

"I'm thirsty, Your Grace. Exhausted from being ordered about by a duchess for the better part of an afternoon and being given no cake." He kept one arm around her waist, pulling her weight into his. "And now I want some of that stale, hardened oat cake." One elegant hand trailed down the length of her hair, twisting a curl about his finger.

That Blythe knew of her accident was no longer up for debate. He obviously did.

She stumbled, but he caught her, pulling her once more against the muscled length of his chest. Estwood's visit, and not knowing what he'd told Blythe, had led to a great deal of snarling and bad behavior from Beatrice. It would probably lead to a great deal more. Having him *acknowledge* and be *tender*—well, it smacked of pity and—

"Don't," she snapped, trying to pull away.

"Drink more ale? I admit, as fond as I am of Chiddon's ale, I would prefer some wine. Fortunately"—he spun her once more—"I had the foresight to stash a bottle of wine with Mr. Gates at The Pickled Duck. I suggest we avail ourselves of that bottle now. Perhaps find a chicken leg or two lying about."

"I don't want a chicken leg." *Or your pity.*

"Your Grace, forgive me, but you become incredibly monstrous when you don't eat properly. I think that's part of the problem. Lady Foxwood probably starved you for years."

Her mother *had*, but that wasn't the point.

"You've probably had a decent amount of ale—you and Mrs. Farthing. I do adore a brazen vicar's wife. At any rate, I'm sure the amount of ale, with no food, is the cause of your behavior. Taking liberties with me while we danced." Blythe made a clucking sound. "For shame, Your Grace."

"I did no such thing," she puffed, somewhat outraged by his suggestion, forgetting all about Blythe pitying her. He was very good at deflection.

"I thought my virtue safe, Your Grace." Blythe led her to a table set back from the others and nestled beneath an enormous tree. "You are as bad as every other young lady, attempting to compromise me."

"You fat-headed peacock," Beatrice fumed.

"Puddles have more depth than you, Your Grace." Blythe pressed a kiss to her forehead. "Don't move." He strolled away to retrieve his wine and possibly a chicken leg. The blood pulsed furiously through her veins at his audacity, making Beatrice feel more alive than she had in years. Maybe in forever.

It was utterly, completely terrifying.

Beatrice stretched her palms along the scarred wood of the table, trying to still the crazy beating of her heart. The skin along her arms tingled. Her breasts ached. And Blythe had barely touched her. She thought of herself at the mill, moaning as she chased her bliss, looking up into the blue of his eyes.

Beatrice pulled her knees together.

The wisest course would be for her to proclaim loudly that she had a headache brought on by her work earlier today. Someone nearby would inform Blythe. She could flee through the woods and be safe in her bed within an hour. Beatrice didn't need to sit here and be tempted by carnal things. No one need ever see her right side, ever again.

"Stop frowning. You'll get lines around your mouth." Blythe's broad shoulders rolled. "At least that is what Lady Blythe claims. Not to me. My sisters."

The wine bottle met the table with a dull thud.

"I suppose I've annoyed you once again, Your Grace." Blythe folded his legs gracefully to sit beside her. Half an apple pie landed next to the wine. "No chicken legs are to be found. I had to arm wrestle a young boy for the remainder of this pie. Quite the tussle. He didn't care in the least I was an earl."

Beatrice took a deep breath. Best to get this over with. No one else was close by. Blythe was facing away from the light so she wouldn't have to see the distaste and pity on his handsome features. "I suppose you'd like to know everything," she murmured. "I think that best."

"About you?" Blythe rolled his shoulders. "I know more than enough, you shallow, ambitious chit." He took a swallow of the wine and made a sigh of satisfaction. "Quite good."

"Blythe—" A weight fell over her chest just thinking of the accident. Castlemare. That bloody riverbed. "You may have noticed I favor—"

"Me?" he interrupted. "Entirely. I can't blame you. Nearly every woman adores me. I'm incredibly dashing. Honestly, I wasn't sure how you've resisted thus far. The mill is what pushed you over the edge. No flowers for my duchess. Only a rotting building in a state of disrepair will do."

He was shameless. *Truly*.

Beatrice placed her hand on his arm, feeling the tug of her heart. "You may have noticed the way I wear my hair. It is because—"

The right side of my face is pitted. Scrapped like a cow's hide at a tannery.

"You like ribbons. I noticed. But you can purchase your own fripperies, Your Grace. I bought you a mill. There were no cups for the wine. Well, there were, but I'm not sure they were clean. You'll have to swill from a bottle like some doxy."

"Blythe—" He wasn't going to let her speak, at least not now. She didn't know whether to shake him or curl up against his chest.

"I see you eyeing the pie, Your Grace. You've always been a greedy, demanding little snob. Very well." He scooped up a portion of the pie. "Open," he commanded in a silky tone. "This is but one of many times I will ask you to do so tonight."

A shiver ran down her spine. When he spoke to her in such a way with such command . . . Beatrice pushed her knees together once more, trying to assuage the ache that had sprung up.

Obediently, Beatrice parted her lips as Blythe put a spoon of apple pie between them, feeling the rush of arousal as her mouth closed.

"Good duchess." The whisper floated over her skin. Blythe was watching her mouth, his hunger apparent.

Beatrice's insides twisted lazily, like honey dripping on to her morning toast. She could grow used to being regarded in such a way. By him.

"Mrs. Lovington has a way with pie." She licked just a bit of apple from her lips, fascinated at the sound Blythe made as she did so.

Blythe straddled the bench, facing her. "If we are to share the wine, we should be closer." He pushed the pie tin away, the spoon clattering along the top of the table. He inched toward her on the bench until Beatrice was securely positioned between the heated muscle of his thighs, then he brought the bottle of wine to her lips. "Try a little, Your Grace."

Beatrice took a swallow, letting the fruity, warm taste fill her stomach. "This is entirely improper."

"It is doubtful the residents of Chiddon give a damn. Vicar Farthing might be the only one to care, but he's far too concerned with currying my favor to dare chastise my behavior. Suppose the decent thing to do would be to find him another post. I could stick him outside of Larchmont, but then I would have to tolerate his presence at my estate. Doesn't Lord Foxwood need a vicar somewhere?"

Beatrice tilted her chin, smiling at the sight of Peg dancing about in Martin Tidwell's arms. "I haven't the slightest idea. Lord Foxwood doesn't write to me often. Or ever."

"And Lady Foxwood?" He tilted the bottle up to her once more. "Does she venture to Chiddon?"

"You have already surmised, my lord, that she does not."

A disgruntled sound came from him, both protective and somewhat frightening. He was angry on her behalf. It warmed her more than the wine.

"I never cared for your parents." Blythe grabbed hold of her waist, nearly pulling Beatrice into his lap. "And there is a drop of wine at the corner of your mouth," he purred, licking sensuously along her bottom lip. "Oh," he said. "There's another." His teeth nipped gently before his tongue once more traced the seam of her mouth.

A low, tortured moan came from deep inside Beatrice. He wanted to seduce her, even knowing she was no longer perfect. Desired her even after pushing him away. Repeatedly. There could be no future with Blythe, not beyond Chiddon. She knew that. But perhaps, tonight, Beatrice might have him for a little while. Have him for a time before Lady Blythe and his responsibilities forced him back to London.

Blythe's mouth swept over hers, claiming every inch for himself. Hunger spilled from his lips as he kissed her, along with a blatant sensuality that had Beatrice wedging herself closer to his chest. Her palms flattened along the lines of muscle, tilting her head so that Blythe could have more of her. Gently, he sucked at her tongue until her fingers curled into his shirt.

Not once did he attempt to touch the right side of her head.

A small cry sounded inside her at the great care he took, even now, when Beatrice was so consumed, so muddied by the feel of his mouth on hers. She would deny him nothing.

The heat of his hand plucked at her skirts.

"It's far too dark for you to examine the daisies along the hem, my lord." Her breath hitched as his fingers toyed with the hollow of her knee.

"I don't care about your skirts. Only what is beneath them." There was a rawness to Blythe's voice, so unlike his usual charming, cultured tones. The sound rasped along her skin, holding her in place. "I cannot be near you, Bea, and not touch."

The hand beneath her skirts inched higher, tracing a circle along the sensitive skin of her inner thigh. The ache which had started earlier pulsed once more to life, startling Beatrice with its intensity. Her nerves felt . . . strained. Taut.

"I think, my lord," she said, sounding out of breath, "that you have explored there before. And we are in public. Perhaps—"

"Spread your legs, duchess."

"I don't—" The words were torn from her throat as the heat of his fingers touched her naked skin. He'd found the opening in her underthings with little effort.

"No more talking," he murmured. "Unless it is to direct the position of my fingers. Though from our previous failed picnic at the mill, I have a good idea of what must be done to please you, Your Grace."

A small gasp came from her. "But we are in full view—" Beatrice looked wildly about. The next table wasn't so far away, filled with the Tidwells and their children. "Oh," she gasped as the pad of his thumb brushed along a very sensitive part of her anatomy. "I—" Her eyes fluttered closed. Blythe stroked and teased with such certainty, promising more of the pleasure she'd experienced at the mill.

"You are very wet, Your Grace. Just here." Two of his fingers drew over her damp folds, drawing out the piece of flesh most susceptible to his ministrations. "I think you like having me touch you with all of Chiddon just steps away." He pressed a kiss along the slope of her neck. "I know I'm enjoying myself."

The place between her thighs gave a delicious pulse. More wetness followed. At the mill, Blythe had been all gentleness. Tender, even. This was far more erotic in nature. Naughty, even. Beatrice bit her lip to stop a moan from erupting.

Blythe leaned over, teeth grazing along her ear. "Imagine the things I could do to you at a dinner party while everyone enjoys the trifle."

The very idea sent another wave of arousal through her.

"You are far too confident in your ability to please a woman. Frivolous rake."

"Ill-mannered viper." He purred seductively against her throat. "Now keep your eyes on me, Duchess of Castlemare, patron saint of Chiddon." Blythe's features remained hidden, cast into shadows so that she couldn't see his expression. "There has been no one but Castlemare, has there?"

"No. But you likely already guessed as much." A soft noise came from the back of her throat as his fingers worked themselves inside her. His other hand casually picked up the bottle and took a mouthful of wine as if nothing at all was happening—

He pressed another kiss to her lips. "I want to put my mouth on you, Beatrice. Here." His thumb flicked purposefully, toying with that small nub, the source of the sensations rioting through her body. "I'll use my tongue. You'll enjoy it."

Beatrice sucked in a breath. She hadn't any doubt she would. "Castlemare once likened me to a corpse."

"You don't feel dead to me."

Her hand reached out and grasped his shoulder as Blythe's finger hit a particularly sensitive spot deep inside her.

"Didn't know what he was doing. Some men have no appreciation for the female form."

"Your Grace. Lord Blythe." Vicar Farthing's voice came from the other side of the table.

"Don't move, Your Grace," Blythe whispered for her ears alone. His fingers slowed but did not stop their torture.

Beatrice was caught, held hostage by the waves of pleasure threatening to burst over her skin at any moment and the appearance of Vicar Farthing. She had never detested the vicar more than she did now. Thankfully, Blythe had wisely settled them at a table far from the circle of lit torches. Farthing, unless he could see in the dark, could only make out their outlines. He couldn't fail to see how closely they sat to each other, but there was no reason to look beneath the table.

"Vicar Farthing." Blythe's fingers slid deeper, then retreated, the tip of one digit circling leisurely at her entrance.

Beatrice's fingers dug into the wood of the table.

"Are you enjoying the festival? I believe Mrs. Farthing is —" Blythe nodded in the direction of the fiddler. "She's dancing just over there."

Farthing never even looked in the direction of his wife. "I do not endorse such frolicking about, unlike my predecessor," Farthing said. "My pursuits are more scholarly in nature. Theological, if you will."

A tiny squeak left Beatrice as Blythe's thumb pressed against her.

"Are you well, Your Grace?" Farthing said. "I will escort you to Beresford Cottage if you wish to leave."

"Yes, I mean no." Blythe's fingers pressed inside her again. "I do not require escort, nor am I ill. A bug of some sort ran across my ankle, startling me."

Another rush of wetness eased between her thighs, giving further credence to Blythe's assumption that Beatrice actually enjoyed being *tortured* so pleasurably in public. She chased that same blissful release she had at the mill, but this antici- pation was different. Stronger. The knowledge that Blythe toyed with her while the vicar and his joyless presence stood across the table did something to her.

Blythe deserved his reputation. Dear God.

"I was wondering, my lord"—Farthing spared her one last glance before addressing Blythe—"if I might speak to you in private? On a small matter."

Farthing was—another soft flick of Blythe's finger against her flesh had Beatrice's fingers atop the table curling into a fist—a bootlicking toady of the highest order.

Oh. Dear.

A quaking sensation swept down her thighs to her ankles, jerking one of her feet. The delicate pulsing between her thighs hummed and spread over her lower body. Beatrice tried desperately to remain still.

"Is it urgent, vicar?" Blythe answered. "The duchess and I were discussing the repairs that must be made to the old Mandrell property. I'm sure you've heard I purchased the mill and intend to restore it for the people of Chiddon."

"My wife made mention."

Blythe appeared perfectly composed, not at all as if he were—

Beatrice bit her lip so hard, she drew blood. She was going to erupt. Explode. Burst into a thousand tiny bits all over the staid, proper Vicar Farthing. The only one who could possibly appreciate this moment fully was, ironically, the vicar's wife. And Blythe, of course.

I'm going to kill him for this.

"Of course, my lord." Vicar Farthing couldn't hide his annoyance at having Blythe put him off. He thought himself far too important to be ignored.

How Melinda had ever ended up with such a—

Oh, good lord.

"Tomorrow then, vicar." Blythe dismissed him. "I'll stop for tea, shall I?"

"My lord." Farthing bowed, glaring at Beatrice before striding away into the darkness.

"You're very close, Bea, aren't you?" Blythe said in a rough tone as his fingers retreated again. "That went on far longer than I supposed."

"I—" Beatrice could barely think let alone answer his question. It was all she could do to stay upright.

Blythe reached over and grabbed the wine bottle by the neck and took several swallows, all the while stroking her.

Did she have a fever? Beatrice was burning up, her hips thrusting across the bench toward Blythe. "Your Grace, don't make a sound." He pressed and pinched gently at the small bit of flesh hidden in her folds. "Press your head to my shoulder. Bite down if you need to."

She did as he bid her, teeth tearing into the edge of his coat as the pleasure Blythe held at bay finally ripped through her, jerking her body against his. A sob came from between her lips.

"Blythe," she gasped.

The sounds of the crowd around them became low and muted as tremors shook her body. She buried her face in his chest, inhaling all that citrus-scented warmth until the fluttering pulse of her blood cooled.

"Not at all like a corpse, Your Grace." Blythe cupped the back of her head, holding her against him, his fingers trailing up and down her spine. "Castlemare was an idiot." Blythe shifted. "Don't worry yourself, Mrs. Tidwell." He fell back a few inches. "The hem of Her Grace's dress is caught on a nail."

Beatrice smiled weakly into the darkness. She could barely make out Mrs. Tidwell's outline as the other woman waved and walked off, leaving Beatrice with a sense of growing mortification.

"This isn't amusing. Get away from me." She pushed at him. "How could you humiliate—"

Blythe took her wrist. "Beatrice, stop. All the things which you are thinking have no place between us. *Stop*."

"The pathetic Duchess of Castlemare," she hissed. "So desperate for companionship, scarred and unwanted. Will you boast of this, my lord?" The words tumbled out of her, every fear she had about Blythe, every bit of pain she still experienced for being exiled from her previous life, came rushing out. "You've always despised me—now you pity me. I'm not sure which is worse."

"I haven't an ounce of pity for you," Blythe stated.

Beatrice slapped at him before jumping up from the bench, sick to the very depth of her soul. Her heart cracked at such vicious treatment. So well-deserved. No matter how she atoned and—

"You do this out of fear, Beatrice. Nothing you are imagining is the least true."

"You've no idea what I think." She marched from him, hurrying toward the path through the woods which would take her to Beresford Cottage where she could nurse her wounds in private. Damn Blythe. Damn her for believing, if only for the space of an evening, that she could have something other than—

The moon lit the path before her, thankfully, for she'd been so determined to flee Blythe she hadn't bothered to grab a lantern or a torch. But Beatrice knew the way well. And no one would dare harm her.

"You snide, spoiled little chit." Footsteps sounded behind her. "I'm sick to death of you dismissing me."

18

Beatrice was absolutely, *positively* not dismissing him again. Or whipping herself up into some ridiculous frenzy where she became convinced that he stroked her to climax out of amusement. Ellis had told her how much he wanted her.

He caught up to her easily, taking her by the elbow, refusing to release her no matter how she flailed.

"Leave me alone. I'll scream."

"Go right ahead. I'm not leaving."

He'd been so busy basking in the aftermath of Beatrice's pleasure, realizing once more that Castlemare, selfish prick, had never properly pleasured his wife, that Ellis had failed to notice the slow stiffening of her body. The way she'd absently patted the thick tail of her hair. The iciness which had suddenly bled into her words. All telltale signs that she was having an argument Ellis wasn't privy to—one calculated to push him away.

Ellis pulled Beatrice roughly to him. Cupping the back of her head, his fingers slid through the thick mass of her hair, pulling out the damned ribbon and the multitude of pins holding the thick mane in place. He pulled at the scarf wrapped around her throat, tossing it into the leaves at her feet.

A horrible, wounded sound left Beatrice, only halting when his mouth fell on hers, hot and urgent. Demanding. She struggled against him, pathetically and without much effort, before a small, feminine growl came from her throat. She nipped at his bottom lip, pulling it between her teeth before wrapping her arms around Ellis, pressing her breasts against his chest.

"I detest you," she said, hurling the words at him.

"You don't. Now lift your damn skirts."

Beatrice twisted, leaning to grab the edge of her dress and pull it up her legs, high enough so that he could just make out the opening in the cotton of her underclothes. The moonlight glinted on the small tuft of hair hidden between her thighs.

"You're beautiful."

"Not anymore." There were unshed tears in her words. She leaned her head so that her hair fell over her right cheek.

Ellis kissed her hard, pushing her back against the tree. "Yes, you are."

Beatrice pulled at his hair, clutching at his shoulders like a wild thing. He breathed into her neck while unbuckling his trousers, knowing that if he let her go now, she might well keep herself from him forever. Intentionally, he cupped her right cheek, feeling the raised scars and pitted holes just beneath her ear, surprised to find her earlobe was missing.

My poor, damaged duchess.

Lifting her leg, Ellis thrust into Beatrice's warmth without preamble, her body clasping his like a sheath.

A sob left her as he cupped her backside, pulling both her legs around him, taking her far rougher than he'd originally intended, but Beatrice needed this. The savageness of being forced to acknowledge she was desirable. Any sign of tenderness from Ellis would be misinterpreted as pity. There would be time to properly make love to her later. This joining was just as it should be. Violent. Furious. Passionate. The result of years of frustrated lust.

He slowed, only enough to catch his body against hers, hearing her moan wildly against his chest. Beatrice grew taut, the heel of one foot digging into his backside.

"Blythe," she sobbed, hands curling into his shirt. "Ellis."

A ball of sensation settled at the base of his spine as he spilled into her, the first time in his life he'd been so careless. But his body already knew what his mind and heart had yet to admit. Beatrice was where Ellis ended and began. There would be no one else but her.

When the last ripple finally left his body and hers, Ellis pressed his face into her neck, hearing the steady beat of her heart.

"*I have drunken deep of joy,*
And I will taste of no other wine tonight.'"

A small sound of surrender came from her. "Shelley," she whispered. "And I've a cramp in my leg."

Ellis pressed his forehead to hers, pressing a kiss to her lips and carefully lowering her to the ground. "Take me home, Bea. I wish to do this properly in a bed."

19

Beatrice could stay here forever, in the forest with Blythe, though the muscles of her leg had started to cramp, and the bark of the tree tore at her back. She wanted to cry out in protest as his body left hers, but she didn't. It was all Beatrice could do not to cling to Blythe and beg him never to leave, like one of those adoring idiots who had followed him in London.

She had developed such a weakness for this man, a man Beatrice could never hope to keep, not for any length of time. Chiddon was a bubble, one she lived in gladly, but Blythe couldn't possibly survive here indefinitely. Nor would he wish to.

"I'm all for trysting out of doors." Blythe raised her wrist and pressed a kiss to her pulse. "But I want you in a bed with me. Now."

She tried to pull away from him, but Blythe held fast. "I'm not done. I don't care if you've got a bloody peg-leg hiding under your stockings or have a tail."

Beatrice ran her fingers through her hair, purposefully pulling the now unbound strands over her right shoulder.

"You don't understand." He couldn't possibly. The light touch of his mouth and fingers along her right cheek had nearly undone her.

"I do not. But you're behaving as if you are an ogre wearing a wig." He jerked his chin. "Or a scarf." He stooped and picked up the discarded scarf but did not return it to her.

A quarter-hour later, Beatrice begged Blythe to leave her at the door of Beresford Cottage. He, in turn, refused politely. The house was dark. She didn't need bruises in addition to everything else. Her entire staff was in Chiddon.

"What if there is an intruder?" He raised a brow, still refusing to release her hand. Leaning over, Blythe's lips grazed her temple.

"The only intruder I've had the entire time I've lived here has been *you*, Blythe. I'm perfectly safe. Mr. and Mrs. Lovington will be back before long. As will Jasper. Peg, I'm not sure of." Her maid was likely getting tupped, possibly in the very woods she and Blythe had just vacated.

"I'm not leaving you."

Stubborn, glorious, preening dandy. "Fine. But your presence here will likely cause a scandal."

"Doubtful. Half of Chiddon is rolling about in the grass as we speak." He waved a hand up the stairs. "Stop trying to get rid of me."

With a sigh, Beatrice reluctantly led him up the stairs. He'd touched her cheek. He had to have noticed she was missing part of her ear. She cast him a sideways glance. None of that had deterred him in the least. But that had been unbridled madness, their passionate joining in the woods with only moonlight to guide them.

This would be far different.

Could she convince him to allow her to remain at least partially clothed? Her hand unconsciously fell to the curve of her right breast, hidden beneath her corset, and her steps faltered. It was one thing to be taken in the woods where the darkness hid her, quite another to be naked with Blythe before the light of the fire.

Years ago, she might have gloried in it.

Blythe pushed open the door and gently nudged Beatrice inside.

He placed her right in the middle of the room while he strolled about, taking in every detail. The bedchamber was large but not lavishly appointed. Pale lavender pillows sat in a pile upon her bed, matching the counterpane with its design of vines and decorated with silver tassels. The furniture was all finely made but slightly outdated. Beatrice saw no reason to send to London for anything grander. She was quite comfortable here. Books littered the table near the fire, just as they did downstairs. There was a stack of notes on what she hoped would be the dressmaker's shop. The ledger, her notebook of sins and atonements, was thankfully in her parlor and out of Blythe's questing gaze.

But her fingers itched to cross off Rosalind Richardson's name from the list.

"Maybe some brandy," Beatrice started. "I'll just retrieve the decanter from downstairs, shall I?"

Blythe's hand shot out, his fingers wrapping around her wrist. "You don't need the brandy. I'll warm you up. And you've twigs in your hair."

"Well, yes," she said curtly, wiggling free of his grasp to wander about the room, unsure of what to do. Castlemare had always appeared in the early evening, lifted her nightgown, and—"You were—"

"Tupping you against a tree?"

"Yes."

"Come here, duchess." Blythe held out his hand. "I'll help you take off your peg leg. At the very least, we can put a ribbon on your tail."

"You are often incredibly unkind, my lord."

"Only to you." His eyes grew solemn, so dark, the blue appeared pitch black. "Tell me what you see when you look at me, Your Grace." Blythe turned in a semi-circle, handsome and glowing before the fire.

Love.

Beatrice turned abruptly to gather her thoughts, fingers twisting together, before facing him once more. Love had never been a feeling she'd considered overmuch. She'd been raised with the idea that marriage was for other, more important considerations so Beatrice hadn't expected much from Castlemare in that regard. And after his death, well, she'd had no desire to wed for those considerations again.

I should just get a dog. Or a cat.

"I see an uninvited guest," she replied in her patented, snobbish tone. "One who charmed his way into my home, taking advantage of my previously stoic housekeeper who now giggles like a schoolgirl at his appearance."

"I do adore Mrs. Lovington." A half-smile pulled at his mouth. "Go on."

"A lover of poetry, though you cannot write a word of it yourself. You have the soul of an artist but cannot create a masterpiece, yet you can mend a plow and take apart a pocket watch." She gave him a sideways glance. "You love pitwheels and old mills."

Blythe's smile widened. "Who doesn't like a haunted mill, Bea?"

A shiver caressed her skin. She liked the name when he used it. "You are unfailingly kind to others, no matter their station. Charismatic. Friendly. Patient."

"Yes, particularly with you."

"You are not a snob."

"My friend Haven would disagree with you."

"You are the most eligible earl in London, though I think you would be just as content as a gentleman farmer."

"All true." Blythe came toward her, lifting his hand to thread the heavy mass of her hair through his fingers until it spilled over his hand, exposing her cheek and neck.

She closed her eyes, unable to look at him as he studied the marks decorating her skin.

"I suppose a pair of earbobs, as a gift, are out of the question." He pressed an open-mouthed kiss to the base of her ruined ear where one of the longest gashes started.

"You are insufferable," she whispered, refusing to open her eyes.

"Did you note, my duchess, that not once in your dissection of my person, did you mention my stunning, golden magnificence?"

"Possibly because I find it annoying." Her eyes snapped open. Blythe's beauty had become the least of the things she had grown fond of. She'd realized that tonight, watching him interact with the villagers in Chiddon.

"Do you find me shallow, Your Grace?"

"No." She trembled as he pressed his lips to the tiny pebble-shaped scars decorating her neck. "You are not."

"It isn't so bad, Bea. Certainly, it doesn't merit you hiding away in Chiddon. I would be proud to escort you anywhere you please in London, with your hair up."

Lord and Lady Foxwood had disagreed with Blythe's assessment. As had the Duke of Castlemare. Beatrice's presence in London, scratched up and dented like an old piece of furniture, would cause talk—the unwelcome kind.

"There is more, my lord. If you leave now, you won't have to see it. Or we can couple fully clothed as we did earlier." Her entire body was shaking, mostly from fear of him actually doing as she asked.

Blythe made an annoyed sound and stepped away from her.

If he left now, they could put this entire evening behind them. The tryst in the woods could be excused away as being brought on by a goodly amount of ale and the festival which certainly lent itself to such behavior.

"Perhaps you should go," she whispered.

"Stop telling me to leave. Dismissing me. I'm bloody exhausted with it." Blythe tore at his coat and tossed it to a chair. Ripped the cravat off his throat. Dusty, muddy boots flew across the fine Persian rug covering her floor. A button popped off his waistcoat as that garment joined his coat. The shirt was next, peeled off and crumpled away like a discarded rag.

Oh.

Now that the shirt was gone, the gorgeous lines of Blythe's torso were on display, the carved muscle hinted at beneath her fingertips earlier now fully revealed. Without looking away, lips drawn tight with apparent fury, Blythe doffed his trousers next, kicking them out of the way. He padded around her, naked, angry, and extremely aroused. She'd felt him, of course, in the woods but—

Castlemare had been deficient in more ways than one.

"You don't need to prance about so bloody perfect, Blythe." She clenched her fists and tried not to look below his waist.

"Always ready with a cutting remark. And I'm not prancing. I'm not a bloody horse, Beatrice. And we are not *coupling*, as you so quaintly put it, with our clothes on. I intend to make love to you, properly, in that bed." He pointed. "And you will be naked."

Beatrice lifted her chin. "I will not."

"You will." Blythe stood behind her, pressing his cock into her buttocks. The blissful fluttering between her thighs returned as he pulled her back against him. A big hand ran over her stomach to cup her sex beneath the fabric of her dress. Squeezing softly, he kissed the edge of her ear where the skin had been torn off. "I promise all will be well, Bea."

"It can't possibly be. Castlemare told me I resembled a lizard."

The grip on her stomach tightened. "Every time I think I've heard the worst of Castlemare's faults, I am surprised by another. Now stay still."

Blythe unbuttoned her dress with excruciating slowness, pulling the fabric apart to trail his lips along the scars of her shoulder. Once the fabric fell to the floor in a heap around her ankles, Blythe started on her corset, releasing her from the garment with practiced skill.

"I'm sure you've untied many a corset," she said in a snide tone.

"Quit trying to dismiss me with a random insult. I'm not leaving."

Beatrice could feel the panic starting to swell within her. "You've already had me once tonight. Made me climax twice, the first time nearly in front of Vicar Farthing. Must you debauch me again?"

Blythe gave her a sad look. "I'm afraid I must."

"Let me leave my chemise on."

"No." He tossed her on the bed, placing his naked body between her thighs. Lifting one leg, Blythe drew the plain silk of her stocking down, pausing only to press a kiss to the skin of her knee. His hand drifted between her thighs, brushing lightly over the soft down.

Beatrice took a shaky breath.

When he finished with both legs, he pulled her up to stand, drawing up the hem of her chemise as he did so, revealing her stomach.

She resolutely took hold of the fabric, refusing to allow him to pull it up over her right side.

"Leave my chemise. You'll get everything else. *Please*, Ellis." The top of her ribs and her breast were the worst of it. One would have thought her stupid corset would have protected both. Instead, a particularly sharp bit of rock had sliced clean through, opening Beatrice up to being dragged further across the rocks of the riverbed. When the carriage tipped, it had pressed her into all the pebbles, rocks, and sharp sticks.

"No," he repeated, pulling it up over her head and tossing the fabric out of reach.

Beatrice turned her chin. Even Peg, when she thought Beatrice wasn't looking, couldn't help staring at times. Taken together with her cheek, neck, and shoulder, it was rather unappealing. Her mother, upon seeing Beatrice the first time, had called for smelling salts.

"This isn't terrible at all," Blythe said. "I've seen much worse inflicted when my sisters argue over a ribbon. Young girls are nasty fighters." His finger lingered over the deepest gash, dipping into the small ravine the rock had made in her breast.

"Only a lecher would continue to try to seduce a woman who doesn't wish it."

"Yes, I felt your disgust for me earlier."

Beatrice looked away from him and into the roaring fire, wishing a flame would escape and burn her to a cinder. "I will understand if you find it necessary to leave, Blythe. Truly. I realize it isn't at all appealing." She tried to sound matter of fact.

Castlemare had gagged the first time he'd seen her naked after the accident. Put a handkerchief to his nose and declared her to be horrifying. Like a skinned rabbit.

"Tell me." Blythe's words were soft and punctuated with

another kiss to her shoulder. "What happened? Estwood only told me of a carriage accident."

"My driver became lost. We were in Castlemare's second best carriage, which I don't suppose had been cared for properly. It grew dark." Beatrice could still feel the carriage seat beneath her rattling, then jerking when the wheels hit something in the road. "I am only grateful that Thomas—"

"Thomas?"

"The driver. He was young and not experienced." An ugly sound escaped her. "I thought at first, we would be fine. The carriage was stopped in its descent down a steep embankment by a large tree trunk. Thomas jumped off and managed to release the horses before—well—" Her words grew thick. "Before everything, including me and Thomas, tumbled down to the riverbed. Parts of the vehicle shattered, and what didn't break apart landed atop me."

"And Thomas?"

"Dead. Thrown against a rock." The image of his bloodied face, eyes open and staring at nothing, would haunt Beatrice until the end of her days. If only she hadn't insisted on defying Castlemare and been so determined to return to London. "It's my fault. Thomas's death. The accident. I was so insistent I return to London because Castlemare didn't want me to."

"It wasn't your fault, Bea." Another kiss was pressed to her ruined shoulder.

"There were a great many splinters. It took nearly a week for the physician to get them all out." Beatrice had screamed as each one was pulled from her abused shoulder and neck. The line of her ribs. "Tiny pebbles were imbedded in my cheek from laying in the riverbed with the carriage atop me. I think it was hoped I'd die from infection." Castlemare had said as much when he thought Beatrice unconscious.

"It must have been painful." He tugged gently on a lock of her hair.

"Don't you dare pity me." Beatrice jerked from him. "I am not some pathetic creature."

"I'm not offering you pity," he snapped back, cupping her breast, thumb running over her nipple until the small peak tightened. "When I fucked you up against a tree like a light-skirt, did that feel like pity to you?"

The zing of sensation shot from her nipple straight down between her thighs. His mouth, wet and heated, fell over the nipple, sucking gently.

Beatrice fell back against the bed, Blythe alongside her, crawling up the length of her body with small licks and bites, grazing his teeth and caressing her damaged skin. She writhed beneath him, focusing completely on the sensations brought on by his touch and forgetting entirely about hiding herself. Instead, she allowed Blythe to worship her. Adore her with his tongue and his fingers, feeling more beautiful than she ever had dressed in the finest silks and surrounded by hopeful suitors.

"Terrible harpy," Blythe murmured, clasping Beatrice's hands above her head as he entered her with exquisite slowness. He moved as though he wanted Beatrice to feel every drag of his cock against the inside of her body. Each thrust teased at a sensitive spot deep inside her. He lifted one of her hips. "There, Bea?"

She nodded, coming apart beneath him in an instant, so shocked at the violent tremors rocking her body that her eyes rolled back in her head. Beatrice barely caught her breath before he flipped her. "On your knees, duchess. Take hold of the headboard."

Beatrice did as he asked, legs still trembling, every inch of her skin so sensitive, the slightest touch of his tongue along her spine had her panting out his name. Teeth nipped at her buttocks. The side of her hip. A gentle caress swept over the line of scars across her ribs.

Wrapping one hand around the back of her throat, Blythe took her again in one hard, punishing thrust. The new angle of their bodies had her gasping. Begging as the pleasure rose once more inside her.

Coupling, indeed.

A calm, tentative word which in no way resembled the way Blythe took her, body bent like a bowstring as he thrust inside her, holding her in place with one hand. She screamed herself hoarse from the sheer intensity of her release, bucking wildly until finally, with a groan, she felt the warm spill of him inside her.

When at last Blythe allowed her to rest, he pulled her exhausted body over him so that Beatrice's body, scars, and all, lay partially draped over his larger one. She moved her leg, wincing as the muscle cramped, probably from their earlier encounter in the woods. Never in her life had she imagined—

"Lady Foxwood instructed me to lie still in the marital bed and allow Castlemare to do whatever he wished. I did, and it brought me no joy." Not like this. "There were times he attempted to—offer me some pleasure. But nothing ever happened."

"Castlemare, as I believe I've said, was an idiot." Blythe's fingers pressed into the muscle of her thigh, easing the knot. "Right here, Bea?"

It sounded very much like his question earlier, when he'd been busy locating the exact right spot. Beatrice blushed in the darkness. "Where did you learn to do that?"

"A lovely girl I met in Paris. I had a strained shoulder from fighting with Haven." He tucked a lock of hair behind her right ear. "Don't be jealous, my duchess."

"I'm not." But Beatrice was. A little.

"Lovely liar." He kissed her once more and curled the

warmth of his larger body around her small, battered one. "Sleep. You're exhausting for a snooty duchess. Insatiable. I'm too tired to move from this bed, so you will have to weather the scandal. And Mrs. Lovington makes a fine breakfast." His arms tightened protectively around her before pressing a kiss to her forehead.

"Sleep, Bea. I'll be here when you wake."

❧ 20 ❧

"You look incredibly refreshed, Your Grace."

"Do I?" Beatrice sipped her tea, wiggling to get comfortable on the settee. She was deliciously sore, especially between her thighs, but overall, she felt rather splendid. Wrapped up in Blythe's arms, Beatrice had slept soundly for the first time in years, with no dreams of Castlemare or the accident to disturb her rest. She'd been so peaceful, in fact, that her scarred cheek and neck had been the last thing she'd thought of as Blythe had kissed her goodbye this morning.

She frowned into her tea.

Though Blythe claimed to not care about creating talk in Chiddon, and despite his blatant adoration of Mrs. Lovington's cooking, he had taken his leave just as the sun peeked over the horizon.

"What is it, Your Grace?" Melinda bit into a scone. "Oh, it's still warm. I can't wait for Milhenney to take up residence, so I won't have to depend on the charity of Mrs. Lovington."

"I fear I had too much ale last night. As did you." She was trying, with little success, not to have doubts about her evening with Blythe. Beatrice didn't want to believe that the sight of her face in the morning light had given him pause. It was one thing to have her injuries glimpsed in shadows, another in sunlight.

She reached up and patted her hair, neatly tied over her shoulder with a green ribbon. Secure as always.

"I may have had more than my share of ale," Melinda answered through a mouthful of scone.

"Who was the gentleman you were dancing with?" Beatrice asked, trying to push aside the sight of Blythe, big and naked, roaming about her bedroom this morning, searching for his discarded shirt.

No wonder he was so arrogant. Blythe was hard to look away from with clothes on, but naked? A small bit of warmth crept up her cheeks. He'd been smiling at her the entire time and hadn't appeared the least distressed to be greeted with scars and pitted skin. So possibly he was only being discreet by leaving.

"I'd hardly call Jake a gentleman." Melinda toyed with another scone.

"Jake?"

"Smythe. Jake Smythe. I'm surprised his lordship didn't introduce you. Jake was brought to Chiddon to run the mill. He grew up near Larchmont, Lord Blythe's estate." Her eyebrows wiggled just a bit. "Big, strapping man, isn't he? The good vicar doesn't dance. Or do anything else which appeals to me."

Beatrice eyed her friend from beneath her lashes. Melinda always hinted around her dislike of Farthing but was rarely so blatant in her disregard. "Discretion, Melinda. I don't think Chiddon or the mill can afford another scandal," she cautioned. Having had a distasteful husband, Beatrice wouldn't judge her friend for finding happiness, but neither did she wish her to become a pariah.

"More discreet than you and Lord Blythe? Most of Chiddon saw him running after you last night. Did he catch you?"

"Possibly." Beatrice took a sip of her tea.

"Was it as magnificent as I imagine? His catching of you?" Melinda took her hand. "You are perched rather awkwardly on the edge of your chair, so I believe I have my answer."

Beatrice swatted her away. "You are incorrigible. I'm a widowed duchess. Affairs with handsome lords are my prerogative. And I've never considered remarrying." She hadn't thought any man would show her interest again, not with her scars.

"I think it more than an affair, Your Grace." Melinda popped her hand open. "Sparks. Remember? He'll want you to go to London with him, I warrant. Show you off. You're wasted in Chiddon."

Beatrice studied her tea. London loomed like a billowing cloud of darkness full of those who would be only too pleased to mete out their opinions of her.

"Chiddon needs me," she finally said. "One night, brought on by an excess of ale, means nothing. We are amusing each other, nothing more. Blythe is only in the country because he is avoiding his duty, which is to wed a suitable girl and produce an heir. Lady Blythe, his mother, is quite determined he do so immediately."

"You're a duchess. Aren't you suitable?"

"Hardly, Melinda. Look at me. I can't even ride in a coach without dissolving into fits. I can't be expected to attend a ball or a garden party like this." Beatrice waved a hand down the right side of her face. "Nor properly wear a pair of earrings."

Melinda chewed the scone, eyes mutinous. "I disagree, Your Grace. But let us continue. Am I to understand you will allow Blythe, magnificent earl, to return to London without you—"

"I can hardly keep him here. He has an entire life full of responsibility. Sisters. Lady Blythe. An estate. Producing an heir." Beatrice thought of his face, so solemn when he'd told her his family's happiness was his responsibility. "Even *if* he were inclined to do so, and I assure you he is not, I would never ask it of him."

Beatrice firmly resisted the idea of London. Blythe belonged there. Melinda couldn't comprehend that holding a title came with a great many obligations. What was Blythe to do, run back and forth between London, Chiddon, and his own country estate?

A wave of desolation swept her. It really was impossible.

"So, it won't bother you to have him wed some well-bred twit instead of you? Make this twit his countess and bed her?"

Beatrice thought of some faceless girl, one who would dangle uselessly off Blythe's arm. She *would* be horribly well-bred. Approved by Lady Blythe. The sort of girl Beatrice had once been but was no longer. "I didn't say I would like it. I won't. I think Blythe bears me some affection—"

"*Some* affection?" Melinda made a puffing sound. "Affection is a mild word to describe the way in which Lord Blythe looks at you, Your Grace. He cannot take his eyes from you, even for a moment. I became quite heated watching the two of you dance."

Beatrice set down her tea. "Blythe would *never* offer for me. Let us say he is hopelessly enthralled by me. Even so, I am unsuitable to be his wife for a variety of reasons." She came to her feet, pacing back and forth across the rug.

"I'm anxious to hear them."

She glared at her friend. Why couldn't Melinda see how bloody impossible this was? It was exceptionally clear to

Beatrice. Physical desire, of which she and Blythe had plenty, was *not* affection. Liking, possibly. But not love.

"I bought you a mill. Doesn't that count?"

A tool for seduction, nothing more.

"Very well, Melinda. First and foremost, there is the matter of an heir. I realize you don't understand the weight of such a thing, but I assure you, it is the most important duty a titled gentleman possesses. I am incapable of producing a child. I could not do so for Castlemare."

An image of Castlemare invading her rooms, tossing back a glass of wine before he told her to lay back, flitted before her eyes. He would grunt and sigh for a quarter hour. Thrust into her. As each month passed and her courses arrived, Castlemare became crueler. Ugly.

Melinda raised one brow. "I see."

"Then there is the matter of my previous existence in London. Yes, I'm still a duchess, but one who is neither missed nor remembered with any fondness." Painful to admit, but true. Lying in that riverbed for two days with her absence not even noted had driven that pertinent fact home. "Given my current state," she said, once more gesturing to her ruined cheek. "Society will await my return with undisguised glee, claws sharpened and ready to tear me to shreds. Which would not be undeserved. I was unkind to a great many people, all of whom would like the opportunity to extract a bit of vengeance. Blythe should not have to suffer for my past mistakes."

"I think him intelligent enough to have already considered your previous reputation, but do go on."

Beatrice waved a hand. "Even so, eventually I would become a burden. A regret. Something he pities but must endure. Eventually, Blythe would be forced to consider discarding his despised mistress—"

Melinda's eyes widened. "Good lord. You really don't think he'd want to wed you?"

"He *could* not, Melinda. Even if he were so inclined. Which I do not believe he is. I can't provide an heir. Poor reputation. Disfigured." She picked off each statement with her fingers. "But let us assume that those issues were of no import. There is still the matter of the Duchess of Granby."

"The Duchess of Granby?"

"The woman I wronged so grievously, whose reputation I took great pains to destroy, is Andromeda Barrington, now the Duchess of Granby. Not only is Granby Blythe's closest friend, but Andromeda's brother is the Duke of Averell. And while the Barringtons are considered—" Beatrice's brow wrinkled. "Let's say, unconventional—one brother is a duke and the other a bastard who runs a gambling hell—the Barringtons survive their eccentricity because of the power they wield. I'm sure they haven't forgotten my horrid behavior, just as I'm certain the gossips have not either. Do you see the complication? Andromeda and her family despise me, with good reason." A vision of Andromeda's mother, the dowager duchess, fiercely guarding her daughter at a ball came to mind. "The Dowager Duchess of Averell, in particular, should not be crossed."

"So apologize to the Duchess of Granby. You could write her a letter," Melinda said. "Or better, pay a call upon her. Send a bouquet with a heartfelt admission of your guilt."

"I cannot envision a time when I would ever willingly visit London, for all the reasons I've given you. Not to mention I would have to contend with Lord and Lady Foxwood." It had taken a great deal of time for her to come to terms with Lord and Lady Foxwood but part of her still longed for their affection. She had no desire to revisit their relationship or see them again.

Melinda bit into a biscuit. "Lord and Lady Foxwood are horrid."

"Melinda."

"Right, right." She stuck a second pink-frosted biscuit into her mouth. "Vicar's wife and all of that. May I offer rebuttal, Your Grace?"

"You may." Beatrice took her seat once more. Her fingers shook just slightly as she smoothed her skirts, likely the result of thinking about her life in London. Castlemare. Her parents. All the parts of Beatrice she had buried in Chiddon.

"First." Melinda held up a finger. "I wish to offer my opinion on your indiscretion with Lord Blythe. I do not think it wise to judge the depth of feeling between you based on your recent acquaintance. You must account for the years preceding it, for I think the basis of the affection he obviously bears you has roots in your past association."

I want you, Beatrice Howard. I have from the moment I set eyes on you.

"Secondly," her friend continued, "I would like to point out that your inability to produce an heir might well have been Castlemare's fault, *not* yours. Much like it is Vicar Farthing's."

Beatrice looked up.

"Surely by now, Your Grace, you've guessed that I bear the good vicar little affection, nor does he have a great liking for me. I had little choice in wedding him. I found myself in a difficult situation, which, ironically enough, resolved on its own." Melinda paused and cast her gaze to the view of the garden outside, eyes shadowed with pain. "My parents, only slightly better than your own, insisted on marriage to Farthing, though I begged them to send me away. But they were overly concerned with their reputation, and so, here I am. He's dead, by the way." Her gaze settled on Beatrice once more with a great deal of sadness. "Or he would have married me. I was forced to settle for Farthing."

"Melinda—" Beatrice's heart broke for her friend. "What can I do?"

"I doubt there is anything, Your Grace." She brushed a crumb off her skirts. "But perhaps, should you ever gather your courage and decide to visit London once more, you might require a companion."

"I'm not going to London, whether Blythe asks it of me or not."

"He *will*, Your Grace. Lord Blythe does not strike me as the sort of gentleman who will keep you as his mistress in Chiddon. Nor do I believe he means to wed another woman when his affections lie elsewhere." Melinda shot her a pointed look. "I believe you are correct in believing Blythe cannot be expected to stay in Chiddon indefinitely. Probably should have gone back well before now, but he stays because of you. Eventually, Your Grace, you will be forced to decide on London."

Beatrice nibbled on her bottom lip. "I have already decided."

Melinda came to her feet, throwing up her hands. "As you say. Forgive me, Your Grace, but I must take my leave. The vicar has requested I review the upcoming sermon for this Sunday, most of which will be directed at me. I am more full of sin than anyone suspects."

"If you ever need—" Beatrice started, rising to see Melinda to the door. "You know if you ever need anything, you have only to ask."

"I would make a fine companion for a duchess were she to visit London. Modest. Discreet. I'd stay in the background and carry your fan." Melinda smiled as she slipped away. "But you must allow me to dance at a ball."

21

I n the weeks following the festival in Chiddon, Beatrice and Blythe fell into a comfortable rhythm.

He breakfasted with her most days, much to the delight of Mrs. Lovington. Her housekeeper bustled about Blythe's handsome golden form, placing the fluffiest omelets and choicest bits of ham on his plate. Beatrice would sip tea and make snide remarks about his appetite, disparaging him for always taking her seat at the head of the table and lamenting over the cost of feeding him.

Blythe's heated gaze would rest on Beatrice, promising a wealth of retribution. Nearly all his reprisals were sexual in nature and vastly enjoyable.

She was always sure to be outraged at breakfast.

Blythe rode out to the mill most days, inspecting the work and conferring with Mr. Smythe, whose acquaintance Beatrice had finally made.

Smythe was attractive in a rough-hewn way, ambitious and intelligent. He treated Blythe with casual familiarity which came from the pair having grown up together. Observing Smythe, it wasn't any wonder why Melinda found him so appealing, especially in comparison to Vicar Farthing.

Beatrice's interest, however, wasn't on Smythe. Or the fine mason repairing the crumbling mill wall. Nor even on dredging the pond. It was on the smiling man, hopping about the rocks in the stream, waving his hands about as he examined the mill wheel.

Beatrice's heart beat fiercely for Blythe. She wasn't at all sure what to do about it.

Before she took her leave of the mill to see to her other affairs in Chiddon, Blythe would pull her behind the building or a wagon, if there happened to be one about, and kiss Beatrice senseless before releasing her. She would go about the remainder of her day in a blissful haze of Blythe-induced intoxication, visiting Milhenney, the baker, who had completed his move to Chiddon. Beatrice would next check in on the cheese monger, the apothecary, and then, finally, The Pickled Duck.

Chiddon ale had already found a home at several prominent taverns in Overton. Gates was overjoyed.

Beatrice would arrive home in the late afternoon to find Blythe awaiting her in the parlor, a brandy in one hand. If there were problems at the mill, he might come later. But he always arrived in time to sup with Beatrice.

Uninvited, but assured of his welcome.

They often read together in the evenings before the fire, Blythe in the chair beside her. He would pause every so often to trail a finger along her arm or take her hand before returning to his book. Once the house quieted, he would follow Beatrice upstairs, strip her of every stitch of clothing and press his mouth to her skin, using his tongue in ways Beatrice had never imagined. Sometimes, he took her roughly, pounding into her with such force, she worried the bed would shatter. Other times, Blythe took her tenderly, trailing his mouth along every scar and piece of pitted flesh until Beatrice was left shaking and near tears from the pleasure of it.

Blythe made a great show of sneaking out of the house just as the light turned misty gray to ride to his own residence, shave, and change his clothing before once more appearing in the breakfast room as if he hadn't been tupping Beatrice upstairs just hours before.

None of her staff were fooled, but they were discreet.

Until Blythe, she had never considered herself to be capable of such passion or carnal appetites. If she had once had any inhibitions, Blythe had fully wiped them away. The sight of him naked, curls tossed about his temples, snoring in her bed, undid her. When he absently ran his fingertips along the scars decorating the edge of her cheek with no disgust, Beatrice wanted to cling to his broad-shouldered form and beg him to never leave her.

Beatrice had found the meaning of happiness. It was Blythe.

Her prior existence as the jewel of London was a pale version of her life now. Even Chiddon, before Blythe, seemed stale and far too dull. Her feelings for the earl, once so filled with anger and bitterness, had grown into something beautiful. Richer. More profound.

But one day soon, this blissful interlude would end, and there was little Beatrice could do about it. They didn't speak of the future, at least not directly. Blythe made vague references to London and an eventual return, but he spoke nothing of his intentions.

Beatrice didn't give voice to her own feelings, too afraid of rejection or that she had misjudged the depth of his attachment to her. Even if Blythe loved her, marriage was out of the question, and the only other option—well, Beatrice didn't think she could tolerate being known as the Earl of Blythe's scarred mistress.

THE DESIRE OF A DUCHESS

Either way, Beatrice had to decide on London. But not today. Or tomorrow.

Which is why, when she walked into her parlor, slightly foxed from having spent the afternoon sampling ale with Gates, she was overwhelmed by her own emotions. Blythe sat before the fire, drinking her brandy and paging through the book he'd been reading. Her heart fluttered softly at the sight, as it always did in response to his presence, and whispered a single word only Beatrice could hear.

Love.

࿇

"MY LORD."

Ellis leaned over the arm of the chair to see his lovely Bea, standing at the doorway of the parlor. There was a flicker of joy across her delicate features before she attempted to hide it from him.

"How unexpected to find you here," she said in a clipped tone.

It really wasn't. Pretending to be irritated by his presence when he was in her bed every night was a game Beatrice seemed to enjoy, so Ellis played along.

He glanced at the blue ribbon neatly tied around the thick mass of curls dangling over her right shoulder. Ellis had coaxed Beatrice to wear her hair up over the last few weeks since the festival, but the results were mixed. On the first occasion, Beatrice caught sight of herself in the mirror, scars exposed, and had ripped out all of Peg's hard work. They'd had quite the row after, he and Bea, ending only when he'd lifted her skirts and pressed his tongue inside her.

The next time Ellis persuaded Beatrice had been better, but only because he'd had her bent over the edge of the settee, her teeth sunk into a cushion so Mrs. Lovington wouldn't hear her scream when she climaxed.

"Good day, Your Grace." Ellis sniffed at the air and stood. "I caught the scent of roasted chicken and came to investigate."

Beatrice gave him a dubious look. "All the way from the mill? You've a keen sense of smell, my lord. I suppose you expect an invitation to dinner. Do you even employ a cook at your own residence?"

He ambled toward her, brandy in one hand. "I adore roasted chicken. I hope there are potatoes." Ellis bent, trailing his lips hungrily over hers. Sparks ignited between them, fusing their mouths together.

He would never, *ever*, tire of kissing her.

"I'm uncertain about potatoes." Beatrice tilted her chin. "My other lovers prefer carrots. Sometimes peas. A turnip, if I'm feeling generous."

Beatrice was bluffing, teasing him deliberately, because there weren't any other lovers. But the thought of another man, even a nonexistent one, touching his duchess didn't sit well with Ellis. Jealousy wasn't a completely foreign emotion for him, but usually his envy was for a poet or a sculptor. Never over a woman. Not until Beatrice.

"Vile creature. You seem to require convincing that I am a most desirable companion." Ellis set down his glass and carefully moved aside the thick tail of her hair. He cupped her chin, his mouth lingering over the scars along the edge of her cheek before moving to Beatrice's lips once more. Everything Ellis felt for Beatrice bled out in that kiss. He no longer wondered why a romantic poem had never flowed from him; Ellis had never had the proper muse until now.

"Any roguish peacock can kiss properly," she whispered against his mouth.

"Yes, but not like me." He tugged at her bottom lip with his teeth. "Harpy."

Beatrice rubbed the top of her head against his chest, like a kitten needing to be stroked. "Agreed. There are some benefits to your presence."

He held her tight for a space of time, relishing the feel of Beatrice's softness against his chest. "I come bearing gifts." Pressing a kiss to the top of her head, Ellis caught the scent of wind and lavender tossed among the strands. He pulled a small package from his coat pocket, wrapped in silk with a neatly tied bow atop. "I had a devil of a time getting the bow correct."

"A gift?"

"You may not think so after you open it."

The gift was a promise of sorts. A decision made. The future would be fraught with challenges. Society must be faced. But Ellis didn't intend to hide his feelings for Beatrice Howard from the world. He'd already taken the precaution of writing for reinforcements.

Beatrice plucked the package out of his hand, carefully untying the ribbon, which she placed on the table holding her books. "It is never a good thing, my lord, to run out of ribbon."

"I see." His heart swelled fuller than it had ever been. She might never be comfortable wearing her hair up or allowing others to see her scars. The actions of Castlemare and the Foxwoods after her accident had given Beatrice a skewed view of her appearance. But he didn't care.

Pulling aside the silk, her eyes widened as she held up the piece of carved wood. Probably wondering what the devil he'd made her.

"You carved me a bee." Beatrice smiled up at him with such joy, one would think he'd presented her with diamonds or gold.

"I did, Your Grace." The carving wasn't exceptional, but you could clearly make out the wings. The tiny eyes. Honestly, it resembled a great many other insects. He was relieved Beatrice saw a bee. The carving, much like the kiss he'd bestowed on her, contained much of his heart.

Standing on tiptoe, Beatrice pressed a soft kiss to his mouth. "Is this bribery for the roasted chicken?"

Ellis's hand trailed down her ruined cheek, the pad of his thumb caressing the marks he'd come to love. "I am glad you are pleased. More so that you see my vision."

Beatrice walked over to the mantel, placing the bee in a prominent position facing the chair Ellis knew to be her favorite. "Mrs. Lovington has already set another place at the table, to no great surprise, but I suppose you deserve potatoes. I will ensure you receive them. Give me a moment." She waved and slid out the door on her way to consult with Mrs. Lovington.

Ellis moved to the sideboard and poured a brandy for Beatrice, setting it on the table between the two overstuffed chairs, making sure Beatrice's glass would be in easy reach once she was seated. A stack of books was piled atop the table.

His eyes fell on the green leatherbound notebook, stuck halfway through the haphazard mountain of essays, novels, and Keats.

Beatrice's ledger.

A ribbon, bright red, had been inserted inside as a bookmark. Curious, Ellis flicked open the cover, surprised to see nothing more than a list of names, some crossed off.

Miss Elkins. Random gossip and malicious behavior.

Ellis recalled Miss Elkins. She was the girl he'd danced with instead of Beatrice at that long ago ball. Because Beatrice had needed a lesson in humility.

I never knew her first name until after she died, which is, frankly, horrid. The small cornerstone repaired at Chiddon's church will read Elizabeth Elkins Summerstone and that of the child who died with her. I've had a rose bush planted in the vicar's garden in her memory.

A line had been drawn through the entire paragraph as a sign of completion.

Mr. Howard Kilpatrick. Footman. Relieved of his position for stepping on the hem of my new gown and causing a tear. Located in London along with his younger brother. A small lump sum along with the offer of employment as butler at Lord Derby's. Wrote brilliant recommendation.

The list went on for three more pages, every entry with notes detailing what wrong each person had suffered at Beatrice's hands.

Miss Rosalind Richardson, now Lady Torrington. Unkind remarks about her figure. Persuaded her to give me the location of Lady Andromeda's rooms, which I then used for malicious purposes.

Milhenney. Not of Lady Torrington's caliber, but it is Chiddon. No one is buying elaborate cakes here.

The baker Beatrice had recently brought to town was Milhenney. Blythe knew Rosalind and her skill at pastries. He had often wondered how Beatrice had ferreted out Andromeda Barrington's penchant for playing modiste. Madame Dupree's shop had nearly been shut down. The scandal had been wielded against the entire Barrington family, along with Beatrice's continued assertion that Granby had ruined Andromeda at the house party. It hadn't stopped until Ellis had advised Granby to assuage Beatrice's wounded pride.

He looked back down at the page.

Lady Andromeda Barrington, now Duchess of Granby. Vile, unwarranted gossip which I cultivated for years. Excessive ruination of her reputation after house party. Kept her from practicing a talent which gave her joy. Inexcusable, especially because she loved Granby, and I never would. Dressmaker to be brought to Chiddon. Possibly a heartfelt letter of apology. I am not brave enough to do more.

Ellis was holding Beatrice's atonements. Recompense for all the wrongs that the other, vain, *terrible* version of herself had committed. Chiddon was penance of sorts, as much as it was her sanctuary. She could have wallowed in self-pity and bitterness at what the fates had dealt her, but she hadn't. Instead, Beatrice had used it as a reason to help others. The riverbed had nearly taken her life, but it had returned to Beatrice a *soul*.

"It makes for interesting reading, does it not?" Beatrice said from the door, hands clasped before her. The cobalt of her eyes wavered, both angry but also afraid. "I didn't mean for you to ever see it, my lord. Rather horrifying, is it not? Reading the awful marks of my character laid out in perfect penmanship. What you must think of me. I'm much more terrible than you could ever have guessed."

"That isn't what I think at all. Come sit, Bea." Ellis held out his hand, wanting nothing more than to wrap his arms around Beatrice and never let her go.

I won't ever let go.

"I promised myself as I lay in that riverbed, looking into Thomas's sightless eyes"—her voice grew thick with emotion —"that no one's life would ever be ruined by my hand again. I made a vow that the creature who lay bleeding in that riverbed would *not* survive. I must try to repair that which is broken. It is the only way to set things right. Balance the ledger, so to speak."

Ellis thought of the church and vicarage. The buildings standing empty in Chiddon which Beatrice was slowly filling back up with bakers, cheese mongers, and apothecaries. Using her influence to promote Gates's ale. Spreading good to balance out the bad.

"Andromeda weighs on me, Blythe. I said despicable things about her even before Granby's house party. And her family." Her lips twisted. "I was so envious, though I didn't know it at the time." A breath left her. "The Barringtons would have looked for Andromeda had she been lying half-dead beneath a carriage." Beatrice pressed a palm to her stomach. "All of England would have been searching." A tiny sob escaped her. "Two days, Blythe. I was there for two days. I don't know what it would be like to have someone miss me. To care enough to wonder where I am."

Oh, Bea. I will always look for you.

"You should write to Andromeda, Your Grace," he said softly. "Duchess to duchess. She will forgive you." Ellis took her hand, threading their fingers together. "No grudge will be held against you, I promise." He raised her wrist to his lips and pressed a kiss to the beating pulse. "I've written to Granby. Told them I am here with you."

She shot him a look filled with betrayal. "You told Granby about my appearance. How pleased he must have been."

"Bea." Ellis drew in a breath, thankful there was nothing sharp within her reach. "You know I must eventually return to London. I have responsibilities. And—"

"A young lady to wed and make a countess, I wager." She took a seat and picked up the glass of brandy he'd poured, refusing to look at him. "One I'm sure of whom Granby approves."

"That isn't—" he started, confused.

"I understand, my lord. You need not be gentle." Her tone was snide, cold. He'd forgotten Beatrice could sound so chilly. She hadn't for a long time, not since before they'd—

"I have been expecting this discussion. Prepared for it. We've had a lovely time together, Blythe, but all good things must end. Your life is in London with your responsibilities, and mine is in Chiddon. Please see yourself out."

A wash of ice trailed down Ellis's spine along with a great deal of irritation. He'd *expected* a protest. That she might fight him on returning to London. He'd been prepared to make concessions until she could grow accustomed to the idea, but for her to assume Ellis would cheerfully skip away without her—

"You're *dismissing* me, Your Grace?" Ellis set his glass down so hard on the table it nearly shattered.

"It seems I am. If you will calm yourself, you'll see I'm attempting to make this easier for you."

"Easier for—have you lost your bloody mind, Beatrice? I wish to understand. I'm to leave you in Chiddon and go off and wed Lady Anabeth Swift without another thought? Maybe make the occasional visit to Chiddon to check on the mill and tup you? Is that correct?"

"I don't expect you'll have much time to visit Chiddon," she murmured.

Ellis ran a hand through his hair in frustration. This wasn't at all how he'd pictured the conversation. He'd only meant to gently coax her to London with him. Ease her discomfort by explaining that she need not worry over Granby or Andromeda. Yes, he'd expected obstinance. Possibly a terrible row after which he'd take her to bed for the remainder of the night and eat roasted potatoes off her bosom.

He had *not* expected Beatrice's icy dismissal.

"Is that her name? Lady Anabeth Swift? I'm certain she's well-bred if Granby approves."

"How flattering that you'll give me over to another woman without so much as a whimper," he bit out.

"I've thought long and hard about London, Blythe." Beatrice stared into the fire and took a swallow of the brandy. "I've no wish to return. You must leave me here."

A thick cloud of fury nearly choked him. "*Must* I? First a saint, now a martyr." Ellis was so bloody angry, he could barely speak. Wounded to the very depths of his being.

"We—have no future together. I've known for some time."

"Well, you didn't bother to inform me, you vile little harpy."

Beatrice flinched. "As you say."

"Contrary to what *you* believe, I have always imagined a future together. I realize a mere countess is a step down from duchess, you bloody snob, but I thought—" He took a deep breath to steady himself before his temper unleashed a torrent of insults, ones he would regret later. Ellis had thought he and Beatrice were of the same mind and heart. Her rejection of him was so incredibly painful. She cared more for the London gossips than him.

"I thought you would try," Ellis said. "For *me*."

Beatrice took another swallow of brandy, tipping the glass up until she drained it.

Ellis glared at her profile, willing her to look at him. "If you are too uncomfortable in town," he said quietly, begging her to listen, "we will find a way to divide our time, or you can take up residence at Larchmont. There's plenty there to keep you busy. The important thing is we would be together, Bea. I won't let anyone disparage you. Nor will I leave your side. I promise."

"Now who is speaking madness?" She finally turned toward him. "You will spend half your life riding over the countryside. It isn't as if I don't bear you a great deal of affection, Blythe. You have made me—" She looked away, throat working. "You've made me happy. But I would not survive London, and you could do little but stand by and watch the vultures pick at my bones. I've no desire to be fodder for the gossips once more." She tapped her cheek. "Nor have my ugliness on display for all to mock."

"Bea, the scars are not so bad. Most are hidden. They'll fade in time."

"Nevertheless."

"Coward."

Beatrice set the empty brandy glass on the table. "Castlemare originally banished me from London because I couldn't provide him an heir. It was common knowledge. Barren Beatrice—that's what he liked to call me. I won't be able to give you a child, Blythe."

"I have a cousin," he roared back at her. This entire discussion had gone completely wrong. "I don't care if you are as barren as that stupid field behind your house."

"Not now, you don't," she said calmly. "But in time, you would regret your decision. Once your lust for me has cooled. I want—"

My lust?

"To hide? Lick your wounds some more?" He nodded at her ledger. "Write in your little book and pretend? You don't even have the courage to apologize to anyone in person. Instead, you run about hiring cheese mongers. You certainly aren't brave enough to confront Andromeda Barrington." Ellis bellowed so loud, the entire household could probably hear them. "I thought you loved me."

Beatrice turned back to the fire with a choked sob. "Stop."

"Clearly, I was mistaken. I would have walked through fire for *you*, Beatrice Howard. Flames searing my flesh. Burned myself to a crisp. And you refuse to even *consider* getting into a damned carriage and going to London with me." His chest heaved. "It wasn't as if I meant to parade you about in Hyde Park."

"You don't understand."

"I think I do. Contrary to reports otherwise, I do possess a decent degree of intelligence. Go on, then. Sit in your parlor and make your notes. Live your life in Chiddon brewing ale with Gates. Maybe you should get a dog. You always say I remind you of one. Your scars are merely an excuse. A way to burrow farther away from the world that may not like *this* version of Beatrice Howard any better than the first."

"Blythe—" Beatrice paled.

He stomped to the parlor door and threw it open, unsurprised to see Mrs. Lovington and Peg standing just outside.

"I've another engagement, Mrs. Lovington. I won't be staying to sup after all. Pity, your chicken smells delicious." Ellis inclined his head to both women before storming out, slamming the front door of Beresford Cottage so hard, he might have torn it from the hinges.

He'd made her a heartfelt carving. Practically proposed, though that hadn't gone well at all. He'd also been unnecessarily cruel to Beatrice, but he'd learned early on not to coddle her. Didn't she know Ellis couldn't possibly leave Chiddon without her? It would be akin to tearing himself in two.

I bought her a bloody mill.

He strode over to Dante and mounted, turning the horse toward the hunting lodge.

When his temper cooled, as it eventually would, and Ellis had gotten over the thought that Beatrice meant to toss him to Lady Anabeth Swift like an extra biscuit she didn't want, he would speak to her once more about London.

He wasn't leaving her in bloody Chiddon. He loved her far too much to do so.

22

Beatrice paced back and forth across her parlor, arms crossed. She looked at the empty chair Blythe usually occupied before dinner, frowned, and paced some more. This room, once a cozy haven, now seemed bleak. Devoid of sunshine. Empty of the one thing that infused life into it.

Don't be ridiculous. I got on quite well without that fop. I will do so again.

She paused in her careful steps to take in the bee on her mantel. Barely a bee. He was terrible at carving. His sculptures in marble must have been quite hideous to behold. Beatrice caught the scent of roast chicken coming from the kitchens. Blythe's favorite. Mrs. Lovington kept expecting he'd just reappear one day. Hopefully he'd bring some brandy because Blythe had drunk all of hers.

Beatrice missed him quite desperately.

Five days had passed since Blythe had lost his temper and stormed out of Beresford Cottage. Imagine how a lifetime without him would feel.

The night of their terrible argument, Beatrice had been

served dinner in silence, Mrs. Lovington making no secret of her disapproval at Beatrice's treatment of Blythe. After dinner, she'd read for an hour or so before deciding to make some notes in her ledger. The green leather notebook fell open, on the very page containing the entry for Andromeda Barrington. Slamming the ledger shut, Beatrice had gone to bed, telling herself that she would feel better about Blythe and her decision in the morning.

Tomorrow would be better.

None of the following days had been better. Blythe's absence permeated Beatrice's entire existence. She'd stopped sleeping through the night. No glorious earl had appeared in her breakfast room, tossing bits of bacon into his mouth while charming Mrs. Lovington into making him an omelet. Even Jasper regarded her with a great deal of judgement.

She had gone about her usual business. Visiting Gates. Melinda. Checking on Milhenney. Riding by the mill, Beatrice had hoped to catch sight of Blythe, but there had been no sign of him. Part of her hoped he would ignore her dismissal. She expected to arrive home and find Blythe sitting calmly in her parlor once more, wondering why there was no more brandy to be had. He would smile and chide her for behaving like a spoiled brat. Kiss her and take her upstairs.

But Blythe had not appeared. Or sent a note.

I may have well and truly driven him away.

Beatrice wiped furiously at her eyes, which were sprouting an enormous amount of moisture suddenly. She paused in her pacing as a sob left her. Then another. Soon she was roaming around the room in a circle, weeping like a banshee. Her stomach roiled and pitched at the thought of never seeing Blythe again.

Peg silently slipped into the room, bobbed politely, and pressed a handkerchief into Beatrice's hands.

She hadn't meant it. But her emotions, swirling like a

terrible maelstrom of self-pity and bitterness, feeding every fear she had over Blythe, had somehow spewed out of her. Beatrice had always operated under the assumption it was better to strike first. Reject before she could be rejected. Blythe hadn't even been given a chance to explain. He might have proposed marriage sometime during their argument. Or at least he'd made a vague reference to her becoming a countess and living at his country estate. He'd given her a poorly carved bee.

A wail left her as she fell to the floor. "I didn't know the bee was some sort of promise. A betrothal bee. And I do not wish to give him over to Lady Anabeth Swift, who I'm certain is merely an insipid, obedient twit. She'll only adore him." Beatrice pounded on the rug, sobbing as if her heart had been torn from her. Because it had been. And now Blythe was gone. "I just don't know if I can get into a carriage. Or let everyone see my cheek. I don't have a bloody ear lobe."

Blythe was right. She was a coward.

"This is unbecoming behavior for a duchess."

Beatrice looked up and wiped at her eyes.

Melinda stood at the door of the parlor, regarding her calmly.

"Go away." Beatrice threw the balled-up handkerchief at her. "Can you not see I am bereft?"

"Temper tantrums do not become you, Your Grace. Nor caterwauling and wailing about like some washerwoman having a fit. Creatures are fleeing the woods. Vicar Farthing claims he hears the devil about to ride to Chiddon. Frankly, you're terrifying."

"Blythe is gone." She hiccupped. "I think he may have returned to London."

"Isn't that what you wanted, Your Grace? Forgive me, but you kicked that magnificent earl away like a small pebble found in your shoe. I suppose you had illusions you were *saving* Blythe so he can wed Lady Fancy Petticoats and have a brood of brats. Or was it sparing him the shame of your association?"

Beatrice collapsed into a heap on the rug. "A hasty decision concocted from my own unwieldy emotions." She pointed to the mantel. "He carved me a bee. A betrothal bee."

Melinda strode over and picked up the carving. "I would have said cricket, but it is the sentiment that matters. A ring would have been more appropriate."

"I thought—" Beatrice dabbed at her eyes with the corner of her skirts. "I thought I was doing what was best."

"Yes, your decision to send away the man you love has brought you great happiness. It is apparent for all to see. Or hear." Melinda stooped down, picked up the handkerchief Beatrice had tossed, and threw it back to her. "Wipe your nose, Your Grace."

Beatrice grabbed the cloth. "Where is your comfort? You are a terrible vicar's wife."

"So I've been told. But I am an excellent friend. Now, shall we see what your glorious earl has to say?" Melinda held up a note. "I intercepted a messenger coming up the steps." A wrinkle took up residence between her brows. "A boy. He said to tell you Mr. Sykes apologizes profusely for the error and begs you not to allow Lord Blythe to sack him. Mrs. Lovington," Melinda called over her shoulder. "I know you're in the hall listening. Will you bring tea please? Some biscuits?" She took Beatrice's arm and led her to the settee.

"I don't want biscuits. My stomach is distressed of late."

"The biscuits are for me, Your Grace. You can hardly expect me to console you on an empty stomach." She held up the note once more, showing the waxed seal. "What an ugly bird."

Beatrice's name was scrawled across the top. Blythe had

beautiful handwriting, much like the rest of him. "It was supposed to be a raven. The legs are all wrong." Beatrice took the note and slid her finger beneath the wax.

Your Grace,

Matters dictated that I return to London immediately. Lady Blythe has taken ill. I apologize I was not able to inform you of my departure in person.

Beatrice looked up at the date of the letter. Blythe had left the day of their terrible argument. Word of his mother's illness must have been waiting for him. "He's been gone from Chiddon for nearly a week, and I wasn't told. No wonder Sykes feared his dismissal. I suppose I should be lucky he remembered to send me the note at all."

I did not leave Chiddon willingly, Your Grace. Not without you.

A deep, rasping sob came from Beatrice at reading the words. Of course, he hadn't wanted to leave her. Even after Beatrice had so brutally dismissed him. He'd yelled. Stomped about. Said some unpleasant things. But Blythe's feelings for her had not faltered.

She had faltered.

"He meant to propose, I think." She wiped her eyes. "And I—I dismissed him and told him to wed another woman. But Blythe—"

"Loves you, Beatrice. Deeply. You are the only one who doesn't realize it." Melinda put an arm around her shoulders. "I doubt you can ever rid yourself of him. Nor do I think you wish to."

"He asked me to *attempt* London, Melinda. *Attempt.* He was prepared to try to live in two places at once for me." Beatrice pressed the palms of her hands to her eyes. "Instead, I told him to go off and marry someone else. Because I may not be able to give him an heir and his friends won't like me."

"And what did Blythe say?"

"He may have called me a vile harpy."

THE DESIRE OF A DUCHESS

"So romantic." Melinda sighed. "Read the rest."

I will look for you, Bea. Always.

Beatrice pressed her forehead once more to the floor and sobbed. Her fingers curled into the rug. Blythe understood, far better than she'd ever given him credit. He did love her, despite what a terrible creature she still was at times. The knowledge sent a fresh wave of tears flowing down her cheeks.

She could not continue to hide from the world, not when Blythe wanted to share it with her.

I will look for you, Bea. Always.

It was daunting, the idea of London. Coaches and balls. Whispers behind fans. The hum of the gossips all deciding a young lady's reputation. Not to mention Lord and Lady Foxwood.

Another cry left her.

I am Lady Beatrice Howard.

Or at least a part of her still was. Jewel of the *ton*. A duchess now, no less. She'd survived that damned riverbed. She could survive a half-dozen snobbish matrons pushing their little nitwits about. So what if no gentleman ever regarded her with admiration again?

It only mattered that Blythe did.

"Beatrice." Melinda took her hand. "Please tell me we are going to London."

"We are," she answered. "You'd best inform Vicar Farthing you'll be gone for some time. Possibly, you'll become my companion permanently and not return at all." Beatrice sucked in a lungful of air and came to her feet. "I'm not even sure I'll survive the coach ride. Bring some laudanum. Don't worry about a wardrobe. I know an excellent modiste." She paused. "I must pay her a long overdue visit upon my arrival."

Her palm pressed along her stomach, begging the horrible pitching to stop.

201

"I'll make an excellent lady's companion, Your Grace. More so than a vicar's wife." Melinda helped her to the settee.

"I've no doubt." She took her friend's hand. "There is no way but through it, is there?"

"I don't think so, Your Grace."

Blythe deserved a woman who was beautiful, unscarred, could bear him children and possessed a more pleasing personality.

Unfortunately, the prancing dandy had already thrown his lot in with her.

The very least Beatrice could do was go to London to fetch him.

❧ 23 ❧

Beatrice left the carriage, relieved as she always was that the vehicle hadn't toppled over on the way to Madame Dupree's. After over a week in London, she still wasn't completely at ease in a carriage. The journey to town had not been a pleasant one. Beatrice had become ill several times, casting up her accounts more than once. Melinda had refused to give her any laudanum, insisting Beatrice must grow accustomed to riding in carriages once more. London was filled with them. She couldn't just take a nip of laudanum every time she ventured out. No one appreciated a dazed duchess except the gossips.

Beatrice had reluctantly agreed.

Castlemare's brother, now the duke, had been informed of Beatrice's arrival. She'd sent him a note before leaving Chiddon, advising him of her intent to return to London and asking if he would do her the kindness of having her house made ready. Beatrice did not mean to cause him any undue embarrassment with her visit.

Beatrice's house had not only been readied for her, but

much to her surprise, it had been made welcoming. Vases of fresh flowers had been placed in the rooms, which all smelled of beeswax. The larder had been stocked. And a small staff had been hastily assembled. All Castlemare's doing. The duke had greeted Beatrice upon her arrival, nodding thoughtfully at the scars decorating her neck and cheek, for she'd insisted on wearing her hair up.

I thought it to be much worse. Should you require it, Beatrice, I am at your disposal.

That was something. The support of her husband's brother. She'd always assumed Castlemare's family detested her.

"Take your time, Your Grace." Melinda interrupted her thoughts by fairly pushing Beatrice out of the carriage. "I've a book and plenty of things to occupy my time."

Beatrice stepped onto the street, pulling the veil across her features and the shawl tighter about her shoulders. Her hair was atop her head, but the shawl covered the worst of it. That was as far as Beatrice was willing to go today.

She walked past the front window of Madame Dupree's, relieved to see that the modiste's shop was nearly empty. Turning around the corner, Beatrice walked down the narrow alley behind the row of shops. A splendid carriage sat waiting near a nondescript back door. The carriage bore the coat of arms of the Duke of Granby.

The footman she'd set to watching Madame Dupree's the past few days had been correct.

Taking a deep breath, Beatrice walked to the door and opened it a crack. Peering in, she ascertained no one was about, slipped through the door, and shut it behind her. The back rooms of Madame Dupree's shop were dark and slightly treacherous given the maze of fabrics one must walk through. Bolts of silk, muslin, tulle, and lord knows what else were stacked haphazardly against the walls. The path between was no more than a sliver.

Beatrice darted quietly along a row of satins, pausing to run her fingers over the fabric.

A male rumble echoed down the hall, followed by the seductive laugh of a woman.

"Good grief," Beatrice whispered to herself. "I hope I don't interrupt them in a tryst. That will hardly endear me to either." The sounds emanated from behind a door, partially ajar. A workroom, she guessed.

"Delicious little shrub." The endearment, for that's what Beatrice assumed it to be, came out in a masculine growl.

I suppose that's better than being called a vile harpy. Marginally.

A feminine sigh followed, one of undisguised pleasure.

Beatrice didn't move. If she ran back out now, she wouldn't have to witness—but the opportunity would be missed. She'd been hoping to catch Andromeda alone at Madame Dupree's without Granby, but she should have guessed he'd be here. Granby wasn't the sort to allow Andromeda, burdened with her pins and sketches, to go about London without protection.

Very well.

Beatrice pushed the door open enough for her to step through. She couldn't see Andromeda, only her hands, which were held by the wrist above her head. Granby's massive form completely hid his wife from view. His dark head was bent over her, murmuring to Andromeda in a foreign tongue. Italian, probably.

If Beatrice were wise, she would pivot and go back the way she'd come. Maybe a note would suffice. A box of chocolates. Or a pastry. She could send a tart purchased from Lady Torrington, who everyone in London pretended wasn't running a pastry shop by the name of Pennyfoil's.

No. I must do this in person. If I survive, I'll still buy the tart.

Beatrice cleared her throat hoping Granby didn't charge at her like some immense bull for the untimely interruption. How Blythe remained such close friends with the stony duke was a source of mystery.

"David." Andromeda's muffled voice came from somewhere beneath all that mountainous duke. "Did you hear that?"

David?

Beatrice had never thought of Granby having a Christian name, but of course he must. Had she known it was David?

How bland.

"I apologize for interrupting," she said to Granby's back.

Granby spun, dropping Andromeda's wrists. A blast of chilly air was leveled at Beatrice for her untimely interruption. He looked exactly as she remembered, big and monstrous. Like an iceberg wearing a tailored coat.

Andromeda leaned to one side, eyes widening at the sight of Beatrice. She patted the arm of her annoyed duke, pressing him to move away, and when he didn't, she stepped around him. Motherhood and marriage agreed with Andromeda. She was a vision, with her lustrous dark hair and those blue eyes with their disarming circle of indigo.

Self-consciously, Beatrice's fingers trailed down her neck.

"Madame is gone for the day," Andromeda said. "She has given us leave to examine some of her fabric for a gown I'm considering. Claudine is up front, I believe. She can help you."

Beatrice spared some annoyance for not being recognized before recalling the veil hiding her features. She flipped it over the brim of her hat. "I'm here to speak to you, Your Grace," she said to Andromeda. "If you have a moment."

Granby angled his body closer to his wife. Protectively. As

if Beatrice were some viper threatening Andromeda. "Beatrice Howard."

"I should like to speak to your duchess on a matter of some import."

Granby's lips thinned in disapproval. His chilly gaze flicked over Beatrice's exposed cheek and missing earlobe.

"Please." Beatrice lifted her chin.

Andromeda pushed at her giant of a husband. "Your Grace, she is unlikely to stab me with a pair of shears. Let us dispense with formal address. We are all well acquainted. Good afternoon, Beatrice."

"Andromeda." There was no gasp of shock from either of them at her scars. Curiosity, yes, but no stammering or looking everywhere but at her cheek or neck. Blythe would have told them everything in his bid to have them accept her.

An ache floated over her chest. Her heart missed Blythe desperately.

Beatrice wished he was here right now, but she had intentionally neglected to inform him of her arrival in London. This had to come first. Blythe would want to protect her, and she had to do this on her own.

"Wait for me in the coach," Andromeda said to Granby, but she didn't take her eyes from Beatrice. "Better yet, send the coach back for me in an hour."

"Andromeda—" Granby protested.

"Beatrice and I need to become reacquainted." She reached up on tiptoe and pressed a kiss to the edge of Granby's chin. "Don't fuss."

A sound came from the duke, that of a disgruntled bear, but he obeyed his wife with no further argument.

Once the door shut behind him, Andromeda turned back to Beatrice with a wary smile. "He's overprotective."

"He's had reason to be," Beatrice countered. "I wouldn't

leave you alone in a room with someone of my character either." She wandered around the table, looking at the drawings strewn about. Andromeda was immensely talented. Her designs were one-of-a-kind. "The gown you created for me—those tiny suns to put in my hair—pure genius. I repaid you poorly and far more cruelly than you deserved."

"I took your duke."

Beatrice shrugged. "Granby was never my duke. He was yours from the moment he saw you, in this very shop. Do you recall? I mistook you for one of Madame Dupree's assistants."

"I do. But I met Granby before that day, at a garden party. Blythe accused me of sketching out his backside."

Beatrice smiled. "That sounds like Blythe." He'd never mentioned meeting Andromeda at a garden party. She took a deep breath. "I have come to make amends, or at least attempt to do so."

"I suspected as much." Andromeda took a step forward. "After speaking to Blythe. Go on then, Beatrice. Give me your apology so that I may forgive you." There was a great deal of patience reflected in Andromeda's lovely features. Empathy. But no pity for Beatrice's scars or the tragedy she'd suffered.

"You are being terribly kind about this."

"I've learned in recent years how difficult change can be for a person, more so when you are groomed with a particular set of ideals from birth. Loss, or the fear of it, provides powerful motivation to become a better person. There is little shame in owning up to one's faults."

Beatrice had the sense Andromeda wasn't speaking of her, or at least, not completely.

She inhaled slowly. It was far harder to apologize when the person stood before you. Easier to merely find a dressmaker for Chiddon.

"I will confess that I have always envied you, Andromeda Barrington. Not only your talents, which are significant, but your ability to walk through life emboldened, unconcerned about what others may think. I envy you your family, who loves you unconditionally. Your beauty, for it is flawless and will never fade because it shines from within you."

"Beatrice."

"Let me finish. *Please*. I was cruel to you for many years long before I ever met the Duke of Granby. I assassinated your character at every turn. I used your cousin Rosalind to discover your secrets. Spread those secrets to Lady Carstairs, whom I knew to be a notorious gossip. When Granby tossed me over for you, I made sure to paint you as a harlot." Beatrice had to look away. "I was—humiliated by his decision, but not heartbroken. Lord and Lady Foxwood encouraged my behavior, mortified that their daughter had been thrown over for a Barrington."

"I surmised their opinion of me early on," Andromeda replied.

"When Granby came to me and offered to put out the story that I had jilted him, I nearly didn't agree. Not because I was enjoying my humiliation, or because Granby had made me such an offer out of any great liking for me. But—he did so for *you*. He loved you so bloody much and couldn't bear for *you* to be hurt even though *I* was the injured party." Beatrice plucked at her skirts. "The hatred I felt for you in that moment, the knowledge that no one would ever love me enough—that is what I must apologize for."

"But that isn't true, Beatrice. Has Blythe never told you? It was he who convinced Granby to make you such an offer." Andromeda took Beatrice's hand. "Not for my sake, but *yours*."

"I didn't know," Beatrice whispered, her heart aching once

more for Blythe. "And I am not groveling nearly as much as I meant to."

"I think you're doing quite well." Andromeda's eyes blazed blue fire at her. "Finish it."

Beatrice took a deep, cleansing breath, feeling all the ugliness, all the bitter taste of acrimony, finally leave her body.

"I am truly, *deeply* sorry from the depths of my soul, Andromeda. For all the wrongs which I have done you." A tear slid down her cheek, and she wiped it away. "I beg you to forgive me and the horrible creature I once was."

Andromeda took both her hands and squeezed. "I forgive you, Beatrice Howard. For all of it."

Beatrice gave a choked sob. "Thank you."

She leaned against the pitted table used to cut fabric. A weight pushed off her chest and floated free. Turning, she sobbed into her hands, trying to stifle the sound before she started wailing away at Madame Dupree's.

"Beatrice." Andromeda gently turned her. "Stop weeping. I insist. You are forgiven, and we need never mention this again. Are we agreed?"

"Must you be so bloody wonderful? I shall try not to hate you further."

Andromeda smiled. "I am rather spectacular. Granby often says so. Now." Her gaze focused on Beatrice's ruined ear. "We'll have to find a way to work around that. A hairstyle with curls that cascade to the right and a subtle rewiring of—"

"What on earth are you talking about?" Beatrice's hand raised to cover her ruined ear. "Stop staring at it."

"Earrings, Beatrice. You want to wear them again, yes?"

"Well yes, but—" She took off the shawl around her shoulders and laid it on the table. "There is also this to contend with."

Andromeda cocked her head, taking in Beatrice's neck.

THE DESIRE OF A DUCHESS

"I'd heard the rumors, of course. Disfigured. So hideous you couldn't be looked at." A snort left her. "Goodness. It isn't nearly as bad as all that. Blythe was right. The scars, at least along your cheek and neck, aren't too deep and will fade with time." Andromeda paced around her. "Blythe told Granby and me, of course. Over a dinner during which he became incredibly foxed. He spouted off terrible poetry about your beauty. I had to have a footman escort him to a guestroom."

"He isn't any good at writing poetry, only reciting another's words." Another ache in her chest. "Blythe doesn't know I'm in London."

Andromeda regarded her shrewdly. "You needed to prove you could do this without his help. I understand. And Blythe did not need to be present for our earlier discussion. That will remain between us, Beatrice." She leaned closer to Beatrice's ear. "I can't hide all of it, but I can hide the worst."

"It becomes more terrible closer to my shoulder and bosom."

"No matter. I can arrange the neckline just so." Andromeda scratched furiously with a piece of charcoal across the sketchbook she held. "To sweep up your right shoulder while leaving the left exposed." She smiled. "I saw a gown similar in design while Granby and I were abroad. Very daring." She circled Beatrice again. "I need to take your measurements."

"I told you the scars become worse." Beatrice lifted her arms obediently as Andromeda started to unbutton her gown. "Don't go screaming or say I didn't warn you."

"I shan't. Do Lord and Lady Foxwood know you are in London? Does Lady Blythe know of your involvement with her son?"

Beatrice shook her head. "I haven't spoken to my parents in some time."

Andromeda gave her shoulder a sympathetic squeeze. "I see."

"And I don't think he would have mentioned me to Lady Blythe."

"Good. I feel certain Lady Blythe could do with a surprise or two. Repayment for her kindness to my sister, Theodosia. Oh, and luring Blythe to London under the pretense she'd fallen ill. She's in perfect health for a tyrant."

Blythe's mother wasn't ill after all. "He must be furious."

"Oh, he is. I'll have to work much of tomorrow to get this done in time." Andromeda measured Beatrice from waist to ankle, pausing only to make a note.

"Time for what, exactly?"

"The party Lady Blythe is hosting, which was planned well before her sudden illness. Thankfully, she has left her deathbed just in time. There will be dancing, of course. Terrible refreshments. Blythe has promised not to depart London until after." She took a hold of Beatrice's shoulders. "He's trying to get back to you."

The thought warmed her. "I wasn't sure I could attempt London. He wasn't either. It isn't as if anyone will welcome me back, pitted as I am like a month-old orange. I include Lord and Lady Foxwood in that number. But I will go. Hold my head up. Brave the esteemed Lady Blythe." A tremble started down her spine, but Beatrice forced herself to straighten once more.

"That's the spirit. Granby and I will be there. Blythe will find you."

I will look for you, Bea. Always.

"I have no doubt," she said with as much bravado as she could muster. "And I will have a friend with me. Mrs. Farthing. Do you have something possibly half-done that she might wear to this party of Lady Blythe's?"

"I do. Bring her over tomorrow. Through the back."

Andromeda helped Beatrice dress once more. "And bring a pair of earrings you wish to wear. I have an idea."

"Andromeda." Beatrice took her hand. "Thank you."

She motioned for Beatrice to follow her back through the stacks of fabrics. "Don't thank me. I'm doing this for Blythe. I don't even like you." She winked before stopping. "How do you feel about blue?"

24

Ellis caught sight of his treacherous mother from across the room, plump form garbed in her usual canary yellow, a color only appropriate for a woman at least twenty years her junior. Floating about, Mother greeted the throng of guests in his drawing room with a smile and a well-placed compliment. She looked quite hearty for a woman who, only days ago, had been at death's door.

A ruse. One concocted by his conniving mother to force Ellis's return to London.

He'd arrived at his hunting lodge just after leaving Beatrice, already having decided he would appear at her breakfast table the following morning and demand she listen to him, only to be greeted by Sykes and a messenger from London. Ellis's presence was required immediately. Lady Blythe had fallen ill. Ellis had immediately packed a valise and sent the messenger ahead. He'd scribbled a note to Beatrice and instructed Sykes to have it delivered as soon as the stable boy could be found.

After traveling all night, arriving exhausted and hungry,

Ellis hadn't even paused to change his clothing before going upstairs to check on his mother.

Lady Blythe had been sitting up in bed, reading the Times and delicately poking at a poached egg. She'd fallen back against the pillows at the sight of Ellis, claiming great fatigue though she was feeling much better. Ellis had sent for the physician and sought out his two younger sisters who had accompanied Mother to London. Their acute lack of concern over Lady Blythe was his first clue that all was not as it seemed.

If one fakes an illness, all parties should be on board.

Lady Blythe's recovery was miraculous, declared the physician.

Mother had claimed the remedy had been Ellis's presence. The following day, she'd informed Ellis she was well enough to continue with the small gathering planned weeks ago. Barely a party. Certainly not a ball. No more than a hundred or so guests. Invitations had gone out some time ago and, thankfully, did not need to be rescinded.

Splendid.

After tonight's party, Ellis was sending Mother and the girls to Larchmont, season be damned. He wanted to be in Chiddon, though he had no idea what sort of welcome would await him. There had been no response from the letter he'd left for Beatrice, and Ellis worried for her. Which was ridiculous since she'd existed just fine without him for several years.

It was *his* existence that was called into question.

Ellis wasn't fine without Beatrice.

Only the presence of Granby and his duchess in London had made things the least tolerable. He'd dined with them the other night, had far too much wine, and might have spouted some poetry. Granby had claimed disgust. Blythe had called him a philistine who didn't appreciate the art of words.

"Lord Blythe."

He cast a dispassionate glance at the approach of Lady Pierce and her daughter, Lady Anabeth. Mother watched from across the room, round face beaming, breathless with anticipation that her *little exaggeration*, as she'd called scaring Ellis half out of his wits, would somehow compel Ellis to offer for Lady Anabeth. No such proposal for the girl before him would be forthcoming. Lady Anabeth was a slim-waisted brunette who barely spoke above a whisper. There was nothing of a vile harpy about her at all.

She bored Ellis to tears.

"Lady Pierce, Lady Anabeth. How lovely you both look this evening." The usual polite, charming words fell from his lips.

Lady Anabeth blushed furiously, regarding Ellis as if he were a large tart meant just for her.

Sorry, a more dangerous creature has already had a bite.

"My lord, we grew concerned at your continued absence from London," Lady Pierce twittered. "I was so pleased to learn you'd be here this evening."

Mother had probably sent a special messenger to Lady Pierce the moment he'd set foot in London.

"Oh, Lady Pierce." Mother appeared in her swirl of yellow silk and took her friend's hand. "There you are. And Lady Anabeth, you resemble a rosebud about to unfurl, my dear. I see you've found Lord Blythe."

Anabeth blushed a deeper red and giggled softly.

Ellis wanted to hang himself with his cravat.

"The musicians are about to start," Mother said in a meaningful tone. "Perhaps Lady Anabeth would care for a dance."

Maybe Granby would be a good sport for once and push Ellis down the stairs. Anything to stop this torture. Not enough to break Ellis's neck, only injure him enough so he couldn't dance. Or speak. "With your permission, Lady Pierce."

"Of course, my lord."

Ellis took Lady Anabeth's hand and led her into the other colorful bits of silk twirling across the floor. Blythe's home didn't have a proper ballroom, but the furniture and rugs had all been thrown back to make room for the dancing. He considered hurling himself into a marble bust in the corner, but at this angle, he would probably only stub his toe.

Certain to keep Lady Anabeth at a proper distance, Ellis made polite conversation about the weather and ignored her blatant attempts to induce him to call upon her for a carriage ride.

"I'll be indisposed," he finally informed her. "Due to the enormous amount of wine I plan to imbibe this evening."

Lady Anabeth stayed silent for the remainder of their dance.

❧

THE CARRIAGE SAT JUST OUTSIDE BLYTHE'S HOME, a footman standing by the door, ready to assist Beatrice and Melinda from the vehicle.

Beatrice looked down at her skirts, soothed by the weave of the iridescent blue silk. The fabric was beautiful, rippling in the light as if stars were caught within. An eye-catching gown, meant for a magnificent entrance. Melinda had helped style Beatrice's hair so that a fall of ringlets hung over her right ear. Sapphires dangled from her ears.

Clever Andromeda had taken a bit of wire and placed it over the curve of her right ear, settling the sapphire earring just over her ruined lobe. Looking in the mirror, not even Beatrice could tell that the earring wasn't affixed to her earlobe. The bodice of her dress was cut at an angle in a departure from the current style and nearly covered all her right shoulder before sweeping across to fall from her left.

The design was bold. The scars along the edge of her cheek and neck were clearly visible, but the worst were hidden. She looked beautiful, slightly snobbish, and very much like the Beatrice Howard she'd once been.

"Stunning, Your Grace," Melinda said from across the carriage. "And I thank you for my own gown." Andromeda had produced a gown of green striped silk which only needed a few adjustments to fit Melinda.

"You're quite welcome. But your thanks are owed to the Duchess of Granby." Beatrice's stomach pitched, though the carriage had stopped moving. "I should have eaten. I don't feel at all well." She thought it was being in London once more and perhaps apprehension about seeing Lord and Lady Foxwood. There was no fear over seeing Blythe, only a gnawing desperation to be with him.

"Nerves, Your Grace. But don't worry. I'll be right beside you, carrying this." She held up a fan. "And the Duchess of Granby is inside, waiting."

After completing the gown in record time, waving away the extreme effort as of little consequence, Andromeda had called earlier today to ensure no further alterations were necessary. The idea of surprising Blythe, and everyone else, with her presence had seemed like such a good idea when they'd had tea. Andromeda had brought the most delicious tiny cakes made by her cousin, Lady Torrington.

"What if I misread the situation, Melinda? Or what if I pushed him right into Lady Anabeth's waiting arms?"

"He'll take one look at you in that gown and put all that aside." Melinda stepped out of the carriage. "Blythe has a lovely home, Your Grace. Very grand."

"It doesn't have a ballroom," Beatrice said with a shrug. "So, by London standards, it is only average."

"I see." Melinda nodded. "Still, much finer than dancing at the village green in Chiddon, don't you think?"

Beatrice would give anything to be back in front of the fiddler and dancing on the grass with Blythe. "I don't think I can go in, Melinda. What if he no longer—" Nausea welled up inside her again. Beatrice had been ill the entire time she'd been in London. She wasn't used to the noise anymore. Or the smell. And all the carriages. Not to mention the pile of hissing snakes she knew awaited her inside Blythe's home.

"Lord Blythe cares deeply for you, Your Grace. I do not think one terrible argument in which you behaved stupidly will put him off. Summon all that sharp, cold superiority you once wielded. March inside and take your place once more."

"My parents are likely here. Lady Blythe doesn't care for them, but Lord and Lady Foxwood are the sort you must invite to maintain appearances."

"All the better. I've looked forward to making their acquaintance." Melinda lowered her voice. "Andromeda is inside. She expects you. I wouldn't dare disappoint her. And Blythe will find you. Ignore everyone else."

Beatrice straightened her spine and lifted her shoulders. Her battlefield was before her. She was a seasoned soldier. Let them make their cutting remarks. Whisper about her. Stare if they wished. She was not the wounded duchess Castlemare had banished. Nor the daughter her parents had manipulated for years and then discarded. "I'm ready."

Melinda stayed just to her right, a pace behind as Beatrice took the steps and walked inside. A servant passing by stumbled, catching sight of her ruined cheek and neck.

Barely noticeable indeed.

Beatrice lifted her chin higher. "You should see my shoulder," she murmured before he scuttled out of her path.

The house was warm, scents filling the air. Pomade, the press of warm bodies, and violets fought for dominance over the vases of fresh roses topping nearly every surface. Beatrice could hear the strains of a waltz echoing along the hall.

Melinda, eyes wide, drank in the sight. "Impressive."

"Not really." Beatrice steeled herself and took in a large portrait of a green pear sitting in a bowl. "Blythe's mother has terrible taste in art. You'd think with his love of such things, he would have tempered her plastering the walls with that." She pointed to the painting. "The pears will be the first things to go."

"That's the spirit, Your Grace."

Beatrice's steps hesitated a fraction as she moved through the crowd. This was no small party. Half of London must be here. Eyes turned in her direction. Fans snapped. Surprised gasps sounded.

I always did like to make an entrance.

She reached into the pocket of her gown, fingers tracing the lines of her little carving. Her betrothal bee. Upon seeing the bee earlier, Andromeda had declared it a good luck charm —one Beatrice must keep with her tonight. It would give her courage and remind her of Blythe.

Wisdom. Another thing Beatrice decided she envied in Andromeda.

Not only for insisting on the bee but also for putting pockets in every gown she designed.

A painfully thin young woman, chin pointed and sharp, wearing a gown full of flounces, stopped right before Beatrice. Struck dumb by the sight of the pitted scars along Beatrice's neck, her thin lips gaped open in the most unappealing way.

What has happened to manners while I've been gone?

Beatrice looked down her nose at the girl and asked in a snide, dripping tone. "If you keep your mouth open, you might attract flies. Now get out of my way."

She stepped aside, red-faced, to take the arm of a

gentleman beside her. He bowed, staring at Beatrice's neck. "Pardon, Your Grace."

The humming grew a great deal louder.

"Remember who you are," Melinda said quietly so only Beatrice could hear.

Beatrice could feel her knees wobbling beneath the silk. She hid her hands in the folds of her skirts so no one could see how she trembled.

Good God. What's happened to her face? I told you the rumors were true.

Not so high and mighty now, is she?

I'd almost forgotten about Beatrice Howard.

Someone should tell Lady Foxwood.

Andromeda stood next to the mountainous Granby at the far end of the room, stunning in a gown of deep indigo. She caught sight of Beatrice and inclined her head.

Dozens of eyes watched the interaction between them, salivating in anticipation. The room grew silent, holding their collective breath. Perhaps hoping for fisticuffs given Beatrice's past with Granby and Andromeda. Or that Granby might cut her.

Granby bowed stiffly in Beatrice's direction. A polite acknowledgement. More than she'd expected. Or deserved.

Just to Granby's left stood Blythe, the burnished gold of his hair shining like a guinea against his dark formal wear. His back was to her, his attention taken by a blob of yellow, like a fattened canary.

The esteemed Lady Blythe.

An adoring young lady stood next to Lady Blythe, blushing and stammering. Lady Anabeth was exactly as Beatrice had imagined. The older woman at her side could only be her mother.

"That's what you were going to leave him to?" Melinda whispered. "Doesn't seem like such a grand idea, does it?" Her friend drifted off a pace. "I think I'll fetch something to drink."

"The punch is always terrible," Beatrice whispered back.

The smile on Lady Blythe's face froze. Tightened. The sight of Beatrice had made her speechless. She placed a hand on Blythe's arm.

The other guests still watched but with much less enthusiasm. They'd all be hoping for a scene between Granby, his duchess, and Beatrice. Lady Blythe—nor anyone who was drinking her terrible punch—did not know of the relationship between Blythe and the widowed Duchess of Castlemare. They did not know that Beatrice loved Ellis Aperton, Earl of Blythe with her entire heart.

Nor that he loved her in return.

But they would now.

Blythe's feelings for Beatrice, as he turned toward her, were stamped in every line of his handsome face. Impossible to miss. On full display. He took one step forward and stretched out a hand in her direction, a silent command for her to come the rest of the way. The sky blue of his eyes shone with pride. He meant to claim her before everyone.

Beatrice took two more steps, extending her fingers.

His hand curled around hers protectively as he brought her to his side.

"There you are." Blythe's words rasped with longing. "I've been looking for you, Your Grace."

25

Blythe purposefully drew Beatrice to his side. "You are full of surprises, Bea." He leaned to press a subtle kiss on her ear. "I thought more negotiation would be required on my part. Another carved insect. Perhaps keeping you naked in your bed for a week or so."

"I could do with a bit more incentive, my lord. Your dubious charms aren't nearly enough," Beatrice replied.

"My lord," Lady Blythe intoned, no longer speechless.

"You recall the Duchess of Castlemare, do you not, Lady Blythe?" Ellis said in a firm tone. "We became reacquainted during my time in the country. I extended an invitation on your behalf."

The plump canary bobbed. "Your Grace. Welcome." She gestured to the two women beside her. "Lady Pierce and her daughter, Lady Anabeth Swift." Lady Blythe, oddly enough, didn't seem terribly upset to find Beatrice at her party now that she'd overcome her shock.

"Delighted." Beatrice greeted both women politely with just the right amount of boredom.

Lady Pierce glanced down at Beatrice's skirts, where Blythe's hand was firmly entwined with her own. "A pleasure, Your Grace. If you'll excuse us, I see Lord Norris has arrived. Come, Anabeth." The two retreated in a flurry of silk, Anabeth casting one last wistful gaze at Blythe before disappearing into the crowd.

Lady Blythe, clearly unsure how to proceed, said, "I must check on the refreshments. Excuse me."

"You've rattled my mother," Blythe murmured once she'd disappeared. "No easy task. I approve of the gown, by the way." He cast a glance at Andromeda who was engaged in conversation with another young lady a few paces away. "You apologized and received a spectacular gown as a reward. I'm very proud of you, Bea."

Beatrice's fingers slid over the small carving in her pocket. "Andromeda is kind in the most annoying ways. Forgiving." She gazed at the Duchess of Granby. "Another thing I must dislike about her."

"You are a cause she has championed. Remind me to tell you the story of Granby's elderly tailor one day. You'll find it amusing." His fingers tightened on hers. "I'll assume your entrance tonight means you won't be handing me over to Lady Anabeth."

"That pale, mousy thing? I can't believe you'd have any interest."

"Well, she's no snobbish harridan, I grant you. But she adores me."

Beatrice rolled her eyes. "*I* adore you. But do not expect fawning of any sort."

"I was prepared to live in Chiddon indefinitely." His voice grew solemn. "It would have been difficult but not insurmountable. Your comfort is most important to me."

Beatrice tightened her fingers around his. "I—have a house here. I will tolerate London for you. Ride in carriages.

Be gossiped about. Have children scream at the sight of me."

A bark of laughter left Blythe. He really was glorious when he laughed.

"It isn't all that bad, Beatrice. Not with your hair styled just so. Barely noticeable. But society will whisper a great deal after tonight. Speculate over the accident. Your mysterious departure from London. How even so, you managed to snare the eligible, charming, and magnificent Earl of Blythe."

"Fop."

"You'll have to show me later how Andromeda managed to give you the appearance of an earlobe."

Beatrice discreetly stepped on his foot.

"Mrs. Farthing doesn't look at all distressed to be away from the good vicar. I found him a post, by the way. Prestigious, but far from London and Chiddon. Cornwall, to be exact."

"In that case, I am in desperate need of a lady's companion. I simply can't release Mrs. Farthing from her duties to me."

Blythe's jaw hardened abruptly, the blue of his eyes becoming frosty.

"I'll tell the vicar, Blythe. I thought you liked Mrs. Farthing." Beatrice looked up at him, puzzled he was so concerned over the state of Melinda's marriage or the vicar's feelings. "I know it's a bit unusual, but I doubt Farthing will care overmuch. Not if you've awarded him a decent post."

"Your Grace." A hesitation. "Beatrice." The voice of Lady Foxwood, crisp as a glass of chilled white wine came from behind her.

Beatrice pressed a hand to her stomach, the contents of which had recently settled with Blythe's presence but now, pitched once more. She'd hoped, foolishly, that Lord and Lady Foxwood might ignore her if they were here. After all, they'd done little else but pretend Beatrice didn't exist since the carriage accident.

She turned to face her mother, who was garbed in rich purple silk. Diamonds dripped from her throat and wrists, glittering in the muted light. "Lady Foxwood."

Her mother made a great show of greeting her, pressing a perfumed kiss to Beatrice's cheek, aware of those watching. "I'll confess I'm delighted to see you in attendance. I hadn't thought to see you in town. You've preferred the country for so long." Her voice carried to those listening with rapt attention.

Lady Foxwood fell back, discerning gaze trailing over Beatrice's hair, the edge of her cheek, and settling on the swath of scarred skin at her neck. "Why, your little tumble healed quite well," she said in a low voice. "Your father will be so pleased."

Her little tumble. Lady Foxwood made it sound as if she'd merely tripped on her skirts, not lain screaming beneath a carriage.

"Will he? As I recall, you hosted a house party rather than come to see to me after my *little tumble*."

"Dearest," her mother reprimanded in an imperious tone. "We couldn't disappoint our guests. Invitations had already gone out."

"And your excuse for not seeing to me since?" Beatrice uttered in a choked tone.

"There you are, darling." Lord Foxwood appeared before her mother could speak, sleek and golden, a glass of wine in one elegant hand. A calculating glance was tossed at Beatrice, eyes trailing over her much the same way her mother's had. He'd written her off, but now he was revisiting her value to him.

Lord and Lady Foxwood exchanged a look.

A wave of nausea rolled through her. It was one thing to

THE DESIRE OF A DUCHESS

acknowledge that ambition and standing would always be more important to her parents than Beatrice, especially when doing so from the safety of Chiddon. Quite another to see them assessing her future usefulness to them in person.

No wonder I became so bloody awful.

Blythe's grip on her hand tightened again, becoming almost painful.

"Ah, Lord Blythe." Her father's lip curled. "I hadn't expected you to be here tonight."

"Why, Foxwood? It's my house."

Lord Foxwood reddened at the rebuke. "You don't spend much time in London these days. First Rome, now the countryside. One wonders what you find to amuse yourself."

"Duchesses and haunted mills," came Blythe's chilly reply.

"Apologies, my lord. But I must speak to you on a matter of some urgency." Lady Blythe interrupted in her jarring bright yellow, fingers plucking at Blythe's arm. "A misunderstanding has occurred, of which you must be made aware." She nodded politely to Lord and Lady Foxwood, not sparing a glance for Beatrice.

Well, that was fine. She and Lady Blythe had never gotten on. The course of their relationship was only destined to get worse. Especially after Beatrice rid the house of pear paintings.

"Your Grace. I'll only be a moment." Blythe's reluctance to leave her with the Foxwoods bled through his words.

"I shall await your return and amuse myself with Lord and Lady Foxwood." She released his fingers, and his hand fell away from her skirts.

Lord Foxwood made a disgusted sound.

"Don't tell me you've taken up with that rogue, Beatrice. As a duchess, you can do better. A stop will need to be put to any further acquaintance. If he calls, we will refuse him." Lord Foxwood took on his usual authoritative manner.

"She's healed well, hasn't she?" Lady Foxwood said to her husband, studying Beatrice's neck. "It looked so much worse when I first saw her. Ghastly, really." Her elegant shoulders gave a shudder.

"I believe you screamed at the sight and swooned across the bed, my lady," Beatrice snapped. "A footman had to be summoned to carry you out."

"Beatrice, you will not speak to your mother in such a tone." Lord Foxwood took Beatrice's elbow. "Your injuries at the time were . . . substantial. We didn't even know if you would survive."

"Nor did you care. You allowed Castlemare to send me to Chiddon." A wave of disgust for her parents, along with all the rage she'd held inside, rolled in her stomach. "You never even visited."

"That dreary backwater?" Lord Foxwood rolled his eyes. "Beatrice, we have *duties*. Social obligations. You embroiled us in an entire host of scandals which had to be smoothed over. First allowing Granby to jilt you, then your little tumble."

"Stop calling it a *tumble*. An overturned carriage," Beatrice hissed, "is not a bloody tumble."

"Do you know how much effort I put forth to keep things quiet?" Her father continued as if she hadn't spoken. "No easy task. And not an ounce of gratefulness from you. The only thing you did was wed Castlemare. That was something." He gave her a pointed look. "But you didn't provide an heir. Imagine what we could have accomplished with a grandson who was a duke." He shook his head.

Beatrice tried to speak, but no sound came out. A few moments was all it had taken for her parents to once more reduce her to nothing more than a disappointment to be borne on their expensively clad shoulders.

"I'll have your rooms at home prepared, Beatrice." Lady Foxwood bestowed a dazzling smile. "We can visit a modiste as soon as possible. I assume we cannot bare both your shoulders, so we'll have to work around that."

"I have a house. I am a widow," Beatrice said in disbelief. "I've no need to take up residence with you."

"Don't be silly. You need your family now more than ever, especially if you are to remarry. Now, the Ralston ball is two days hence," Lord Foxwood said thoughtfully. "There's a marquess this season. A widower. Henley."

The arrogance of Lord and Lady Foxwood, the sheer self-serving nature of the two people standing before Beatrice, astounded her. That they could possibly think she would cheerfully return to their London home and pick up as if Castlemare and her accident had never occurred. Pretending as if the last few years had never happened.

"You stand before me without a word of welcome or concern. Behaving as if we have not been estranged. You abandoned me," Beatrice said quietly. "Discarded me. I appear unannounced. Not nearly as disfigured as you imagined. And you expect me to just — "

"Yes, Henley," her mother interrupted, patting Beatrice's arm. "Older. A bit of gout. He won't mind." A graceful hand fluttered over Beatrice's cheek. "A few imperfections, darling. You're still quite beautiful, *especially* at a distance."

The Foxwoods were horrible, terrible people. She was ashamed to be related to them.

"Better connected than Castlemare," her father agreed. "Quite a catch."

"I don't have a right earlobe. Are you sure Henley won't mind?" Beatrice's tone was brutally sarcastic. "Perhaps he enjoys a lady's ears."

"Henley isn't terribly fussy," Lady Foxwood said with assurance. "You can be wed by the spring, I think."

Where was Blythe? She glanced over at the refreshment table and saw Melinda flirting outrageously with a young gentleman. Her friend looked up, saw the Foxwoods, and set down her glass of punch, features hardening in an instant.

Oh dear. Melinda was going to come to her defense and cause a scene.

The light scent of citrus caught in Beatrice's nostrils. Warmth, comforting and solid, suffused her back.

There he is. Relief flooded her. Bravery could not be sustained by her indefinitely. She'd done rather well, considering. But her parents—Blythe tended to coddle her, but just now she was grateful for his protection.

"I disagree about a spring wedding," Blythe joined the conversation. "Rains quite a bit. You don't want that spoiling the day, do you? What do you think, Beatrice?"

Lord Foxwood snapped to attention. "You will not address my daughter with such familiarity."

"I must remind you once more, I am a widow, my lord. You've no say over any aspect of my life, including how Blythe addresses me. Your gentle care of me ended some time ago." Bile filled her throat. "I'm not living with you, listening to you, or being introduced to a marquess so you can further your own connections. How dare you assume that my appearance tonight is for your benefit." She leaned toward her mother. "And by the way, Mother, the scars are much, *much* worse the farther down you go. Just ask Blythe."

Lord Foxwood's lips pursed. "Now see here, Beatrice."

Unable to endure the horror of her parents another moment, Beatrice wobbled, placing a hand over her mouth. Bile surged up her throat before it could be stopped. Stomach pitching like a ship in a storm, she cast up the contents of her stomach at the feet of Lord and Lady Foxwood, in clear view of Lady Blythe's guests.

Lady Foxwood shrieked as her splendid gown and matching slippers were ruined.

Lord Foxwood fell back with a gasp, jumping behind his wife attempting to avoid the worst of the splatter.

"Oh dear," Beatrice muttered as the room swam around her. "My apologies."

Strong arms, Blythe she supposed, caught her collapsing form just as the edges of her vision grew dark.

🦊 26 🦊

Beatrice opened her eyes, blinking until she could see only one Blythe hovering over her.

"Dramatic, Bea." He wiped her forehead gently with something cool. "Clearing a room in such a fashion."

"I like to make an entrance," she whispered. "Have all eyes on me."

"You succeeded, Your Grace." His lips tilted in a grin. "I will carry the appalled look of Lady Foxwood in my mind forever. Lord Foxwood shrieked as if he were a virgin on her wedding night. Pompous idiot."

"I suppose Lady Blythe is horrified."

"Completely," Blythe assured her before lifting a glass of water to her lips. "Drink slowly. It is a pity you fainted, though I'm sure you can read all about tonight's events in the gossip columns tomorrow. Mrs. Farthing came running forward, brandishing your fan like a sword, ready to defend you against the vile Foxwoods. I thought she might stab your father."

Beatrice sighed. "I really cannot force her to return to Vicar Farthing. She detests him. I must keep her with me."

"Agreed." Blythe pressed a kiss to her forehead. "Mother's guests shrank back in horror at the sight of a duchess *spewing* so profusely." His shoulders shook as he tried not to laugh. "Andromeda rushed over, demanding you needed air. Granby growled about, waving his massive hands, pushing everyone back." A snort left him, no longer able to contain his amusement. "When I picked you up, shocking everyone with my overly familiar behavior, the curls around your ear fell away exposing your lack of earlobe. Lady Foxwood, already barely conscious, gasped and fainted. She fell to the floor, and your father tripped over her."

"I did warn her." Heat flew up Beatrice's cheeks. "Humiliation is a state I am accustomed to. I suppose tonight's events are all anyone will be able to speak of for some time." She closed her eyes with a sigh. "But it serves the Foxwoods right for already trying to wed me to a marquess, *who isn't terribly fussy*," she mimicked her mother. "Less than a quarter hour after seeing I did not resemble an ogre."

"Good god. You sound exactly like Lady Foxwood. Don't ever speak that way again." Blythe snuggled next to her on the settee, his larger form taking up all the available space.

Beatrice didn't mind. She pressed her nose against his chest.

"Lord Foxwood kept insisting I take my hands from your person when I carried you away. Hovering about me like an annoying horsefly. I did think Mrs. Farthing might punch him. He finally left off after being informed of some rather pertinent facts. Suffice it to say, the introduction to Lord Henley, who isn't terribly fussy, is now moot." Blythe's palm settled on her stomach.

"My father's arrogance is rather shocking, isn't it?"

"Completely. I summoned a physician. Mrs. Farthing repeated her concerns over your health to the good doctor since you were indisposed."

"I was examined?" Beatrice tried to sit up. "While unconscious."

Blythe shrugged. "A cursory examination. Dr. Wells took one look at you after Mrs. Farthing recited her findings to him and agreed with her conclusions." Long fingers stretched possessively over her abdomen. "Apparently you are *not* as barren as the field behind Beresford Cottage."

"No, I can't possibly—" She thought back to the last time she'd had her courses. Before Blythe had ever arrived in Chiddon. The shock of him being there had distressed her, that was why she hadn't—there hadn't been any worry because she was barren. Everyone had said so.

"My sugar beets have taken root in your heretofore barren field."

Beatrice swatted him. "You are terrible with words. Awful. Poetry is definitely not where your talents lie." She trailed her fingers over Blythe's hand, cradling her stomach. The joy Beatrice felt was insurmountable. Pure. Magnificent. A part of Blythe dwelled within her. "I cannot believe." Moisture gathered in her eyes. "But—"

"No buts, Your Grace. No waffling over whether you deserve the happiness that marriage to me will undoubtedly bring. And I already know what a terrible creature you are so you cannot use that excuse. London, at least part of the time. Agreed?"

"Agreed." She would do whatever Blythe asked of her. "We don't have to return to Chiddon, but I would like to visit on occasion. Check on things. I don't wish to abandon the village. I cannot."

"I do not expect you to. Mother will give you control of Larchmont. She has my two sisters to launch at any rate. I've been gone from my estate, and it needs tending. There will be enough to keep us busy when we aren't in London."

"Lady Blythe must be disappointed." No matter her feelings for Blythe's mother, he loved his family. Beatrice would make every effort to ensure a peaceful existence. After she got rid of the pear paintings.

"My mother is annoying, controlling, and overly determined, but she is not unintelligent. Cunning is a better word, I think." A thoughtful look entered his handsome features. "She wasn't terribly surprised to see you, the reason for which I'll share later." The pad of his thumb brushed softly against the scars along her cheek. "Besides, she is getting exactly what she wanted. Now, close your eyes for a bit." His warmth left her as he sat up. "I'm having the carriage brought around. I sent Melinda home in yours."

Her hands curled in his coat, suddenly panicked. Ridiculous, really. "Blythe."

"Don't worry, Bea. I won't leave you." He carefully plucked her fingers from his coat. "Not tonight and not ever. I'm only going to see to the carriage and make an attempt to be discreet as I see you home. A wasted attempt, I'm sure. The gossip is already spreading. Dashing Blythe finally meets his match in the snobbish Duchess of Castlemare. I can hear the disappointed sighs of every young lady in England. They might storm your front door. Demand you give me up."

A smile curved Beatrice's lip as her eyes fluttered shut. The evening had been exhausting. "Prancing fop. I love you."

"You should. I bought you a mill. Carved you a bee."

"My betrothal bee." She sighed. "Melinda expected a diamond or sapphire. She's disappointed."

A rumble of laughter shook him once more. "I love you, Beatrice. You need never worry that you'll be alone again." He pressed a kiss to her temple. "I will *always* look for you."

EPILOGUE

Lady Blythe tapped her fingers on the edge of the pew, trying to appear as if she were moderately put out when, in fact, this might be the happiest day of her life. Excepting the birth of her only son, of course.

Ellis was *finally* marrying. An enormous relief. Better still, an heir had already been sired. She didn't entirely approve, of course. One could never applaud improper behavior, but it was still rather splendid. She adored Cousin Randolph, but she wouldn't have relished seeing the earldom pass out of the direct line of the Apertons if Ellis hadn't wed. It wouldn't have been what her husband would have wanted.

"My lady, may I join you?"

"Good morning, Mr. Estwood." Lady Blythe looked up at the handsome man bowing before her. "Please." Her eldest daughters were seated behind her with their families. Her two unwed daughters were farther down the pew. She could easily make room for Estwood.

"Thank you." Estwood was attractive, though not of good birth. She'd grown to depend on him while her son was busy attempting sculpture in Rome. Perhaps she might help Estwood make a good match.

"They make a lovely couple, do they not?" A smile graced her lips as she took in her son and his bride. The woman who had once been the jewel of society, Beatrice Howard, was absolutely stunning in a gown of ice blue silk. The design was one of Madame Dupree's, London's finest modiste, and the heavy silk hid the small mound of Beatrice's stomach.

Madame Dupree. Lady Blythe had it on good authority that the wedding gown of her soon to be daughter-in-law was actually the work of the Duchess of Granby.

The duchess dabbled as a modiste. Everyone knew, but it was not discussed.

"I have never seen Blythe so happy," Estwood said. "You were right in your estimation, my lady. I admit, I was hesitant when you requested I make observations in Chiddon."

"I know my son. He would never have lingered so long in the country if he hadn't formed an attachment," she said. "Though I was as surprised as you to find out the attachment was to Beatrice, of all women. I know you didn't care for my methods, but I stand by them." She waved a gloved hand toward the front of the church where Ellis and Beatrice had joined hands.

Estwood. Such a good man. When he returned to London with the news that Ellis *might* be involved with Beatrice, she'd known exactly what must be done. Yes, she'd had to be devious. Pretend to be ill, something for which Ellis still hadn't forgiven her. But in her heart, she'd known that if Beatrice truly loved Ellis, she would follow. Still, she hadn't anticipated Beatrice arriving at the ball like she had. She'd imagined a more *private* reunion. And Beatrice's scars were a little worse than she'd expected.

Goodness, what a scene. She might never live it down.

But in the end, the results were happy. Ellis was joyful.

She hadn't even had to go to the Duke of Granby for assistance, which she'd been fully prepared to do.

She studied the bride, her daughter-in-law, who was absolutely radiant. When Beatrice's hair was styled correctly, you could *barely* see the scars. Castlemare, nearly all of London agreed, had exaggerated. Lord and Lady Foxwood stayed silent on the matter. Which was just as well, for Beatrice didn't care to associate with them. The Foxwoods hadn't even been invited to the wedding.

Ellis recited his vows in a clear, confident voice, looking very much like his father. Handsome and golden, with his hair curling about his temples, promising to love Beatrice for eternity. Lady Blythe's heart sighed with pleasure. The two of them were so attractive, their children would resemble angels.

Today was most definitely the happiest of her life.

৩১৯

I HOPE YOU ENJOYED READING **THE DESIRE OF A Duchess** as much as I enjoyed writing it. **If you did, I'd love a review!**

The Beautiful Barringtons isn't even close to being over.

Coming Soon
The Taming of a Scandal

IF **THE DESIRE OF A DUCHESS** IS YOUR FIRST Barringtons book, start at the beginning with **The Study of a Rake.** Marcus Barrington meets a young lady reading the

Iliad beneath a tree and decides to become a better man. **CLICK HERE TO GET A FREE COPY OF THE STUDY OF A RAKE.**

But if you haven't yet read The Theory of Earls...

"Chemise. Stockings. Piano." Those three words, uttered by the beautifully rakish Lord Welles, leave Margaret Lainscott speechless. His improper request, that she play the piano for him in her...*underthings* is as shocking as it is titillating. Welles is one of London's most committed bachelors, known for his notorious dealings with women and his part ownership of one of London's pleasure clubs. Welles is *certain* Miss Lainscott will not entertain his improper request despite the attraction burning between them.

A young lady such as Miss Lainscott would *never* ruin herself willingly, would she? **START READING THE THEORY OF EARLS NOW.**

If you love reading my books spread the word! Join my reader group on Facebook, **Kathleen Ayers Wicked Wallflowers** or sign up for my newsletter at www.kathleenayers.com and be the first to see my cover reveals, announcements on new books, fabulous contests and more!

Visit www.kathleenayers.com for a complete list of my books.

AUTHOR NOTES

Glowworms or glow-worms are the British version of a firefly or lightning bug. I spent hours on the internet trying to decide whether to go with the American name (so as to avoid confusion) or stay with the British term. This is what writers do. We agonize over a word or term we use ONCE.

Chiddon Ale is a figment of my imagination. I could have gone into detail about porters, half and halfs, pale ale etc., but decided to keep things simple for Beatrice and Mr. Gates. Cask beer (which is what Gates brews) reaches maturity in the basement of a pub or tavern rather than a brewery.

The Piazza di Spagna where Blythe lives and attempts to become an artist, is located in Rome and is the location of the famous Spanish Steps. During the 19th century the piazza also became an area known for English tourists. Keats did live in a house next to the Spanish Steps which is now the site of the **Keats and Shelley Museum**. **Babington's Tea House**, another British institution is nearby. I've visited both and highly recommend.

And lastly, this is a work of fiction. I strive to keep my

historical facts correct, but I may sometimes bend them now and again for the sake of the story.

Made in United States
North Haven, CT
20 March 2023

34333722R00146